PENGU

WA

Krissy Kays was born in Oxford in ....
clubs, festivals and parties. This is her first novel.

WASTED

Krissy Kays

PENGUIN BOOKS

PENGUIN BOOKS

Published by the Penguin Group
Penguin Books Ltd, 27 Wrights Lane, London w8 5tz, England
Penguin Books USA Inc., 375 Hudson Street, New York, New York 10014, USA
Penguin Books Australia Ltd, Ringwood, Victoria, Australia
Penguin Books Canada Ltd, 10 Alcorn Avenue, Toronto, Ontario, Canada m4v 3b2
Penguin Books (NZ) Ltd, 182–190 Wairau Road, Auckland 10, New Zealand

Penguin Books Ltd, Registered Offices: Harmondsworth, Middlesex, England

First published 1997
1 3 5 7 9 10 8 6 4 2

Set in 11/13.5pt Monotype Bembo
Typeset by Rowland Phototypesetting Ltd, Bury St Edmunds, Suffolk
Printed in England by Clays Ltd, St Ives plc

Chapter One

Ellis rolled over and groaned, wanting to sleep but needing to piss. Hazily, he crawled out from his bender. The sun struck him across the face and breathed on his naked body. He stood on the edge of the roof and squinted at London as he peed. From up here he was comfortably detached and could remain cocooned in sleep. Below, in the alley, a man looked up and wondered why a single stream of water was pouring from the sky. Ellis shook his willy and drifted back to sleep.

Two suits (a surveyor and a developer) stood on the roof. The surveyor peered at Ellis's bender, wondering what a tarpaulin was doing up there and why it was draped over a couple of poles. It looked almost like a tent, he thought. He walked a little closer and looked inside. He saw some clothes, a blanket, a wooden box with a candle melted on it, and a body. The body had no clothes on and was snoring lightly. The surveyor quickly withdrew his head. He turned to the developer and exclaimed in finest Queen's English, 'I daren't believe it, there's aactually someone living hare.'

Saul woke and shook the king-size duck-down duvet from him. Joss smiled as he kissed her. He slipped out of bed and into his dressing-gown. It was full-length turquoise satin with a hood, boxer style. The power shower pummelled the last drops of sleep from his body. After drying himself off, he made two cups of tea and took one in to Joss. She was sitting up in bed, leaning against three puffed pillows and rolling a spliff.

'Ready to party?' Joss lit the spliff.

'Sure am. Doppingdean here we come,' said Saul.

Doppingdean was a small village somewhere outside London that was invaded once a year by hippies, junkies, travellers, trendies, ravers, raggas and a few punks who hadn't realized the eighties were over – all with one thing on their minds – fun.

Saul opened the door to his wardrobe and slid the hangers along the rail, trying to decide what to wear. Sometimes it could be so hard. Perhaps he had too many clothes? No, you could never have too many clothes.

Finally he decided on an outfit and laid it on the chair by the bed before dressing. The shirt was a deep blue Vincent Giggliano. The distinctive VGG emblem was embroidered on the top left-hand corner in silver. His trousers were sand-coloured Classicos made of light cotton. The belt was dark brown leather, handmade. His trainers were Cults, a week old, also in deep blue, with Cults' double-chevron trade mark laid out in white leather on the outer side of each shoe. His socks were clean that morning. His pants were navy Ermanios, also clean that morning.

Once dressed, Saul took his drugs from where they were hidden under the carpet behind the bed. He brought them through to the living room and counted out 250 pills, 100 trips and weighed up half an ounce of coke and a quarter of skunk. He chopped out a couple of lines.

'Want one?' he asked Joss as she came in.

They snorted one each.

'Right, we ready?' Saul put his head back and sniffed.

Joss nodded and picked up a bag she'd packed. Saul put a bag of drugs down his balls and gave Joss the rest. She put them up her bra.

Saul's car was a brand new Suberescoo, red in colour. The

engine was a 1.7 speed-assassin turbo. He had taken her up to a cruising speed of 130 mph. The tyres were TR 2s, the windscreen was laminated with DP 3 and the seats were covered with SLC. The car was fitted with twin airbags and ABS brakes and the keys worked using a code which changed every time the door was opened. Saul hoped he never lost the keys or locked them in the car.

In the boot were three full changes of clothes, a jacket, a warm coat in case the weather turned cold, a four-man tent, a couple of sleeping bags and ten cases of premium lager to sell.

They cracked a couple of beers and steamed on their way.

Ellis was trying to find his boxers. They had to be here somewhere. He looked in his jeans but they weren't there. Under the blankets? No. Bollox. Where were they? Ah, there they were. They had slid down one of the legs of his jeans. He pulled them out and inspected them. They were covered in stains, and stank. Hygiene was not Ellis's strong point. But there were limits, even for him.

'Sorry, Billy,' he said to his willy as he chucked out the shorts. 'No knickers for you today.'

Billy shrugged his foreskin. He didn't fancy the idea of banging against those jeans all day without any protection. But what could a willy do?

Ellis clambered out of his bender and looked at the sun, wondering what the fuck the time was.

'Bet I've missed my lift,' he thought.

On the street he asked a woman for 10p for the phone – he was totally skint. She must've heard him but she stiffened and walked straight past. Ellis asked a suit, but the suit kept his buttons facing forwards and carried on marching. 'What's everybody so scared of?' Ellis wondered.

'Boo!' he said to the next person. He jumped, looked around

nervously and hurried on. Finally a pair of trainers stopped and handed Ellis 10p.

'Cheers, mate. Try'na get to Doppingdean but think I missed mi lift,' explained Ellis.

'I'd give ya a lift but mi car's full, see,' said the trainers. 'Sorry, mate.'

'No problem,' replied Ellis. ''Av' a good time anyway.'

'Cheers.'

The phone rang and rang and rang and rang. Ellis hung up.

'Hitch or bunk the train?' he said to himself.

Saul's car was taking a rest at a service station. They stocked up on petrol, fags, skins and Ribena.

'Want another line?' asked Saul.

'Yeah, why not?' said Joss.

You had to start these weekends how you meant to go on. They cracked another couple of beers and cruised on down the motorway.

Ellis looked up, dolefully, at the ticket inspector.

'But she really *is* dying.' He tried to squeeze some tears from his eyes. Bastards never came easy when you wanted them.

The ticket inspector looked down at him. He was not going to fall for that one again (not twice in the same week).

'Off at the next stop.'

All around Doppingdean the roads were clogged. Saul hated driving slowly. But it was a good feeling to look the pigs in the eye knowing he had nuff drugs down his balls to make their day, their whole career even, but that there was no way they'd search him here.

Saul had been given a vehicle pass and was able to drive right on to site. Him and Joss slid their windows down and shouted, 'Beer, Es, trips, Charlie.'

Joss began to sing, 'Anything you want, we got it', until some bloke came up to her and leered.

'That include you, luv?'

By the time they found the others, they had sold two crates of beer, twenty pills, a few trips and a couple of gs of coke. Saul had four hundred and fifty quid in his pocket.

Hitching wasn't so bad, thought Ellis as he stood on the side of the motorway, at least he could get a suntan. He thought hitching was even better as a car pulled up fifty or so yards down the road. Only 'bout the third that'd passed him. Things were looking up. He ran towards the car and stopped beside it, trying not to pant too loudly. He was just about to say, 'Doppingdean', when the car drove off. The bloke in the back seat was waving two fingers at him and grinning as though he'd never seen anything so funny. Ellis found it hard to believe that such tossers existed. Surely this alone was proof that God didn't exist, in case anyone was still in any doubt?

Ellis had been waiting so long, his thumb was beginning to ache. He looked at it closely and was sure he could detect a hint of blue that hadn't been there before. He was clearly suffering from Hitchers' Thumb. Although common among the hitchers of the world, the disease was little studied. All the same, Ellis knew the first symptoms – a blue tinge, a tingling sensation, eventually causing the thumb to drop from the rest of the hand. In some cases, the condition had even been fatal.

Car after car drove past. God, people were stingy. Why the fuck couldn't they stop? None've the cars were full. 'N' most've 'em were probably going near Doppingdean. Were they scared? What did they think he'd do? Steal from them? Rape them? Kill them? Why was everyone so scared? Scared if you asked for 10p in the street. Scared if you asked for a lift. Too scared to trust anyone.

A Gleamer drove past and shrugged as if there was nothing he could do. How could he possibly help?

A Bainge Bover put his thumb up, mimicking Ellis.

'What does he think I'm doing?' thought Ellis. 'Asking if he's okay?'

The most expensive cars never stopped. 'Sad fuckers,' thought Ellis, looking at his thumb and wondering whether Hitchers' Thumb was curable. He wiggled it around and stretched it and didn't even notice a red Ligorleni pull up. The Ligorleni beeped. Ellis looked up and then ran towards it, half-heartedly, expecting it to drive away as soon as he got close. But it didn't. Instead, the window slid down and a woman looked over at him from behind a pair of shades and asked, 'Going to Doppingdean?'

'Yeah.' Ellis jumped in the car. 'You going too?' he asked the woman when he was sitting comfortably in the cream leather seat.

'Yeah, I'm singing down there.'

They had not gone far when the woman handed Ellis a cigarette packet and said, 'There's a piece of charas in there if you fancy skinning up.'

After he handed her the spliff, she asked him to chop out a couple of lines of coke.

'What a lift,' thought Ellis. This was outrageous. He couldn't have asked for more.

When Ellis left the car, they were on Doppingdean site. The woman leant over and said, 'Hang on a minute, do you want this?' She reached down behind her seat and handed him a bottle of green liquid. 'Methadone.'

★

Ellis took a swig of the methadone but it wasn't really what he wanted. It'd send him to sleep. He wanted some beer.

'Swap some methadone for a few cans?' he asked a bloke selling Special Brew. The bloke was skinny and looked like a smacky. Ellis was sure he'd want it.

'I want money,' Skinny said.

'Go on,' said Ellis. 'I haven't got any money an' I really need a Brew.'

Skinny looked moody but then relented, 'Alright, then.'

Skinny didn't drink much of the methadone. Wasn't a party drug. He could do with some acid.

Saul had taken a trip a while back. He had his eyes shut and was trying to explain to some woman that he couldn't fuck her, even though she was so beautiful. He was seeing Joss and he really loved her.

'Oi, mate.' It was Skinny.

Saul opened his eyes and blinked. The woman was sucked back into his imagination, like a bursting balloon.

'You got any acid?' Skinny asked.

'Yeah, how much you want?' Saul reached into his pocket.

'A couple. Only thing is, I ain't got any money,' Skinny lied. 'Swap it for this?' He held up the methadone.

'Mm.' Saul was tripping too heavily to argue. He was trying to concentrate on ripping off two trips. It was hard to see, the world spiralling before him.

He handed the bloke a couple of trips – at least he hoped it was only two – and took the methadone.

'Got an eighth, Saul?' the kid asked.

Saul didn't know him well. He was not even sure what his name was. Perhaps Jamie. Yeah, that was it, Jamie. Saul knew the kid's brother better.

7

'Sorry, mate, ain't got any,' said Saul.

'What's that?' asked the kid, seeing the bottle of methadone in Saul's pocket. 'Methadone?'

'Yeah.'

'How much d'you want for that, then?'

'Dunno. Fiver?' suggested Saul.

'Yeah, alright,' agreed the kid.

'Don't drink it all at once,' said Saul as he gave the kid the bottle.

The kid laughed and handed over the note. Saul took it. He reached inside his pocket and pulled out a wad of money. It was folded over on itself. He wrapped the note around it and put it back in his pocket.

'You're such a lightweight, Jamie,' Tim said.

'Fuck off,' retorted Jamie. 'You haven't just drunk two cans've Brew.'

'I hate the shit, that's why,' replied Tim. 'Fuckin' chemicals.'

'What's this if it ain't chemicals?' Jamie held up the bottle of methadone and took another gulp.

'Who's got some skins?' Richie was trying to skin up but it was becoming increasingly difficult to control his body.

'Lightweight,' said Tim.

Tim was beginning to piss Jamie off. Sometimes when he got on a theme, he'd go on and on till everyone was bored. Jamie opened the back of his throat and glugged the liquid down. He thought he might be sick but he held it down. The world swam before him. Tim's face looked spotty and dirty. Richie was fiddling with a Rizla and fag, not making much progress. They were talking. Jamie couldn't really hear what they were saying, just the odd word. 'Party . . . pills . . . bass . . . losin' it.' The world drained away before him and slipped into white. He tried to focus but the image slid away to nothing.

8

'Told ya he was a lightweight,' said Tim, looking at Jamie's body. 'He's passed out.' Tim shook him. 'Oi, Jamie, ya lightweight.'

'Come on, let's go.' Richie had given up on skinning up and wanted to get to a party. He didn't want to pass out as well and miss out on anything.

'What about him?' Although he took the piss, Tim rated Jamie and he wanted him to be there with them.

'Leave him,' said Richie. 'He can find us later.'

'Yeah, alright.' Tim paused for a moment. He'd had an idea. 'Hang on. You got a pen?' Richie checked his pockets.

'Yeah, 'ere ya go.' He handed Tim a Biro. 'What ya doin'?'

Tim was writing on Jamie's forehead. Richie leant over and read the word, 'lightweight'. He took the pen from Tim and wrote 'dickhead' on Jamie's cheek. They looked at him and laughed and then went to find a party.

Saul jumped over the fence into the copse. The trees swam before his eyes. Branches, leaves, bark blended and danced in a single flowing form. Everything was connected. Everything was living. Each block of colour formed a small piece of a geometric pattern, a huge Altair. The pattern as a whole rose and sank back, like the ebb and flow of the tide.

Saul walked on, forgetting what he had come for. He walked down where the land began to slope. His bladder twinged and he remembered why he was there. He undid some of the buttons on his flies and pulled out his dick and pissed. When he was done, he pushed it back inside his trousers and turned and began walking back up the slope as he did up his flies.

The slope was steep. On the last few paces at the top of it, Saul reached down and touched the ground to help push himself up. He felt something soft and stony cold. He pulled his hand away and looked down. It was the boy he'd sold the methadone to. His face was brilliant white. There was something written on it. It took Saul some time to focus and make out the words 'lightweight' and 'dickhead'.

'Jamie?' said Saul, unsure whether that really was his name. He reached down and touched his face again. It was cold. Saul knew he was dead.

Saul felt his whole body drain. A shiver ran down his spine. He closed his eyes briefly and drew a sharp breath like half a hiccup. Then he became cold and he began to shiver. He could not stop himself. His head jarred in spasms. His arms twitched and then lashed out, uncertain what to do.

He ran, he walked, he stumbled back to the party. The trees' twisted bark laughed at him. Beneath him the forest floor writhed with maggots and contorted faces. He watched blindly, falling and picking himself up. His lungs heaved at the air as though it was thick and heavy to suck. He did not think. He did not feel. It was as though all sensation had been knocked out of him, leaving him numb and empty. Nothing meant anything. Nothing was right. He could not do anything except shake uncontrollably.

As he came out of the copse, there were a couple of people Saul did not know. He climbed over the fence clumsily. His shirt became caught on the barbed wire. He stood, trying to unhook himself. The woman came over.

'You alright there, mate?' she asked Saul and began helping him unhook his shirt. Saul was mumbling, trying to say something.

The woman unhooked the shirt and Saul looked up at her and said, 'He's cold. He, he's dead.'

The woman looked back at Saul, not sure whether it could be true. But she saw how pale his face was and how he shook. She knew it was true. 'Paul,' she screamed over at the bloke she was with. He ran over. He had never heard her voice stretched tight like that. 'Dead. Somebody's dead.'

The people nearby heard and began to say to each other, 'Somebody's dead. Somebody's dead.'

'Who?' said Paul. 'What's going on?'

'Jamie. Jamie's dead,' said Saul.

People had started crowding round. There was a buzz of voices. All Saul could hear was, 'Jamie's dead. Jamie's dead.' The words spinning around and around.

The woman saw Saul shaking. She took off her coat and gave it to him. He didn't seem to know what to do with it, so she helped him put it on. Then she stood with her arm around him saying, 'It's alright, mate. It's alright', because she didn't know what else to say.

Someone pushed through the crowd. It was Jamie's brother, Pete.

'Saul, it's not my brother, is it? It's not my brother.' He was up close to Saul, pushing his shoulder, trying to make him speak.

Saul looked up. 'He's dead. He was cold. He was cold when I touched him.'

Pete crumbled and cried. His shoulders hunched and he sobbed violently.

'Jamie, Jamie,' he called his brother's name, losing it to his tears. 'Saul, where is he? I wanna see him. Where is he?' His tears half swallowed his words. 'Saul, where is he?'

'I'll show you,' Saul replied. He turned and climbed over the fence. Pete followed. Saul walked back to where Jamie was. He thought he might not be able to find the right place. Or he hoped Jamie would not be there. He hoped he had made a mistake. But he remembered the sight of Jamie's dead face and the cold touch of his skin too clearly for it not to have been real. Saul found him. He was still dead.

Pete looked down at his brother's body. 'Jamie, Jamie you stupid prat.' He slumped down on the ground next to Jamie's body and saw the writing on his face. 'What have they done to you? What have they done?' Pete spat on his sleeve and rubbed at the ink. His brother's head shook loosely as he rubbed. 'What's Mum gonna say? You bastard. You stupid bastard.' He gathered his brother into his arms and rocked his body, like a baby, and cried.

'Hello, Saul,' someone was calling. Saul could not understand. 'Saul,' the voice called again.

'Yeah,' Saul called back.

A moment later four ambulance men were there with a stretcher. One went up to Pete and put a blanket around his shoulders.

'You're his brother?' he asked.

Pete looked at him and said, 'He's my little brother. He's dead', and collapsed into tears once more.

'It's alright, son. Just come over here with me while we put him on the stretcher.' He shepherded Pete away.

Saul shut his eyes. He heard the ambulance men putting Jamie on the stretcher. 'Let's do this in as dignified a way as possible.' Saul could see Jamie's body, rotting flesh peeling from his bones. 'Take it easy, and one, two, three.' The other man was asking Pete Jamie's name and address and how he could contact his parents. Then Saul heard Pete scream, 'Just get that writing off his face, for fuck's sake.' He began to sob, gasping, 'My mum, don't let her see him like that. Get it off. Get it off.'

Saul opened his eyes. The ambulance men were lifting the stretcher and walking back. Pete was following. He was shaking violently and had not yet stopped crying.

When they were out of the copse, Pete saw Tim. He had seen him with Jamie earlier.

'You left him to die,' Pete said, stopping crying. 'You wrote on his face and left him to die.'

Tim looked at his feet, scraping one boot against the other. His mouth quivered as he tried to hold in the tears.

'We were just havin' a laugh,' he whispered. 'We didn't know he was gonna die.'

Pete punched him in the head and then kicked him as he lay in the dirt.

'Just havin' a laugh,' he said, sobbing loudly. He kicked Tim again and turned away.

Saul turned away too. He didn't want to see any more. He had to get out of here. Half stumbling, half walking, he tried to find his car. He walked towards the main circuit of marquees. Everything around him was going on as usual. People were laughing, dancing, eating. The stalls were selling. The music pumping. The drugs were still flowing freely. The boy was dead but the world carried on rolling, undisturbed. Somehow he thought it would all have stopped. Saul's own life seemed to have stopped. Since he'd seen that boy's face, everything was held in limbo.

Saul carried on walking. All around him, he heard noise. But he felt quiet and distinct, unable to speak even if he'd wanted. The world tumbled on around him as he tried to find his way. A woman screaming, 'Don't forget the toaster. Don't forget the toaster.' A kid, about ten, on the back of a motor bike. ''Ash for cash. Es. Es. 'Ash for cash.' A drooling Alsatian, growling, lurching into his face. He pulled back. A couple of men. 'You fuckin' . . .' squaring up to 'fuckin', you know you fuckin' did' to fight. Big men. Pierced. Wobbling with spilling cans've Brew. A woman drawling. 'No, you can't 'av' it. He fuckin' needs it. He'll get the shakes soon.' 'Don't forget the toaster.' Kids, white-faced, eyes bulging. Jaws grinding endlessly. 'Lost. Fink we're lost.' 'Do you know where we're going?' 'I'm sure it was this way.' 'I jus' wanna drink. I jus' wanna drink.' A whiff of urine. Thought he might puke. Where's the fuckin' car? Jamie rotting. Don't think about that. Just find the car. Where the fuck is it? Just find the car. Two girls with bindis and fluoro clothes. The colours leapt out and slapped him in the face. Techno bass banging. People dancing. A robot on stilts jarring. Little kids in combats mounting a teddy. 'Shag it. Go on, shag it.' 'Fuck it senseless.' A teepee. A bongo beat. The deep vibrations of dub. Where's the fuckin' car? Panting. Slightly shaking. And then there it was. There was the car.

Where are the keys? They've gotta be here somewhere. Looks in his pockets. In his trousers. In his jacket. Where the fuck are they? In the back pocket of his jeans. They won't be there. Maybe. Never know. No. What the fuck? All I need. Jacket. Jeans. Christ, they've gotta be here somewhere. Rubs his face. Please God. Just gotta get out've here. Jeans. Jacket. What the fuck? Inside pocket. Looks at the jacket. It's that woman's. Still got that woman's jacket on. Keys in my jacket underneath. Here. Here they are. Fumbles. Pulls them out.

Can't focus on the key. Can't see it properly. The key. Is the key the right way up? Holds it up to his face. It looks the same both sides. Can't really see. And then Jamie's face. His face beginning to rot. Shudders. Shakes. Shakes himself free from the image. Don't think about that. Don't see it. Get the key in the door. Fuck's sake. Get out of here.

And finally somehow it works. The door unlocks. And a miracle – the key slots easily into the ignition. The world spiralling before him. Sinking and rising, like a sleeping chest that heaves steadily. Gonna be okay. Take it easy. Drive slowly. Concentrate. Find Joss. Turn the stereo on. Get into the music.

Saul drove slowly around the site looking for Joss. Snapshots of what was going on outside flitted through the windscreen but he managed to keep the picture of Jamie at bay. He turned the music up loud and let it take him on a journey, floating with it. He found the system where he thought Joss would be. He didn't want to get out of his car again, so he opened the door and beeped his horn, long and loud. Again and again.

A man walking past said, 'Shut up, for fuck's sake.' Then he saw the look in Saul's eyes. It was crazy like a caged animal. He kept quiet and carried on walking.

When Joss heard the horn beeping, she knew it was Saul. She wasn't sure how, but she knew. She stopped dancing and pushed her way through the crowds. As soon as she saw him, she knew something was wrong. He was biting the knuckle of his thumb. The palm of his other hand pumped against the horn in the steering wheel. He was staring ahead, fixedly.

Joss got into the car and shut the door. Saul looked at her. It seemed to take him a couple of seconds to see her and remember who she was. When he did, he stopped pushing the horn and flung his arms around her, saying, 'Joss, Joss.' The gearstick dug into his side but he didn't notice. He felt her body, soft and warm and that was all that mattered.

'He's dead. He was cold. He's dead.'

Chapter Two

Sometimes everything seemed to go right for Ellis. He had been looking at the wallet on the table for some time, without actually looking to see what was inside. He had not been sure whose it was and there had been too many people around to risk picking it up. But now he was on his own, he opened it and several crisp notes stared him in the face. He counted them. Seventy quid.

'Just enough for a gram of coke,' he thought and plodded off to find Garth.

Ellis had a theory about money. If you had some, you worried about it. Worried about the best way of spending it. Or about losing it. Or about making more – no one ever had enough, however rich they were. But if you had none, there was nothing to worry about. So he reckoned it was best to get rid of any money you had as quickly as possible. Spend it. Have a laugh. Stop yourself worrying. Once skint everything he needed would usually come his way.

Ellis handed Garth sixty quid for a gram and a tenner for an eighth.

'Skint again,' Ellis thought, chopping himself out a line inside one of the marquees. 'But I've got everything I want.' He snorted the line with a bit of paper rolled into a tube. 'Everything except alcohol,' he thought as he blagged some skins and a fag. He rolled a spliff and bimbled off outside.

Then in front of his eyes was alcohol, and not just any old

alcohol. It was a bottle of finest Scotch, still three-quarters full. Ellis picked it up and took a swig. His insides glowed.

'Nothing like a wee dram to warm the cockles o' yer heart.' He sighed to himself contentedly and wandered on.

A man finished pissing and turned to find his bottle of whisky. He was sure he had left it there. He looked about. It must be there somewhere. And then he realized it was gone.

'Oi,' he shouted. He was a chunky man who could bellow like an airhorn. 'Oi. Who's got it? Who is it?' He strode into the crowds like a bulldog. He carried his elbows high and his fists clenched. He was ready for a fight. 'It's you, ain't it?' He picked on a tall skinny yuppie, carrying a bottle of wine under his overcoat.

'No. I . . . er . . . I don't know what . . .' squealed the yuppie.

The bulldog hooked him up by the lapels of his coat. 'Come on, let's see what that is.' He reached under the yuppie's coat. The yuppie protested feebly. When the bulldog pulled out the bottle of wine he nearly punched the yuppie all the same. Perhaps it was a trick. Maybe the yuppie had hidden the Scotch somewhere.

But Ellis and the whisky were long gone. He bumped into a girl he knew from London. Her name was Alison. She was quite young but Ellis had always fancied her. She looked pale and her pupils were swallowing the colour in her eyes. All the same she looked pretty cute.

'Fuckin' hell, Ellis, am I glad to see you,' said Alison. She always talked fast but especially when she was off her head. 'I lost all mi mates an' I'm rushing like a cunt.' Alison sucked in through her teeth. 'I only went to go for a shit. Fuckin' bastards didn't wait.' Alison paused for a moment and then was off on another tangent. 'But those bogs, I mean, Christ almighty, they're grim as fuck. Course I had ta go an' look down one've em. I tell you, I won't do that again in a hurry. Rank, ain't it? Turd upon fucking turd.'

'Yeah, right,' said Ellis, glugging at the whisky and hoping Alison would spare him all the details.

But there was no stopping Alison. She was on a roll now. 'Bloody tampons on top. Like the icing on some gross cake. An' the smell . . . I got in there an' I didn't need a shit any more. I jus' chucked up everywhere instead.' Alison suddenly noticed the whisky. ''Ere, gi' us a go on that.' She grabbed the bottle off Ellis. Ellis thought he might have a reprieve but no such luck. Alison was off again. 'D'you know, last year some bloke fell into the bogs? I fink he was a bit overweight. Whole thing jus' collapsed under him. He was lying in that shit for hours before anyone fished him out.'

'Ner.'

'I'm tellin' ya, it's true,' insisted Alison. 'He died later in hospital.'

Ellis suddenly felt Billy wake up, ready for action. Billy always got excited at the most unexpected moments.

'Wanna go up there and watch the sun set?' asked Ellis, looking up at a platform raised on scaffolding. Behind, the sun burnt amber into the sky.

'Alright.'

They clambered up the scaffolding. There was a bloke already up there.

'Shit,' thought Ellis. But the bloke got up when he saw them and began to climb down, not wanting to feel like a small green fruit.

'Not kicking you off are we?' asked Ellis, relieved the bloke was going.

'Ner, mate, you carry on. Enjoy yerself.' He winked and was gone.

Left behind him were a couple of blankets, a used johnny and one still in its wrapper. Ellis picked up the used one and flicked it at Alison, like flicking an elastic band.

'Piss off,' she said.

He tossed it over the side of the platform and picked up the new one.

'Think this is some kind've sign?' he asked Alison.

'Maybe,' she said and leant forward and kissed him. They snogged for a while and then she pulled back and asked, 'Want a pill?'

'Yeah.'

Alison pulled out a bag with a few pills in it. They took one each, washing them down with whisky and then settled down for a session of starlight sex, by the end of which Ellis was adept at reusing a condom.

The woman slapped Ellis round the face. He came to with a start, wondering what was going on. He looked around, slowly remembering that his name was Ellis and he was at Doppingdean.

The woman was screaming at him, 'Who the fuck d'you think I am, some kind a tart?'

Ellis looked at himself. He had no shirt on, his feet were bare and his knob was hanging out, one hand clutching it, as though it might fall off at any minute.

What the fuck was going on? Where was Alison? Where were all his clothes? And what had he said or, heaven forbid, done to that dog-ugly woman? Hurriedly he pushed his knob back inside his trousers and mumbled some kind of apology.

'Don't think you're gonna get away with it this easily,' the woman whined.

And then there was her other half. A great hulk of a man who was striding over towards them, gritting his teeth and forcing his chest out, as he shouted. 'What, what's up, luv? What's going on? What's 'e bin doin' to ya?'

Ellis wouldn't have minded finding out himself but he wasn't gonna wait to be introduced to the hulk – and his fists. He ducked behind a tent and ran, his heart pumping as he panted. Now Ellis wasn't much of an athlete – never had been – but at times like this he surprised himself at just how fast and easily he could run. The wonders of adrenalin. He could hear the hulk, loaded with excess baggage, gasping behind him. He was still shouting, 'Come back 'ere. I'll teach you to talk to my woman like that.' And it was all going so well. Ellis was striding away. The hulk didn't have a hope in hell of catching him. Ellis dodged a couple of people, hurdled a gas bottle and – crashed to the ground as he tripped on a tent rope. The hulk pounded closer. Ellis picked himself up and tried to run. Suddenly the Olympic hero was gone and he was his old self again. He was weak and wobbly with a malcoordinated body that could barely walk, let alone run. His only hope was to hide.

There was a car pulled up ahead of him. He tried the door to the back seat and, thank God, it opened. He curled himself up on the floor behind the passenger seat. Outside the hulk was cussing, 'That fuckin' piece of shit. I'll break his fuckin' head open.'

'Is he looking for you?' a lad in the driver's seat said, turning to Ellis.

Ellis hadn't noticed him before. From his hiding place Ellis could just see him. He had a skinhead and a six-inch scar across his face. He was dressed in full combat gear. For a moment Ellis thought he might have jumped from the frying-pan into the fire.

'Er, yeah,' he replied quietly.

The lad paused and then said, 'D'you drink beer?'

Ellis thought this was like asking if birds can fly and then, remembering not all birds can fly, thought maybe it was more like asking if fish could swim. 'All fish can swim, can't they?' he asked himself. 'Yeah, definitely – except dead ones.'

'Yeah,' he said to the lad, thinking it best not to involve him in his rambling thoughts.

'Found an artic full o' the stuff. Want me to show you where it is?'

'Yeah,' said Ellis. Out of the frying-pan into the brewery. Yeah, sometimes everything seemed to go right.

As the car drove off, Ellis pulled himself up, sat on the seat and stretched. It wasn't long before they stopped next to a truck. Ellis jumped out. It was true. The thing was full of beer. He went up to it and jumped inside. There were cases and cases stacked up in towers. Must've been hundreds. A chain of people was passing them out the back. Other people were breaking into cases where they lay in the truck and cracking open cans. There was even a couple of people sat on top of one of the towers. It was an alcoholics' paradise. It was everyone's paradise. Ellis had never seen anything like it. There was a crazy carnival atmosphere. Everyone was laughing and shouting. 'Can't believe . . .' 'Can you believe it? 'What a touch!' 'Is this really happening?'

Ellis felt dizzy with disbelief. He blinked. Was this real? It couldn't be, could it? He blinked again. The beer was still there. Who needed money when you could find truckloads of beer lying around, ready for the taking?

'Is this what heaven's like?' he said to a girl standing next to him.

'Ellis!' The girl was Alison. 'What happened to you? Woke up and you'd gone.'

'Ain't got a clue. I woke up with some woman slapping me round the face and mi knob hanging out.'

Alison laughed.

'Let's grab a couple of cases and get out of here,' said Ellis.

Once they were out of the truck, Alison said to Ellis, 'Here, look, I found this earlier, d'you know what it is?' She handed him a wrap. She had tasted it earlier but couldn't tell what it was.

Ellis had a taste but even he, with his vast repertoire of pharmaceuticals, didn't know.

'Fuck knows,' he replied.

'D'you wanna try a bit?' asked Alison.

Ellis was up for it, so they ducked into a marquee and Alison chopped out a fat line each.

'Wha' cha doin'?' cried Ellis. 'Haven't you seen *Pulp Fiction*? Just do a little bit if you don't know what it is.' He cut one of the lines in quarters and they both did a quarter.

A while later Ellis still couldn't feel any effect. He asked Alison if he could take a little more. She didn't mind but she didn't want any more herself. Ellis took a bit more, a lot more in fact.

'Fancy a sauna?' asked Alison.

They were outside the sauna tent. The sun was getting hot. The drug was beginning to kick in. Ellis was finding walking increasingly difficult. He felt dislocated from his body. His body was wobbling. His head was bubbling. 'Ketamin,' he was thinking. 'It's Ketamin.' The last thing he wanted to do now was sit naked in a burning hot room.

'Ner, 'm alright,' he slurred back.

'Well, I think I'm gonna.' Alison slipped inside one of the tents and began to undress. In the sauna, a man was asking a young girl to beat him with a branch.

'Harder,' he was saying. 'Harder. Harder.'

Alison wasn't sure if this was quite her scene.

Ellis was in the changing tent. All around were bundles of clothes. Just what he needed. He wobbled over. There was a black and silver top he liked. It was difficult getting it on though. One of his arms felt longer than the other. The sleeve seemed to form an endless, inescapable tunnel. The other arm plunged through the neck hole. He tried again. His elbow stuck in the other arm hole. There seemed to be no way out except by bending it back on itself. Finally the top was on – back to front. Fuck it. That'd do.

Ellis teetered but stayed upright, feeling like a Weeble. Weebles

wobble but they don't fall down. He delved into another pile
and pulled out a Vincent Giggliano jumper, which he wrapped
around his waist. And then he saw his favourite trainers of all
time – Kenzys. Black with silver reflective strips and bubbles on
the soles for extra bounce. They were to shoes what Jeeps were
to cars. Ellis pulled one on to his foot. This took some time. His
foot seemed much further away than in fact it was and for a long
time he was trying to put the right trainer on the wrong foot.
He teetered and tumbled to the floor, a trainer still in hand. He
lay there, looking at the world sideways on. He would only fall
over if he tried to get up, so he just lay there. He felt his limbs
swell and recede as though he were a cartoon character made of
balloons. Sometimes he felt the same when he was trying to get
to sleep and was still conscious, but had lost all sense of space
and body.

Alison had given up on the sauna. She was beginning to notice
the Ketamin. She hadn't taken it before – horse tranquillizer had
never seemed like her idea of fun. Now all she wanted was to
lie down in the shade. She stumbled back into the changing
room. Ellis was lying on the floor in someone else's clothes, one
shoe on, one shoe off. Alison managed to pull on some of her
clothes before she lay down and shut her eyes.

Ellis's body had stopped feeling as though it was being inflated
and let loose. Now it felt still and numb. In fact Ellis did not feel
as though he had a body at all. He felt as though he was floating,
as though he was slipping up and away. He turned and looked
down and saw his body lying below and Alison lying near him.
He had never seen himself like this before. It was not like looking
in a mirror. This was something quite different because he was
separate and distinct from his body, rather than entangled within
it. Because he was distinct, he could see himself clearly. He could
see the deep rings pressing beneath his eyes and his lids flickering
open and shut. He could see his grimy complexion, the white

gunge around the corners of his mouth and the dirt around his toes. He didn't like what he saw.

He floated out of the tent. He was free from his body. It was a strange feeling. It was difficult to feel anything at all because he could not tell whether this was really happening. But when he looked down and could no longer see his body, he knew it was real.

He began to enjoy the feeling. He was free, completely free. No pain, no stress, no strain. He felt light and full of space, almost a part of the sky.

The festy stretched out before him. In the distance he could see his mates dancing at a system. He went over to them. It was easy to move. He simply thought of where he wanted to go, and he drifted there. The air was cool as it breezed through him. He had never felt anything like this before. It was a cross between flying and dreaming, a soft sensation.

Everyone was off their heads, dancing manically. They looked crazy. Their eyes, he could see it in their eyes. Suddenly it seemed ridiculous. What were they doing? Why were they here? Ellis knew they were just havin' a laugh, enjoying themselves. He'd done it himself a thousand times. But now he wasn't part of it, it seemed mad. Hollow, unreal.

'Funny, ain't it?' a voice said.

Ellis turned around but there was no one.

'Course you can't see me,' the voice said. As it spoke, Ellis felt warmth rustle through him. 'I'm like you.'

'What?' Ellis was suddenly confused. What was he? 'Are we dead?' he asked.

'Dunno 'bout you but I am,' said the voice.

'How d'you know?'

'Went back to my body, didn't I? But I couldn't get back in. An' I saw them carting me off in an ambulance.'

'Shit,' said Ellis, a bit shocked. 'What d'you die of?'

'Methadone. Fuckin' OD'd.'

'Mental.' Ellis paused. 'What was it like? Dying, I mean.'

'Oh, it was alright. Well, I missed it really. Too off my head. Just went to sleep an' when I woke up, I was looking down at mi body. An' mi brother was there, wailing. Tried to tell 'im I was alright, but he wouldn't listen.'

'Shit,' said Ellis, unsure what else to say.

'My fuckin' mates'd written on mi forehead.' The voice sounded a bit pissed off. 'Wankers.'

'What'd they write?' asked Ellis, surprised that people could still be angry even when they were dead. He'd thought you suddenly became all peaceful.

'They wrote "lightweight" and "dickhead".' The voice sounded indignant. 'I mean "lightweight". Fuckin' died of an overdose, didn't I? Can't get much more hardcore than that.'

Ellis paused and then suddenly asked, 'What about heaven? Is it, is it real?'

'Dunno,' the voice said casually. 'Haven't looked for it yet. No one tells you what's what up here. And there ain't no signposts or nofing.'

'Are you gutted? I mean about dying.'

'Ner. Quite exciting really. I mean it's all new, ain't it?' The voice paused and sighed and then said, 'But I wasn't finished with life. Could've done with a bit longer. I mean seventeen years. Not enough, is it?'

'Ner,' agreed Ellis.

'I'd only left school last year. Fuckin' sixteen years of school. One year of freedom and then dead.' The voice was quiet and then its tone became more serious. 'Don't waste yours. Your life. There's so much to do and see. Don't waste your time. There's more to life than that, that's for sure.' They looked down at the party below. 'It's fun an' that. We all know it's fun. But there's more to life than that. Don't waste yer time.'

'But aren't I dead?' asked Ellis. The voice seemed to know more about all this than he did.

'I dunno. Have you tried to get back into yer body?'

'Er, no,' said Ellis. 'I've only just got out.'

'Well, you'll know you're dead if you can't get back into yer body.'

'Well, shit,' replied Ellis, suddenly feeling nervous. 'I'd better go an' try.'

'Yeah, unless you wanna die.'

'Ner, I don't wanna die,' said Ellis with certainty.

'Well, you'd better go then.'

'Yeah, right,' agreed Ellis.

'If you are dead, come back 'n' find me. Maybe we could go 'n' check out heaven or som'ing.'

'Yeah, yeah alright,' said Ellis, hoping he wasn't dead.

'See ya.'

'Yeah, cheers.'

Ellis could see the sauna tent in the distance. As he floated towards it, he was drawn up into the sky. It seemed to envelop him. He was sucked into it and became a part of it. He was beckoned upwards. The sky became white, bleached of any colour. White, only white and he flew towards it. He was thinking over and over, 'I'm dying. I'm dying and it doesn't even hurt.' All there was, was white. Even if he had wanted to go back, he did not know which way to turn, for everywhere was white, sharp, almost painful. 'This is it,' he thought. 'This is it.'

Then suddenly he knew he did not want that and he cried out, 'But I don't wanna die.'

The white light shot back. There was blue and a cold breeze flickered through him. The festival lay beneath him, full of life and colour and rhythm. He seeped back into the tent and saw his body lying there, twisted and dirty.

'Am I glad to see you,' he thought and slid back inside.

Chapter Three

Dead. He's cold. He's dead. Don't forget the toaster. You're worthless. Nothing. Cold. One, two, three. *Joss*. Dignified as possible. Not my brother. Not my brother, Saul. Dickhead. Don't drink it all at once. Es. Es. 'Ash for cash. Don't forget the toaster. One, two, three. Jamie's dead. He's dead. Dignified . . . Don't forget . . . Worthless. Lightweight. Name. Address. Cold. Your brother. Not all at once. Lightweight.

Images in his head. Jamie's body lying on a mortuary slab like the murder victim in some detective show. The autopsy. A knife butchering his body. Green liquid spilling from it. Hanging in chunks from meat hooks.

'Joss,' Saul said. 'Joss, are you awake?'

It was early but he had been awake for some time listening to the voices in the dark.

'Urh,' Joss groaned and flung her arm out from under the duvet. 'What?'

'Joss, will you hold me?'

There was something serious about the way Saul spoke. Joss opened her eyes gently. The light filtered blue through the blinds. She could not see Saul clearly, but she could see his body shaking slowly. She moved close to him and slid her arms around him. As she held him, she could feel him begin to cry.

★

When Joss woke, Saul was still asleep. It was morning. The pillow was damp from his tears. Joss rolled over and kissed him softly on his forehead. He moved his hand to brush her away but remained asleep.

'I bet it was cos of that kid,' she thought as she pulled on her clothes. 'Probably still in shock. I hope he's forgotten about it today.'

It had felt strange holding him like that, feeling him cry. She tried to remember if she had seen him cry before. She must've done but she could not remember.

Joss wanted Saul to start the day well. She picked up a bag and went down to the supermarket. The supermarket was nearly empty and there were no security guards. Stealing was easy. Joss shoved a packet of smoked salmon down her jeans. She put a couple of bottles of champagne in the bag. At the checkout, she paid for a loaf of granary bread, a pack of unsalted butter and a lemon.

'Thanks.' She smiled sweetly at the cashier. They had such mind-numbing jobs, Joss thought the least you could do was smile and, besides, they were much less likely to suspect anything if you were able to look them in the eye.

''S okay,' replied the cashier.

The bottles in the bag clinked together as Joss tried to get some money out the pockets in her jeans. Joss saw the cashier look quizzically at the bag.

'Champagne,' Joss explained. The cashier nodded. 'I'm getting engaged,' Joss continued.

The cashier broke into a smile and felt a little glow in her heart.

'Oh, how romantic,' she said.

By the time Saul and Joss got out of bed for the day, they were full of champagne, salmon and sex. Saul could feel a headache hanging at the back of his head, waiting to kick in. He wouldn't have minded staying in bed a while longer but some people had rung, wanting to buy some hash. They said they'd be round in a bit. Joss left him to it and went round to see Chelsea.

Chelsea was Joss's oldest friend. She had known her since she was ten. Chelsea lived a few streets from Saul in her own two-bedroom flat. She owed her flat to her dad. When asked, he would say he worked in television. His work, he said, was essential to the smooth running of the BBC, Channel 4 and numerous production companies.

'Take me away,' he often boasted, 'and the entire television industry of Britain would collapse. They'd be lost without me.'

Sometimes he would get particularly carried away. 'I am the oil in the engine of television. Without me, the engine would seize.' What he in fact did was deal cocaine.

Chelsea also owed her name, Chelsea F.C. Minnoela, to her dad, to her dad's support of the football club, to be precise.

Initially her mother had not been overwhelmed with enthusiasm for the name, which was unusual – Mrs Minnoela was enthusiastic about almost everything, even the most seemingly trivial things. For example, a friend might say incidentally that she had just bought some eggs.

'Eggs,' Mrs Minnoela would exclaim. 'Oh, that's marvellous. Absolutely fantastic. I simply adore eggs. So versatile. Scrambled. Fried. Poached. Boiled, with soldiers. Never forget the soldiers. Omelettes. Simply adore them.'

Her enthusiasm was of course aided by her passion for cocaine and dry white wine or, preferably, champagne.

But for her daughter's name, Mrs Minnoela had found no enthusiasm, only small comfort that her husband had not supported Leyton Orient or, heaven forbid, Arsenal. It would not have taken long for even the most unimaginative schoolgirl to think up some ghastly nickname from the name Arsenal F.C.

But Mr Minnoela had insisted and Mrs Minnoela had, after many a violent argument, eventually given in. She had in fact grown to like the name. It had a certain aristocratic ring.

Chelsea owed her vivacious dress sense, her flamboyant gesticulations and her enthusiasm to her mother (not to mention her fondness for cocaine – something of a family trait).

When Joss arrived, Chelsea was chopping out a line on the coffee table.

'Want one?' she asked.

'Cheers,' replied Joss.

They each did their line and then sat back into the sofa.

'Have a good time at Doppingdean?' asked Chelsea.

'Yeah,' said Joss, not looking at Chelsea. She was thinking of Saul and Jamie. It was probably the worst weekend of her life. But she had said to herself she wouldn't tell Chelsea. Chelsea had a way of making a drama out of a crisis. But how could Joss chat about it as though nothing had happened? She had to tell Chelsea. 'You know Pete's brother?'

'Yeah, Jamie. Came round here the other day. Not bad looking.' Chelsea flicked her fag with straight fingers.

'He's dead.' Joss did not know how else to put it.

'Dead?' Chelsea was still. She could see the boy's face in her mind. For a second she thought she might laugh. 'Fuck.' A shiver ran down her spine. It could happen so quick. One minute someone's there, the next that's it, game over. 'How'd he die?'

'Methadone.'

'He overdosed?' Chelsea inhaled sharply on her fag.

Joss nodded. 'Saul found him.'

'You're not serious.' Chelsea's imagination was running away with her. She was trying not to picture Jamie dead but she could not help herself. Her imagination worked like some tacky B-movie. She saw his body, a grey shade of blue, and a trickle of blood spilling from the corner of his mouth. 'Oh, that's terrible,

30

simply dreadful.' She stubbed out her cigarette. 'Awful.' And covered her eyes with her hands, breathing deeply as though taking a toke. 'When'd it happen?'

'Sunday night. Saul was tripping.' Joss looked at Chelsea. 'He saw Jamie's body decay.'

'Fucking hell.' Chelsea shook her head. It was strange but terribly exciting. 'Is he alright?'

'Sort of. He kinda thinks it's his fault.'

'How come?'

'He sold it to him,' explained Joss.

'What? What was Saul doing with methadone?'

'Dunno. Someone gave it to him or something.'

'Doesn't make it his fault, though.' It made Chelsea quite irritable to think of Saul blaming himself. The idea was so ridiculous.

'I know,' agreed Joss.

'He can't go blaming himself. I mean, I mean it's insane.' Chelsea was trying to think how to explain it. Then she hit on an analogy. 'It's like selling a car. I mean if you buy a car and you crash it and kill yourself, well, that isn't the salesman's fault, is it? I mean, not unless the car was faulty. It's your fault because you were driving.'

'Yeah, I know. I mean, I tried to tell him but he was tripping. He just got stuck on the idea. He should've come to his senses today.' Joss hoped.

'I mean we're all at it, we're all living dangerously,' continued Chelsea. 'If we fuck up, we've got no one to blame but ourselves.'

Saul weighed out the hash in front of Jack and Sam. He used to enjoy all this wheeling and dealing, having cash in his pocket, always out and about meeting new people, standing out from the grey faces in grey suits who pushed to work each morning and pushed home each night. He had looked at those people with pity. They were trapped in a life sentence of routine boredom. But he knew things didn't have to be like that. He was young and full of energy. He could do what the fuck he wanted. He could be free.

Dealing had been the alternative. Easy money in a crazy scene. It'd whipped him up into its flow like a tornado. He enjoyed it. There was always somewhere new to go, new people to meet, new parties to check out, new drugs to take. There was never time to feel bored and there was never time to doubt. He'd had everything he'd wanted. He had made it all for himself. He had been free. He had never imagined wanting to change. This was his life. It was fun, fun, fun. Why would he ever want to stop?

Now suddenly it all seemed empty. The people all seemed the same. They didn't wear suits but there was still a dress code. The routine of parties and drugs seemed as much of a trap as a nine-to-five job. People said the same things over and over. Nothing seemed to change except the amounts of drugs people took. What'd once been so exciting, now felt dull. Once it'd seemed liberating, now it was enslaving.

As Saul chatted with Jack and Sam, he thought he must've heard that same conversation a hundred times. A million times. They talked about the hash. How they liked the colour and the texture and the smell was good but Jack preferred weed . . . Saul felt like screaming. He wanted to get up and kick them both and say, 'Buy the shit and get out or find something else to talk about.' On and on about the same old shit. But he listened to himself and he could hear how he was as bad as they were.

'You've gotta get out of this,' he said to himself. 'You've gotta get out.'

It was evening when Joss came home. Saul was alone. Music was playing. The telly was on but the sound was off. There was the smell of skunk.

'All alone?' Joss kissed Saul.

Saul grunted in reply.

''Spect everyone's still at Doppingdean. Should be back tonight though.' Joss was talking fast, sniffing and wiping her nose. She'd been at the coke all day. 'Chelsea's had a mad weekend. Got wined and dined by one of her dad's mates. Some producer. Reckons she should go into acting. Ha!' Joss laughed falsely. 'Worst thing you could say to Chelsea. She's full of herself now. Even more than usual. But he was just trying ta get in her knickers. He gave up on the idea as soon as she refused to go back with him. Well posh restaurant that they went to, though. Three-course meal, champagne, the lot. Funny thing is he used to go out with her mother.' Then Joss remembered, 'Oh, champagne.'

She went into the kitchen and took out a couple of glasses and a bottle of champagne from the fridge – they had only drunk one in the morning.

'You alright, my love?' she asked as she opened the bottle. Saul seemed ever so quiet.

'Yeah,' said Saul, unconvincingly.

'What's up? Not still thinking about that kid, are you? I told you it's not your fault. You'll drive yourself mad if you sit here and brood.' The champagne overflowed into the glasses. 'Here, have some champagne.'

'I don't want any, Joss. Alright?' Saul snapped.

'Sorry, I'm only trying ta help.'

'You're not fucking try'na help. You're try'na get pissed cos you're off your head on Charlie,' Saul shouted.

'Don't take this out on me, Saul. This hasn't got anything to do with me. I'm try'na talk to you an you're just sitting there stoned, watching the fucking television and grunting like a caveman.'

'Fuck off, Joss.' He spat with venom.

'Don't tell me to fuck off. This is my flat too.'

'Bet you've bin round there gossipin' 'bout it.' Saul stood up. 'Haven't you?' He thrust his face at Joss and grabbed at the air, his fingers curled with tension.

'Yeah, we talked about it.' Joss did not back off.

'I don't want you fuckin' talkin' about it, alright?' Saul leaned into her face again.

'I'll talk about what the fuck I like.'

'Not about that.' Saul narrowed his eyes. 'Not to her. Not to anyone.' He pushed Joss hard on the shoulder.

Joss was forced to take a step back. How dare he push her? She wasn't gonna stand there and get pushed by him and do nothing. She chucked her glass of champagne in his face.

'What the fuck ya doin'? My Giggliano.' Saul looked down at his shirt.

'I don't give a fucking shit about your Giggliano. You've got nuff of them. 'S all you care about's your clothes.'

Saul wanted to hit Joss but he did not. He held himself back and looked at her. She was charged, ready and waiting for him.

'Sorry,' he said.

Joss was not expecting to hear that. She was ready with her next insult. For a moment she didn't know what to say and then she said, 'I'm sorry.'

Saul wrapped her in his arms. She could feel his wet shirt pressing against her cheek.

'Sorry 'bout your Giggliano,' she said.

'Doesn't matter. You're right. I've got plenty more.'

Saul sat down on the sofa and held Joss's hand, leading her to sit down on his knee. She sat down and put her arms around his neck.

'I keep seeing his face, Joss. I just can't get it out of my head, and touching him. I keep remembering what he felt like.'

'Just don't think about it. Do something different every time it comes into your head. Think about something new.'

'And his mum, Joss.' Saul couldn't think about anything else. 'His mum. What did Pete say? How the fuck did he tell her?'

'Maybe he didn't have to.'

'But how, how can she deal with it? That's her kid. And he isn't coming back. What would she think of me if she knew?'

'It's not your fault, Saul. He was old enough to know what he was doing.'

'It's not that. I know it's not really my fault. He didn't have to take the stuff. But it just makes me think.' Saul paused. He did not know what he was trying to say.

'What? What, Saul?'

'It just makes me wonder what the fuck I'm doing with my life. I'm twenty-four. What have I done with my life? I haven't done fuck all.'

'You've had a laugh. You've made a lot of money.'

'Who gives a shit? I haven't done anything. I haven't got anything to show for it. A flash car and a load a clothes that'll be out've fashion in a couple've years. That's it.'

'But you've had a laugh, haven't you?'

'Yeah, suppose.' Saul sounded tired. 'I'm just sick of this scene. Drugs, drugs, drugs. 'S all anyone can talk about. No one ever does anything except take drugs and recover and then take more drugs.'

'Listen, Saul. 'S not only this scene. People always have doubts about what they're doing. No matter what they've done. You always look back and think how things might've been.'

'But I've fucked it up. It's too late. I've done nothing.'

'Don't be stupid. You're still young. There's plenty of time. Least you're thinking 'bout it now. There's still time to find out what you wanna do. Some people don't think about it till they're fifty. Spend their whole lives locked into jobs they hate. By that time they're bitter, used to disappointment. Or comfortable with a dull routine. Too scared to take any risks.'

'But you're alright, Joss. You've got your singing and music. I haven't got anything.'

'I'm not making any money doing it, am I? It's not like it's leading anywhere.'

'But it's something, isn't it?' Saul looked at Joss, with dull, dying eyes. 'Something you really wanna do. Y'know, keeps you alive. I haven't got anything like that.'

'You've got yourself. You've got more talents than most people. Start using them. You can do whatever you want.'

'I dunno. I dunno.' But he had an idea. He wanted to paint, draw, create. It was what he had always wanted to do. Always done, until recently. And what he had always been good at. What had kept him alive. 'I wanna draw an' shit, y' know.'

'So get on and do it. There's nothing stopping you but yerself.' Joss smiled and kissed Saul. 'Come on, stop moping and come out for a drink.'

All Saul and Joss's mates drank at the Diver's Tavern. No one knew why they went there, except that everyone else drank there. It was a grim place to drink. The walls were red, screaming at you to fight. The floor was smudged with tacky gob and fag ends. The smell of last night's vomit lingered.

When Saul and Joss arrived, the pub was, as always, full of people they knew. Everyone was just back from Doppingdean, still fucked and looking decidedly the worse for wear after a weekend of abuse.

'Alright, Ellis,' Joss called over to him.

Saul bought Joss and Ellis a pint each and they went to a table in the corner to sit down. Ellis was already pretty pissed.

'Weirdest thing happened to me at Doppingdean,' he said loudly. 'Fuckin', really weird. Had this, like, outa body experience.'

'What'd you done?' asked Joss, smiling to herself.

'Um. Ketamin. Couple a pills. Bottle a whisky. Little bit a methadone. Few cans a Brew. Er ...' Ellis paused. What else had he done? 'Oh, yeah, an' a bit a coke,' he remembered.

'Don't you think that had something to do with it?' laughed Joss.

'Well, yeah, course it did, but the experience was still real. I'm serious, Joss, stop laughin'.'

'Sorry, mate.' Joss tried to pull herself together. She managed to stop herself laughing but she couldn't get rid of the smirk. 'So, what was it like?'

'Mad, I'm telling you. Fuckin' well freaky. I kinda like floated up into the sky. An' it was all white. I really thought I was gonna die. But I kinda pulled myself back, y'know, an' I . . .'

Joss laughed again.

'Look, I know I'm pissed,' continued Ellis. 'I know I'm pissed an' I was fucked at the time but it was real, alright? I wouldn't be tellin' ya otherwise. An' y'know how I know it was real?' Ellis paused, waiting for a response.

'How?'

'Because I saw that kid. The one that died.'

Joss inhaled sharply and looked at Saul. Saul would not look at her. He looked at his pint and then looked away. 'I can't get away from it, can I?' he thought.

Ellis saw something had happened. And then he remembered – it was Saul that'd found the kid. He thought, 'Shit, why did I mention it?'

'Sorry, mate. I forgot you found him.' Ellis wasn't sure whether to stop talking or carry on. But he was pissed. It was easier to carry on. 'Y'know, I talked to him when I was out of my body. I didn't know he was dead till later. But I talked to him. Must've bin real.'

'You serious?' asked Saul. It made him feel better to think of the kid talking after he was dead. At least that wasn't it. At least there was something more.

'Yeah, he was alright about it, I mean dying.' Ellis was finding all this quite hard to explain. He hadn't really meant to tell anyone cos he knew it sounded weird. But it'd just kind've happened an' now he'd started telling them, he wanted to explain it properly. So that they understood and he didn't jus' feel like a freak. 'He said it didn't hurt or anything an' he felt kinda free. But still, he wished he'd done more with his life.'

'Doesn't everyone?' said Joss and she looked at Saul.

'S'pose,' said Ellis. 'I dunno. Just got me thinkin'. That's all. Y'know,' Ellis couldn't find the words to say what he meant. 'I mean, I dunno.'

'I know what ya mean. It does make you think, doesn't it? When someone dies.' Saul was relieved that someone else had been affected by Jamie's death.

'It's jus' like there's so much to do with your life, I wanna get out there and start doin' it. I don't wanna be sitting here in ten years' time.' He looked around the pub. 'I wanna get out there. Get living. Go straight.'

Joss could not believe she was hearing this, from Ellis of all people. But he was serious alright.

Saul smiled, perhaps the first smile since he'd found Jamie's body. Someone else understood what he was feeling. 'To going straight.' He raised his glass.

'Going straight.' Ellis banged his glass into Saul's.

A few pints later, Saul felt enveloped in a cloud of alcohol. He felt alone. Joss and Ellis had gone off to talk to some other people. He pushed through to get to the bogs. All he could hear was people talking about Jamie.

'Did you hear? Kid died . . .' 'Methadone . . .' 'Methadone it was . . .' '"Lightweight" written on his forehead . . .' 'And "dickhead" . . .' 'Kid died . . .' 'Jamie he was called . . .'

'Dickhead . . .' 'Methadone . . .' 'Found him . . .' 'Stone-cold dead.'

Saul pissed and then stood there looking at the floor, his knob still hanging out. He didn't want to go back to the pub. He didn't want to hear any more. The door opened. Two men came in and stood, pissing, next to Saul.

'D'you hear about that kid?' one said to the other. 'Methadone overdose.'

'Gotta get out of here,' thought Saul. He found Joss.

'I'm going home,' he said.

'You alright?'

'Yeah, just tired. I'll see ya later.'

'Yeah, see you at home.'

Saul pushed his way to the door.

'Going straight,' yelled Ellis from the other side of the bar. He lifted his drink heartily, slopping half the contents on to the woman next to him.

'Some hope,' thought Saul.

Chapter Four

Ellis didn't get home till the next morning. He'd woken up, naked and wondering who the fuck the woman next to him was and how he'd ended up in bed with her. One look at her severe acne and mushroom-like hairstyle and he was making a fast exit.

When he did get home, it was no longer his home. There was a man boarding up the windows.

'Alright, mate,' said Ellis.

'Alright,' nodded the man.

'Listen, er, I used to live here. All my stuff was up on the roof. D'you know where it is now?'

'Yeah, 's all bin cleared out. Wasn't much there.'

'No, there wasn't much there,' thought Ellis. 'But it was all I had.' Still, didn't matter. There was only a couple of things that meant anything to him. The rest – well, easy come, easy go. Wasn't the first time he'd lost everything, wouldn't be the last.

'Cheers, anyway,' said Ellis.

'No problem.' The man hammered in the last nail.

Ellis wandered off to go 'n' see Chelsea.

'Maybe it's a sign,' he thought. 'New beginning.' He remembered chatting with Saul the night before. 'Going straight,' he repeated. 'Can't be that hard. Just cut down slowly. No class As during the day. Can't be that difficult. If Chelsea offers you a line, just say no.'

He was walking with a lazy step, toes turned in, almost tripping over his feet. His jacket (picked up at Doppingdean) slipped slack about his shoulders and hung down low over his wrists.

'No,' he thought, practising for when he saw Chelsea. '*No.*'

He looked up and saw the wind sifting sun through the leaves of the plane trees. It caught his breath for a moment and his feet tripped on without him. Something about the way the tips of the leaves met between the trees, the cavernous arch billowing open and the sky behind, puffed and expanding, filled him with a sense of space. He almost felt himself being sucked into it, floating up towards the shivering lights.

His eyes fell back down to the pavement and then out to the street. It was broad with tall terraced buildings painted a range of pastels: honeysuckle yellow, lilac, lime, baby blue, barley milk, pale pink and others flaky white. On the other side of the street, there was a man fishing around in the bin. He was a large middle-aged man with a ruddy complexion. Tufts of white hair stuck erratically to his head. He was wearing a thin cotton jacket, cravat and what looked like a Viyella shirt. Ellis imagined him lazing under his panama watching an Oxford river slip by or aboard a yacht as it pulled smoothly into a Mediterranean port or, rifle in hand, creeping through the jungle of some colonial outpost.

'No,' he was thinking. 'It can't be so difficult.' He found Nancy Reagan's weather-beaten, all-American smile glowing at him. 'Just say "No!", kids,' she was saying, overflowing with empathy for the drug users of the world. Ellis watched his feet slop against the pavement, 'No, no, no.' He looked up and saw a woman with a pushchair staring at him. He wondered whether he had been talking out loud. He grinned at her and tried not to feel like a freak.

'Darling, hello,' said Chelsea giving Ellis a huge hug and a peck on each cheek. 'Got some rarely good new stuff.'

Ellis could feel his resolve weaken.

'Pablo's just come back from Colombia,' Chelsea continued. 'Excellent stuff. Rarely good,' she sniffed. 'Fancy a line?'

'Yeah, alright,' Ellis crumbled. He could see this going-straight business was going to be harder than he'd thought.

Through in Chelsea's sitting room, Ellis found everyone engaged in what at first appeared to be an intense political debate on the state of the NHS. It soon became apparent, however, that the conversation was in fact about drugs. Could anyone talk about anything else? Did they know there was a world not connected with drugs?

The link with the NHS was the decrepit state of Jeremy's nose. Due to a sustained cocaine habit, the bit in his nose that separated his two nostrils had collapsed. It seemed his nose might be in need of some internal scaffolding. Everyone agreed it was outrageous that the operation was no longer available on the NHS.

'What, so you have to pay?'

'It's the Tories, ain't it? Labour'd never've let things get this bad. They knew what was important.'

'Should've got into coke when they were still in power.'

It was then that Ellis's dad turned up.

'Power,' he said, just catching the end of the conversation. His pupils were pinned and his eyelids fluttered like the shutter on a camera with the batteries running flat. Ellis watched as he staggered across the room. It seemed touch and go whether he would remain standing.

'Does anybody know . . .' he paused, concentrating to remember what it was he wanted to say. 'Does anybody, does anybody know what the date is?'

'The date?' Chelsea piped up.

Ellis's dad nodded slowly and then carried on nodding as though he had lost control of the muscles in his neck.

'It's the thirtieth of June.'

'June,' slurred Ellis's dad. 'I do know what month it is,' he said, clearly irritated. 'You'll be telling me what year it is next. Think I'm stupid,' he mumbled and toddled back to the front door.

Ellis shook his head and thought, 'Did he come round just to ask that?' He sighed. He loved his dad an' all that. But it was embarrassing seeing him in such a state. Living in a hostel. Skint. Nothing but gear in his life. Would he end up like his dad? He hoped not. But could he stop himself? He was so similar to him. Perhaps it was inevitable. Fate drawing him in against his will to tread a life path already beaten. No. It couldn't be like that. He *did* have a choice. He was in control of his own life. 'Gotta sort myself out.'

'Chelsea, d'you know anyone that's got a job going?' he asked.

'A job, what do you want one of them for?'

'I'm serious,' insisted Ellis.

'Only babysitting. Mate of my mum's.'

'I don't care, I'm up for anything.'

'I don't know if they'd be up for you,' said Chelsea.

'What are you saying?' Ellis was indignant. 'Think I can't look after a baby? For God's sake. It's natural, ain't it? Paternal instinct an' all that.'

'Er . . .' Chelsea remained unconvinced.

'It's just that hair,' said Joss, looking at Ellis's hair. It was shaved except for two mini-Mohicans, dyed red, that stuck out from either side of his head. 'Not exactly typical of a baby-sitter.'

'Well, I'm not a typical babysitter.'

Chelsea and Joss looked at each other.

Ellis insisted. 'Christ, if my dad managed to look after me, anyone can do it.'

Chelsea was unsure. But in the end she gave in and phoned up her mum. Mrs Minnoela had always had a soft spot for Ellis, rather fancied him in fact. She phoned up her friend and spoke about Ellis in glowing terms. Ellis had his first job.

Ellis had taken to heart what Joss had said about his hair.

'D'you reckon I should do something about my hair?' he said to her later in the afternoon when only her and Chelsea were left in the flat. And then he said defensively, 'But I'm not cutting it.' Just to set the record straight.

'You can borrow some of my bleach if you like,' suggested Chelsea.

'You reckon it'd be better if it wasn't red?' asked Ellis.

'Can't get much worse,' smiled Joss.

Ellis hunted down the peroxide in the bathroom cupboard. He mixed it up and spooned it on his head.

'Darling, darling,' Chelsea said excitedly to Joss. 'Haven't told you, have I?' She paused dramatically, waiting for some encouragement from Joss.

'What?' said Joss impatiently.

'I'm getting married.'

'What!' Joss exclaimed.

Chelsea nodded knowingly, scratching the back of her head, and then whispered hoarsely, 'For money.'

'Ner, really?' Joss screeched. 'Ha!' She was imagining Chelsea as a bride.

'Isn't it exciting. I might even fall in love with him, like in *Green Card*. He might be incredibly rich and whisk me off to some Eastern palace.'

'Yeah, right,' said Joss. 'How much d'you get paid?'

'Two grand at the wedding and two when he gets his visa.'

'So, when you gonna meet him?' Joss asked.

'Next week. I'm so excited. I mean it might not be for love or anything. But it's still a wedding, isn't it? I want everyone to come. Have a big party.'

'What you gonna wear?' asked Joss.

'Haven't thought. Not white. Imagery's all wrong. I mean, I'm not a virgin, am I?'

'We should go and find you something nice to wear. What d'you reckon?'

'Why not?' Chelsea adored clothes almost as much as she adored cocaine.

Ellis was just about done when Chelsea came in.

'Me and Joss are going out. Wanna come?' she asked.

Ellis did wanna go. He didn't feel like staying in on his own. But he wasn't sure about wandering round London with a headful of bleach.

'Think I'll stay here, if that's okay,' he said.

'Sure,' replied Chelsea.

Yes, Chelsea loved clothes shopping, especially at Fitzroy's. She squealed with delight as she tried on dress after dress. The only problem was, it was ever so difficult to decide which suited her best.

While Chelsea was deciding, Joss found a shirt she liked. She pulled off the tag and put the shirt on over her T-shirt.

Chelsea finally narrowed down her choice to a sky-blue sun dress and a little black and white polka-dot number. The sky blue made her eyes shine out, whereas the polka dot was rather sophisticated. It was impossible to decide. She'd have to have both. She pulled off the tags and put both the dresses on over her own. She thought it looked rather stylish – only the other day she'd seen a woman in a colour supplement wearing several dresses, one on top of the other.

As they were about to leave the shop, one of the sales assistants came up to them and said, 'Have you paid for those clothes?'

'Which clothes?' asked Joss, so confidently that the sales assistant suddenly felt a little uncertain.

'The clothes you are wearing,' she said tentatively. Chelsea stared scornfully. The sales assistant began to mutter and stutter. 'The, the dresses and the, the shirt.'

'I don't think that's any of your business, do you?' Chelsea looked down her nose at the woman.

'I mean, you're not trying to steal them, are you?'

'Steal them?' exclaimed Joss, loudly.

'How can we steal our own clothes?' Chelsea was beginning to sound angry.

The other customers in the shop could not help hearing what was going on. Some were staring outright. Others, more bashful, were pretending to look at clothes but listening intently all the same.

The sales assistant wasn't sure what to do. They were definitely trying to steal the clothes, weren't they? She wasn't so sure now. No, of course they were. She must stand her ground. She could see one of them had three dresses on, two from the shop.

'No, really, I, I don't think you've paid for those clothes. I think I'd better call the manageress,' she said, sensing things were out of her control.

'I think you better had,' said Joss.

'Yes, we demand an apology. Do you treat all your customers this way? Or only those who are related to Mr Fitzroy?'

At that, the sales assistant squirmed and hoped she had not made some terrible mistake. The other customers were not even pretending to look at their clothes now. They were all transfixed by the scene.

The manageress stepped up.

'What seems to be the problem?' she asked.

'This woman is accusing me of stealing,' said Chelsea.

'Can't believe it,' rejoined Joss.

'Simply outrageous,' finished Chelsea.

This had turned into rather an embarrassing situation. The

manageress wanted to see the end of it as quickly as possible.

'I think she simply thought it was a little odd that you were wearing several of our dresses at once,' she explained in an attempt to diffuse the situation. It did not work.

'Odd?' cried Chelsea. 'Not content with false accusations, you are now calling my dress sense "odd". Didn't you know I am on the frontier of fashion in London, Paris and Milan?'

'You *are* fashion,' Joss embellished. 'I don't think they realize who you are.'

'But they must do,' Chelsea sounded astounded. 'Don't they read *Tatler*?'

The women in the audience certainly did read *Tatler*. They took another look at Chelsea and thought back to the last edition. A couple of them thought she did look rather familiar, now she came to mention it.

'You do know who I am, don't you?' Chelsea stared at the manageress.

The manageress felt herself burn. Why hadn't she renewed her subscription?

'I am Vanessa Fitzroy.' Chelsea overflowed with self-importance. 'Claude Fitzroy's daughter.'

Astonished whispers rumbled through the customers.

The manageress was silent. 'Oh, God,' she thought. 'This can't be happening. One of my shop assistants accusing the designer's daughter of shoplifting. She'll have to be sacked. But please, dear God, can I come out unscathed?'

'Well, please, accept our humblest apologies.' Grovelling was the only way out of this one.

'Huh,' Chelsea grunted as though she would never overcome the affront of the woman. 'Shamed in public,' she said.

'I am terribly sorry,' continued the manageress. 'I . . . I . . .'

'What is your name?' Chelsea snapped, pursing her lips to stop herself smiling. 'I shall have to report this incident to my father.'

'Jean Dorman.' The manageress felt like crying. Why did this have to happen just as she was making such progress in her career?

Chelsea turned to go, exclaiming loudly to Joss, 'I don't know what Daddy's going to say when he hears.' But then she turned back to the manageress, as though relenting. 'Maybe it is best if we just forget this ugly incident.'

'Thank you,' said the manageress wholeheartedly. 'Thank you so much.'

The manageress sighed. What a relief! But her relief turned to embarrassment later when she found the tags for the shirt and dresses. She sacked the sales assistant all the same.

'Oh, my God.' Chelsea's shriek woke Ellis.

He sat up on the sofa. What was going on? His head felt like it had been dipped in acid.

'My sofa,' exclaimed Chelsea. She stormed up to look at it. A large patch was tinged with black and brown. 'You've burnt my sofa with that bleach.'

The sofa was not the only thing that was burnt.

'My head,' moaned Ellis.

'Your hair,' laughed Joss. In places it was pink. Other patches were crispy white. Strands of hair were falling out and his scalp had turned beetroot red.

Ellis went and rinsed his head till the worst of the burning was gone. Then he smothered his scalp with moisturizing lotion. He looked in the mirror. It was alright. He did look sort of respectable. It was better than red anyway.

'So would you trust me with your baby?' he asked Joss and Chelsea.

They looked at each other and burst out laughing.

Chapter Five

Puffing on a spliff, Saul took out a pencil and found his sketch pad. He turned to a new page. The clean white sheet stared at him as if daring him to make a mark. He paused for a moment, wondering what he should draw. Jamie's face came into his head but he blocked it out successfully. His mind was as blank as the paper. Perhaps he could just draw and something would happen. He made a mark on the paper and then, dissatisfied, got up to find a rubber. Finally he found one lodged behind some books on the shelves. He rubbed out the lines he had drawn and sat looking at the blank page once more.

Saul remembered drawing as a child. Images had always flowed freely from him. The images had almost drawn themselves. He had seemed to be merely a conductor. He had never had to sit down and struggle to draw something, as he was doing now. And the worst of it was, he had always been good. Not just good, but one of the best at his school. If he was going to draw now, it would have to be good. He couldn't draw something he didn't like.

He let his eyes slip and tried to see an image. Nothing happened. Saul gave up and went to find a picture from a magazine to copy. The phone rang. It was Chris. He was on his way round.

By the time Chris arrived, Saul had the image of a face on the page. He didn't like it. The forehead appeared to bulge and the mouth was all wrong. Saul tore out the page, screwed up the paper and tossed it in the bin. Dealing was easier.

'So, did you go to Doppingdean?' asked Chris as he sat down in the living room. He looked over at Saul.

Saul was unsure what to say. He thought it must be a trick question. Didn't everyone know he'd been to Doppingdean? Didn't everyone know what'd happened? Didn't they all know about Jamie? The other night at the pub, it'd seemed to be the only thing anyone was talking about. Was Chris taking the piss? Was he trying to fuck about with Saul's head, make him talk about Jamie when he didn't want to?

Saul paused for a moment and then said guardedly, 'Yeah, I went.'

Chris thought Saul sounded slightly defensive. But then it didn't make sense. After all, he was only asking if Saul had been to Doppingdean. Everyone went to Doppingdean. It was the biggest festival of the year. So to ask Saul if he'd been was hardly like asking if he'd been to a meeting of the Ku Klux Klan. Chris ignored Saul's tone. Maybe Chris had imagined it anyway.

'Have a good time?' Chris went on.

'Sly bastard,' thought Saul. 'He's trying to wind me up. He's waiting, seeing if I'll say about that kid. He knows. Of course he knows. Everyone knows. He probably thinks I'm to blame. Probably thinks it was my fault the kid died. Thinks I killed him. But I know I didn't. I won't say anything. I'll play along with his game and pretend I don't know what the fuck he's talking about. Just like he's pretending. I won't talk about it unless he mentions it.'

'It was alright,' replied Saul. He looked away and stayed quiet.

Saul was being really moody, thought Chris. People were so funny. Especially in this scene. One minute they'd be all hugs and kisses. Or handshakes and laughs. The next they'd be quiet and sulky. And they'd walk past you in the street and blank you or, if you were lucky, grunt hello. Perhaps it was him. He hadn't known them all as long as they'd known each other. And his parents weren't in the same scene. Most people had grown up this way. Caning drugs since they were thirteen or fourteen. Dealing since they were fifteen. Sometimes he felt out of place. Perhaps he didn't really fit in. But if he didn't fit in here, where did he fit in? Were all groups of people this moody or was it something to do with the drugs or London or that tough image people tried so hard to keep up? Chris thought he was alright. He wasn't a complete twat. But then sometimes the way people treated him made everything about him seem wrong.

There was an empty silence. Chris filled it by beginning to skin up. Saul put a record on.

Saul sat back down and listened to the tune. It soothed him. He didn't give a shit. He really didn't give a shit what the fuck Chris thought.

Chris was thinking, 'Might as well get those pills and get out of here.'

'So, Saul, have you got those things?' he said. The words were lost as the doorbell rang.

Saul got up to answer it. He had heard what Chris had said but the doorbell was a good excuse to ignore it. He didn't want to talk to Chris.

Chris thought, 'Bet he heard. Why can't he be fucked to answer me?'

Saul answered the door. It was Dave. They greeted each other and then, as Dave followed Saul down the corridor to the living room, Dave said, 'You go to Doppingdean?'

Saul froze inside but his body carried on walking. What the fuck was Dave talking about? He knew Saul'd gone – he'd bought some pills off him. Saul thought about turning around and smacking Dave in the face but he stayed quiet.

Dave realized he'd seen Saul at Doppingdean. 'Oh, yeah, you sold me those pills, didn't ya? Yeah, they were alright, they were.'

In the living room, the record had finished playing. Saul selected another, put it on and sat down to listen.

'Alright, mate,' said Dave when he saw Chris.

'Alright,' replied Chris, feeling some tension released by Dave's presence.

'Just asking Saul 'bout Doppingdean,' said Dave. 'You went, didn't ya?'

'Yeah, had a wicked time,' Chris replied, with a grin. At least Dave was talking to him.

Saul saw that smile. They were *both* talking 'bout Doppingdean now. They'd probably arranged to meet here. To talk about it. To torment him. Dave had acted surprised to see Chris. Too surprised. He wasn't that good at acting. Saul could see through it. Or was Saul just being paranoid?

'Go to that party Sunday night?' asked Dave.

'Which one?' said Chris, trying to remember which party he'd been to.

'Alien Sounds,' Dave replied. He saw Chris still looking unsure so he said, 'The one by the copse.'

It was obvious now. There was no question. Saul wasn't being paranoid. It was a set-up, he knew. They'd probably planned what they'd say to wind him up. Because they knew. Of course, they all knew. And the copse. That was where Jamie'd died. Saul saw his body again and the ambulance and heard those voices. He thought Dave was his mate. And Chris had always been alright. Up until now. What had Saul done? Why were they doing this to him?

'Yeah, I went to that one,' said Chris. 'Fuckin' excellent, weren't it? They were playing some top tunes later on.' He had some vague memory 'bout a kid dying or something. But shit, he'd been so off his head he couldn't remember much. Now the night was just a series of dim flashes. He couldn't be sure if any of it was real. So he didn't say anything about the kid.

'Went to the Juna party in the morning,' said Dave. 'That was wicked too.'

'That was the one Joss was at,' thought Saul. 'He must've seen me there. Seen me cry. Seen me scream.'

'Ner, didn't make it,' said Chris. 'Was it good?'

'Yeah, classic. Some bloke had found a load of beer. He was giving it away.' It was a night Dave would remember.

Saul couldn't hack this. He wanted them out of his house.

'So you want half an ounce, then, Dave?' he said.

Dave thought Saul sounded a bit abrupt. But he didn't really care. He liked Saul. Saul was probably just coming down from the weekend. He'd been pretty quiet when they were talking about Doppingdean.

'Yeah, cheers, mate,' Dave said.

'An' you wanted, what, ten blue and greens?' Saul looked at Chris.

Saul went into the bedroom to find the drugs. He almost didn't want to leave Dave and Chris alone together. What would they say while he was out of the way? Probably say how well it was going. They were really winding Saul up. Saul heard them laugh. Yeah, they thought it was great, didn't they? Playing with his head. Talking around the idea of Jamie's death, without ever saying anything specific, so there was nothing Saul could do.

Saul saw his green UB40 card.

'Fuck, still haven't signed on,' he thought. It was a good excuse to get them out of his house. He gave them their drugs, took their money and then said abruptly, 'You've gotta go. I need to sign on.'

Chris was glad to get out. Dave thought as he left, 'Saul ain't himself.'

As soon as Saul got out the house, he felt his head clear. He was suddenly not so certain that Dave and Chris had been taking the piss. In fact, the more he thought about it, the more ridiculous the idea seemed.

'You jus' got stoned,' Saul told himself. 'You got para.'

How could Dave and Chris have planned that? It was mad to think they had.

Saul believed that it *was* just his mind playing tricks but a little doubt lingered. It was so much easier to think thoughts than to unthink them. He remembered some of the looks Chris and Dave had given each other. It'd seemed as though they'd been in on some scheme. A scheme that Saul had no idea about and every time he tried to figure it out, he was always left one step behind.

One part of Saul was clear and cool. It was saying, 'Don't worry. You were just being stupid. Just stoned. Paranoid. Forget it. Get on with your life. Get on with enjoying yourself.'

But another part of him nagged on. 'You saw that look. They knew. They knew. Tormenting you.' And then it would change its mind, yet still be as negative. 'Even if they weren't taking the piss, you acted so weird, they'll think you're crazy. How can you talk to them again? How can you ever see them again and be normal?'

'Shut up, for fuck's sake,' he said to the nagging voice. 'You'll drive yourself mad. Shut the fuck up.'

A black bloke was walking towards him. He was thickset and wearing a puffa jacket that made him look all the more thickset. He was storming down the street with huge strides. His head was turned down and his wild eyes stared at the pavement. As he brushed past Saul, Saul heard him say, 'No, Charlie, don't. Don't jump out the window, Charlie. Don't.'

'At least you're not as crazy as him,' thought Saul.

It seemed everyone in London was crazy. You couldn't go out your flat or get on the tube without seeing some nutter talking to themselves. Perhaps it was something to do with London. Did it send you mad? Wouldn't be surprised. All those people crammed into such a small space. All those poor people. Skint, trying to survive. All those frustrated people, trying to do what they wanted to do. All those lost people, trying to work out what it was they wanted. All those confused people trying to understand what the fuck it was all about. It was easy to understand those guys who went nuts and slaughtered people on the subway or in MacDonald's. Surprising more people didn't flip out. Wake up in the morning and freak. Find that automatic and blow it all away. All the poverty, the frustration, the confusion.

Saul stepped over a pile of vomit, into the dole office. There must've been about ten people waiting to sign on in Cycle P. Saul joined the end of the queue.

Ahead of him were a couple of black blokes who knew each other. One had dreads. The other's head was shaved. Both had mobile phones.

'What you got then?' said the dread.

'I told you. A Marron. Lightweight. Fifteen gears,' replied the one with the shaved head.

'Hot?' asked the dread.

'What d'you expect for that price?' The shaved head tutted. 'I mean, fifty nicker.'

'Not from round 'ere?' The dread checked.

'Ner, man.' The shaved head sounded a little irritated.

'Why am I so desperate to go straight?' thought Saul. 'Everyone's at it. Bet there isn't a single person in 'ere that's not doin' some sort've scam.' He looked around. There was a white bloke who couldn't have been anything but a builder. He was wearing a dusty work shirt and boots that had traces of cement plastered on them. A scrawny blonde woman was slouched in the corner, clearly off her head. The bloke with her, a little man with a skinhead, was trying to haul her up off the floor but wasn't having much success. Across on the other side of the room was a tall skinny bloke with a pony-tail and goatee beard. He hadn't turned his phone off. It rang. He answered it.

'Yeah, yeah, yeah, garden's fine . . . Just signin' on, then I'll pop rawnd to sort ya awt.'

'Yeah,' thought Saul. 'We're all at it.' He wondered how many people weren't breaking the law in some way or other. I mean you had to, didn't you? Just to survive. Christ, no one could live off forty quid a week. It wasn't possible. And a job? What was the point? You were no better off. Thirty quid a day if you were lucky. You'd be working two, maybe three days just to pay yer rent. Another day would be money equivalent to yer dole. So you're working three or four days before you're any better off. It made no sense doing that. No sense at all. You were better off letting the government pay your rent and a little pocket money and then working for cash or peddling stolen goods or drugs. Whatever you could do. At least then your time was your own and you were free. And who gave a shit about ripping off the government? Who gave a flying fuck? They ripped you off left, right and centre. Tax, tax and more tax. And all the while, you knew they were lining their own pockets.

There was no way Saul could get a job. He totted up in his head how much he'd spent last week. About four or five hundred quid. No job'd pay him that kind've money. He had no qualifications. No experience. And he was used to being his own boss. He was an employer's nightmare. But how could he take a job for shit pay? He was so used to being comfortable, having a nice flat, new clothes, meals out. How could he suddenly stop spending that kind of money? No one could ask him to do that. He couldn't ask it of himself.

He reached the front of the queue and signed his name.

As he left to go home, he wondered why he'd been getting so worked up. 'Emotions are strange,' he thought. 'So out of your control.' His life was alright. Things would work out. It might take some time but he'd find something in the end. And dealing? Dealing was alright for now.

Chapter Six

Ellis was not quite what Mrs Crispin had expected. His hair was shaved to the scalp except for two stripes that ran from above each of his eyes to the nape of his neck. Where it was not shaved, the hair stuck out in irregular spikes. And was that a hint of pink she could see? His scalp was blotchy. Mrs Crispin tried not to stare, thinking that perhaps Ellis had a rare skin disorder. She hoped, however, that it was not infectious. His eyes were sunken and black-ringed and he had not bothered to do up his shoelaces. But he did come highly recommended and Mrs Crispin had always tried not to judge people by their appearances, so she put her qualms aside and asked him in.

'Nice gaff,' said Ellis without thinking.

'Thank you,' said Mrs Crispin. 'It was all my own design. Come upstairs and meet Barnaby.'

'Isn't he asleep yet?'

'I thought it was better that you got to know each other first,' Mrs Crispin explained.

'Get to know each other?' thought Ellis. Get to know? Christ, the thing was only a baby; was bonding really necessary?

Barnaby was sitting in his play-pen. Ellis wondered whether it was legal to keep babies fenced in like that. But then again, he thought, you needed some way to keep them under control.

'Ellis,' said Mrs Crispin, lifting Barnaby up out of the play-pen, 'this is Barnaby.'

She handed the baby to Ellis. Ellis took him awkwardly. Was there a special way to hold babies? Women had hips to rest them on. Ellis wasn't sure what to do with him but he had to give some semblance of being professional, so he slung Barnaby over his shoulder, jiggled him up and down and said, 'Cudgy, cudgy, coo, coo.'

Barnaby puked on Ellis's shoulder and began to cry.

'I think he's been sick.' Ellis felt his shoulder but wished he hadn't as his hand touched the vomit.

To Ellis's relief, Mrs Crispin took Barnaby back.

'I'll show you where the bathroom is. You can clean up,' she said.

She did not blame Barnaby for his reaction to Ellis; after all his appearance had shocked her somewhat. But she did like to keep control of her son. She did not want him to grow up a wimp, so she said firmly, 'That's enough. Stop crying now.'

Barnaby stopped crying. Ellis was amazed. He had been slightly worried about the idea of the baby crying and never stopping. But this one was easy. All yer had to do was tell it to stop crying and it stopped. It was like those alarm clocks you shouted at to stop the alarm going off.

When Ellis had finished in the bathroom, Mrs Crispin showed him to the nursery.

'Everything you need for him is in here. Clothes, nappies, baby wipes, et cetera. I'm going to go and get ready. Could you just change his nappy and get him ready for bed? His jym-jams are there. And put the dirty nappy in the bin there. Bring him downstairs for his milk when you've finished, okay?' Mrs Crispin was a little apprehensive but she would just have to trust Ellis and let him get on with it.

'Alright,' said Ellis, as Mrs Crispin went downstairs. 'Nappies,' he thought. 'Shit.' He had not thought the baby would need a change of nappy. He was only looking after it for one night.

Ellis began to undress Barnaby. It was the first time he'd looked at him properly. He really was an ugly baby. Ellis was not over fond of babies in general but most babies were kind've cute. There was nothing cute about Barnaby.

Ellis pulled the sticky tabs of Barnaby's nappy and unpeeled it from his body.

'Shit.' It was indeed shit and plenty of it. Ellis had always thought nappies soaked up shit and the baby stayed clean. Wasn't that what happened in the adverts? Wasn't that what all those experiments with blue dye were about? New top sheet for drier bottoms and wetter nappies.

But oh, no. Not here. Both the bottom and the nappy were covered in shit. Ellis couldn't believe so much shit could come from such a small baby. Did he shit like this every day? Or had he been storing it up, waiting till it was Ellis's turn to change him?

Ellis pulled one of Barnaby's legs up, so that his bum hovered in mid-air, and slid the nappy out. He chucked it in the bin with a shudder and a vow never to have kids himself. He grabbed a handful of baby wipes, enough so that he wouldn't have to get too close to the shit, and wiped Barnaby's bum vigorously.

'Hope you appreciate this, Barnaby, mate. Are you watching? I am actually wiping the shit off your bum. You owe me one.'

Ellis took a clean nappy and wondered which way round it went. 'I should've looked how the last one was put on,' he thought. He tugged at one of Barnaby's legs and lay the nappy under him. That seemed to be right. But it did seem a bit big. Ellis did not really care. After all it wasn't him that had to wear the thing.

He unpeeled the sticky tabs, pulled them over and stuck them down. They stuck for a second and then sprang back up.

'Must be a dud nappy,' Ellis thought and threw it in the bin.

On his fourth nappy Ellis was beginning to think it must be something to do with his technique rather than the nappy. He wondered how women knew how to change nappies. Were they taught how to do it during pregnancy? Or was it something to do with their hormones?

Ellis was on his fifth nappy and the bin was nearly full. He thought he'd better change tactics. Perhaps if he could get the nappy to stay on long enough for him to get Barnaby's Babygro on, the Babygro might hold the nappy in place.

Everything was going well. One side of the nappy was stuck down firmly. The baby's legs were in the Babygro. Ellis just needed to do up the poppers that ran down the inside of each leg. It was harder than it seemed. Whichever way he started, the poppers never seemed to match up. Did women get lessons in this too? Or was this just more hormones?

Ellis'd just about finished when Mr Crispin walked in.

'You must be Ellis,' he said, trying not to sound disapproving.

'That's right.'

'So, how's Barnaby?' Mr Crispin picked up his son. 'Nappy's a bit loose. Perhaps you could put another one on.'

'Are we seriously going to let him look after our son for the evening?' Mr Crispin said to his wife as she pottered around in the kitchen. He had not been able to believe the sight of their babysitter. 'Can't even put on a nappy.'

'I'm sure he'll be fine.' Mrs Crispin tried not to let her anxiety filter through into her voice. 'Anyway, dear, we mustn't judge a book by its cover.'

'I am not judging a book by its cover,' Mr Crispin snapped. 'I am judging a young man by his quasi-punk hairstyle and the fact that he seems to know very little, if anything, about the job in hand.'

'What do you want us to do?' retorted Mrs Crispin. 'We can't tell him to go now.'

'Why on earth not?' Mr Crispin did not see a problem.

'Anyway, the Griffins are expecting us.' Mrs Crispin side-stepped his question.

'My son's life might be in danger and you talk about social etiquette,' exclaimed Mr Crispin.

'Don't be so melodramatic,' said Mrs Crispin. 'He'll be fine. He's a friend of Mrs Minnoela.'

'As if that counts for anything.' Mr Crispin sounded as though he was about to start sulking.

'Barnaby's a tough little cookie. I'm sure Ellis can't do too much damage,' Mrs Crispin said, trying to sound confident. She faltered as Ellis walked in. How much had he heard? 'Ellis,' she exclaimed, determined to sound pleased to see him. 'Didn't have any problems, did you?'

'Oh, no,' said Ellis. He hoped the lace that was holding up Barnaby's nappy wasn't done up too tight.

'I've just got his milk ready,' said Mrs Crispin. 'So if you give him that, he should drop off pretty quickly. Then just tuck him up in bed. Help yourself to whatever's in the fridge. Oh, yes, I'll turn the baby-com on so you can hear what he's up to in his cot. He should be fine.'

'I hope I am,' thought Ellis, but he smiled and tried to look in control of the situation.

'We'll be back around one. So see you then.' Mrs Crispin tugged at her husband's hand.

'Bye. Have a good night,' said Ellis as the Crispins shut the door.

Mr Crispin refused to say goodbye. They drove around the corner in the Gleamer. The Suberescoo was being serviced.

Putting Barnaby to bed was much easier than changing his nappy. He was asleep before the bottle was empty. Ellis tucked him up in the cot in the Crispins' bedroom and went downstairs to see what was in the fridge.

Ellis couldn't believe his eyes. The fridge was not only full, which made a change from most fridges Ellis got to see, but one shelf was stacked with four bottles of champagne and numerous bottles of white wine. Ellis debated briefly with his conscience. But really there was no argument. Mrs Crispin'd said, 'Help yourself to whatever's in the fridge', and clearly the bottles were in the fridge. Every job had its perks. This was just one of those perks.

Ellis selected a bottle of champagne, found a glass and popped the cork. Ahh! Babysitting wasn't such a bad job after all.

Ellis wandered through into the living room, put his feet up and picked up the phone.

'Jazz? Alright? It's Ellis. You gotta come round. I'm babysitting. I've got a fridge full of food and champagne. All free. Come over.'

'Ellis, where's the baby?'

'Oh, the baby's alright,' said Ellis, confidently. 'It's asleep.'

'It? You don't call babies "it",' said Jazz.

'Are you coming round or what?'

The champagne was going down well. It complemented the salmon nicely, and the cashew nuts and the M&S salad, 'ready chopped for your convenience', and the king prawns, Chinese style, and the pasta with pesto and the Häagan Dazs ice-cream. The Chardonnay wasn't bad either.

'What's that noise?' said Ellis.

'What noise?' asked Jazz. They stopped and listened. The baby-com cried.

'That noise,' said Ellis.

'Baby's awake,' laughed Jazz.

'Jazz,' said Ellis, softly, ready to suck up. 'Will you go 'n' see to him?'

'No.'

'Go on, you're good with kids,' said Ellis.

'I hate them,' said Jazz firmly.

'You're a woman, you can't hate kids.'

'It's your job. You do it,' Jazz insisted.

Ellis went upstairs.

'Barnaby, stop crying,' said Ellis, standing over Barnaby's cot.

Barnaby looked at him spitefully and carried on crying.

'Listen, mate. I'm sorry about the nappies but gi' us a break,' Ellis pleaded. 'Jazz is downstairs. I don't need you crying.'

Barnaby took no notice. Ellis picked him up, tentatively, and took him downstairs. Women always knew what to do with babies.

'I don't know what to do,' said Jazz indignantly.

All women that is except Jazz.

'Tickle him maybe,' she suggested.

Ellis tickled Barnaby but his wailing continued. It was really beginning to grate on Ellis's nerves. He could understand why people hit their babies.

'Or throw him in the air.' Jazz tried again.

Ellis chucked Barnaby in the air and caught him successfully. It wasn't too difficult. And it was working. Barnaby wasn't crying much.

'You see,' said Ellis tossing Barnaby up in the air again and looking over at Jazz, 'women always know what to do . . .'

Barnaby slipped through Ellis's fingers, bounced on to the sofa and then cracked on to the floor. He lay there, eyes shut, head tilted awkwardly on one side. He was utterly still.

Ellis didn't move. His hands were still in front of him, ready to catch Barnaby. He looked down at Barnaby and thought, 'Fuck, I've killed their baby.' He wiped his mouth with the back of his hand. His body felt hot. He was shaking very slightly. 'Fuck.'

Ellis turned on Jazz. 'What the fuck did you tell me to throw him in the air for? For fuck's sake.'

'This isn't my fault. You're the one who dropped him.' Jazz was trying not to cry. Her face was taut with the strain.

'He's turning blue,' cried Ellis. 'I'm gonna go.'

'Where?' Jazz was kneeling over Barnaby, trying to find his pulse.

'Anywhere. This is murder. I've fuckin' killed it.' Ellis screwed up his eyes and rubbed his knuckles against his forehead and then rubbed his open hands on his jeans and breathed deeply.

'Don't be a twat. They know who you are.' Jazz couldn't find the pulse. She wasn't sure she was looking in the right place but Barnaby's chest wasn't moving, and when she put her face near his, she couldn't feel or hear his breath. She thought she should try mouth to mouth. She wasn't exactly sure how to do it but she'd seen it on TV before. She put her fingers in Barnaby's mouth to open it and looked to see if there was any vomit blocking his air passage. It was clear. She put her mouth over Barnaby's nose and mouth and blew very gently. Then she took her face away from his and breathed out and in again. She breathed into Barnaby, a slow shallow breath.

Ellis was quiet. He watched Jazz and sweated heavily. He couldn't help thinking of Pamela Anderson in *Baywatch*.

Jazz breathed about five breaths into Barnaby and then Barnaby breathed a breath for himself and began to cry. Jazz gathered him up into her arms. She sat on the sofa and cuddled him against her tits. Nothing had ever felt as good as this. Barnaby's tiny body felt so warm and full of life despite his tears. She wondered whether this was what it was like giving birth.

Ellis leapt up and kissed Jazz and then kissed Barnaby.

'I love you. I love you, Jazz. Will you marry me?'

'Don't be stupid.' Jazz laughed. 'Course I won't.'

'I love you. I love you. And Barnaby, mate, I'm sorry I thought you were ugly. You're the best baby in the world. You're a miracle. That's what you are, a miracle.' Ellis kissed Barnaby and Jazz. 'And you can cry as much as you want. Go on, cry. Wa, wa, wa. I don't give a shit.' Then Ellis said to Jazz, 'I think we need to celebrate properly. I'll open another bottle of champagne.'

Half a bottle of champagne later, Barnaby was asleep and Ellis and Jazz were slaughtered.

'Let's put him to bed,' said Jazz.

'Bed, I'll take you ta bed,' slurred Ellis, suddenly feeling Billy the Willy wake up.

'Come on.' Jazz led the way upstairs with Barnaby in her arms. She laid him down in his cot. Ellis stood behind her and put his arms around her. He began kissing her neck and nibbling her ear. She nuzzled into him, watching Barnaby.

'He's quite cute really,' she said.

'Not as cute as you.' Ellis could be so corny when he was pissed and horny.

Jazz turned to face him. She started snogging him. He put his hand under her shirt and squeezed her nipple, hard, so it nearly hurt. She undid his flies and held Billy in her hand and Ellis walked backwards towards the bed. His trousers slid down his legs. He felt the bed behind him and lay down on it. She lay on top of him.

'Thanks for savin' the baby,' he said. 'And savin' me.'

' 'S alright, any time,' she said and carried on kissing him.

The Crispins were having a fine time at the Griffins'. The Peterses and the Montagues were there – all very useful people to know and not such bad company either. The pheasant and cranberry sauce was delicious – Mr Griffin had shot the pheasant himself – and everyone agreed the blackcurrant tart was simply divine. So, after a few glasses of wine in such pleasant surroundings, the problem of Ellis had ceased to be quite so much of a worry for Mr and Mrs Crispin. They even told their friends about him and made something of a joke out of their 'tearaway babysitter', as they had dubbed him.

The evening's entertainment was further enlivened when Mrs Peters began to hear what sounded like a parrot talking on the baby-com. (The Griffins also had a young child and always found the baby-com most reassuring.) The Griffins assured everyone that they did not have a parrot and that their child was fast asleep and, in any case, he did not squawk like a parrot, even though at times Mr Griffin found him infuriatingly difficult to understand.

The mystery was solved with a little gossip from Mrs Griffin and the technical minds of the men. Mrs Griffin remembered that the Burtons, who lived around the corner, had a baby, a baby-com and a parrot. Mr Peters rapidly deduced that the baby-com receiver to which they were listening picked up signals from all the baby-com transmitters in the vicinity. Everyone agreed that must be the answer. However, it took Mr Peters and Mr Crispin a further fifteen minutes of scientific debate to agree on the exact physics involved. The intensity with which they debated the subject illustrated their keen search for knowledge, or, as Mrs Peters tentatively suggested, their reluctance to allow the other person to appear to know more than they did.

It was after the blackcurrant tart that the emissions from the baby-com took on an altogether different tone. First there was a crackle. Then there was a hum. Then a woman's voice cried out quite clearly, 'Oh, I love it when you do that.'

Everyone heard it. Should they ignore it or . . .

'Do what, I wonder?' said Mrs Montague, without thinking. There was no chance of ignoring it now.

Mr Montague scowled at his wife. Mr Peters cleared his throat and took a gulp of wine. Mrs Griffin looked down the table at her husband, caught his eye and burst out laughing.

'Mmm,' enthused the woman on the baby-com. 'Oh, don't stop now. Oh, God, keep going.'

'What *is* she doing?' asked Mrs Montague, wide-eyed. Her husband muttered to himself.

'Sex,' said Mrs Griffin. She was not afraid of the word. 'She's having sex.'

Mr Griffin looked at Mrs Montague and wondered how they had managed to have three children. Was it through a hole in the sheet? If it was, she must have wondered what the hole was for.

'Suck it,' the woman on the baby-com was saying. 'That's right, suck it.'

Mr Griffin looked at Mrs Montague, hoping she would not ask what the woman was doing now or more to the point what was being done to her. Mr Griffin did not like the thought of his dinner party degenerating into an impromptu sex-education class.

'I think we should turn this off,' said Mrs Crispin. 'It's verging on pornography.'

'I think it's interesting,' said Mrs Griffin who had started on the G and Ts at about four o'clock.

'Amanda,' said Mr Griffin, sternly.

'What?' said Mrs Griffin. 'Haven't you always wondered what other people say when they're having sex?' Nobody said anything. 'Well, haven't you? I do, I do all the time. I bet you all do. It's human nature. Curiosity.'

'Well, my dear, curiosity killed the cat,' said Mr Montague smugly.

'God, they are all so boring,' thought Mrs Crispin. All these boring bloody dinner parties. With boring bloody people. At least the woman on the baby-com was enjoying herself.

Mr Montague was beginning to picture the woman and a man with her. His imagination could be quite vivid at times. He could feel the blood surging in his trousers. 'Think of something utterly unsexy,' he said to himself. He thought of John Major. Rather worryingly, his penis stood firm.

'I think we should turn this off before it gets any worse,' he said.

No one replied. Everyone was longing to listen but knew they should not.

Mr Peters imagined Mrs Peters screaming these things to him in the height of passion. The trouble was there never was any passion. Hadn't been for a long time. 'Has there ever been?' he wondered.

'Oh, Ellis,' screamed the woman on the baby-com.

'Isn't your babysitter called Ellis?' said Mrs Montague, looking at Mrs Crispin. Mrs Crispin laughed affectedly, in an attempt to avoid the question. 'But he is, isn't he?' insisted Mrs Montague. 'Your "tearaway babysitter".'

'Ellis,' screamed the baby-com.

Mr Crispin stood up. 'I think we had better go home,' he said to Mrs Crispin.

Ellis heard the door slam.

'Oh, my God, they're back. They're early. Shit.' He pulled up his trousers and ran downstairs. Jazz followed.

'Hi, Mr Crispin,' Ellis smiled. 'This is a friend of mine, Jazz. Hope it's okay she . . .'

Mr Crispin was halfway up the stairs. He forced his face into Ellis's and growled, 'Have you been screwing this whore in my bed?'

'I'm not a whore,' piped up Jazz.

'Where's my son?' shouted Mr Crispin. 'I'll be surprised if you haven't killed him.'

'Ner,' Ellis smiled weakly. 'He's fine. He's asleep. He's alright.'

Mrs Crispin came out of the kitchen in floods of tears. 'The kitchen's a pigsty. It looks like a bomb's hit it. Oh, my God, treating my house like a hotel.'

Ellis wondered why all mothers came out with exactly the same phrases. Was there a phrase book for mothers?

'I'm really sorry, Mrs Crispin. I would've cleared up, only you came back sooner than you said . . .'

'And all that champagne . . .' Mrs Crispin forced the words out through her tears.

'You did say, "Help yourself to whatever's in the fridge",' replied Ellis.

'Bonking in my bed,' boomed Mr Crispin.

Ellis and Jazz retreated to the front door.

'I'll come back for my money another time,' Ellis suggested and left with Mr Crispin still shouting.

Ellis shut the door on the Crispins and on his career in babysitting. He turned to Jazz and said, 'And that's all the thanks we get for saving their baby's life? Unbelievable.'

Chapter Seven

'I owe you some money, Saul. I've half now. But, I dunno, I thought maybe you'd want this.' Loopy Liz fished around in her bag and pulled out a gun. 'I thought it might be useful. I mean, I never use it.'

'Where the fuck d'you get that?' Saul could not believe his eyes. Liz of all people, what was *she* doing with a gun?

'I dunno, picked it up somewhere and kept it.' Liz giggled. 'I've had it a while. You know, I felt safe with it in the house. Just in case.'

Saul held the gun. It was cool and dark. Just to have it there in his hand made him feel good.

Liz was not sure what Saul was thinking. He was staring silently at the gun. She needed him to take it. There was no other way she'd be able to pay him back. She hated owing people money.

'It's worth some money,' she said, trying to persuade him. 'I'm not sure how much but I know it's worth something.'

But Saul didn't need persuading. He was already sold on the idea.

'Yeah, alright, I'll take it.'

When Liz left, Saul sat on the sofa and held the gun in his hand and turned it over and smiled to himself.

'She what?' Joss did not believe it. 'Not Loopy Liz? She gave you a gun? I'm surprised she hasn't shot herself by mistake. What was *she* doing with a gun?'

'Dunno. She didn't really say. Said she'd picked it up somewhere.'

'Is that right? Well, let's see it then.'

Saul rolled back the sofa. There was the gun. Joss picked it up.

'Proper little gangster, aren't you?' said Joss, laughing.

Saul raised his eyebrows and looked at her and then looked down at his feet.

'Thought you were try'na go straight?' laughed Joss. 'This is what straight people do, is it, keep guns under their sofa?'

'Yeah, well, I didn't go out looking for it. She just gave it to me. I can always flog it or som'ing.'

'Drug dealer turned arms dealer.'

'Joss, give it a rest,' Saul snapped. 'I've got the thing now. What am I *supposed* to do with it? Chuck it away?'

'Sorry, mate. I'm not havin' a go. I jus' think it's quite funny, that's all. I mean, Christ, a gun. We're not exactly livin' in LA.'

Saul went into the kitchen.

'Cuppa tea?' he shouted back to Joss.

'Yeah, alright,' Joss shouted.

Joss was holding the gun, turning it over in her hands, examining it. She was transfixed, just as Saul had been when he first held it.

Saul came in with two cups of tea and a spliff hangin' out his mouth.

'Stick 'em up.' Joss was pointing the gun at him, arms out-stretched.

'What the fuck ya doin'?' roared Saul. 'Thing's loaded.'

'Is it?'

'Put it down for fuck's sake. Stupid cow.'

'Don't fuckin' call me a stupid cow,' Joss shouted back. 'I didn't know it was loaded, alright? You're really touchy about that thing.'

'You'd be touchy if someone pointed a loaded gun at you,' said Saul, unwinding.

'I'm sorry. I mean I wasn't gonna shoot it or anything.'

'Glad to hear it.' Saul came over to her and took the gun and put it up on the shelves.

'But don't call me a stupid cow. I can't stand it. Next you'll be asking why ya dinner isn't on the table when you come in.' Joss put on her best slob accent. 'And givin' me a good slappin', just to let me know who's boss.'

'Joss, I wouldn't ever do that.' Saul kissed her neck and lay flat out on top of her, pinning her to the floor. 'Never. I won't ever hurt you.'

'Urh,' exclaimed Joss as the breath was squeezed out of her. 'Now me, on the other hand, I've been looking for the chance to blow your brains out.' Joss started laughing.

'Oh, yeah?' Saul tickled her. Joss squirmed and giggled.

'Have you ever fired a gun?' she asked a moment later, when her giggles died down.

'No.'

'We should take your gun out and shoot it.' Joss suddenly sounded animated.

'Shoot what?' Saul lifted himself off Joss and sat up next to her.

'I dunno.' Joss shrugged. 'Pigeons, squirrels. Anything.'

'Anything that moves,' Saul joked.

'I mean it,' insisted Joss. 'What's the point in a gun if you never shoot it? It's like a car you never drive.'

Saul thought about it. Joss was right. Why did he have the gun if he didn't want to shoot it? He did want to. He just didn't have the guts to admit it. That's what he liked about Joss. She always knew what she wanted and she always went for it. Him, on the other hand, half the time he didn't even know what he wanted, let alone how to get it.

'Come on, then,' he said.

The sky was grey and spitting slightly, so the park was not busy. By the time they arrived their hair stuck to their heads in clods.

Saul had the gun in his pocket. On the walk round to the park, he'd felt it jarring against his leg. Every now and then he'd reached into his pocket to touch it. It was strange how good it made him feel. It made him strut and look the raggas in the eye and think, 'Fuck you'. When they went into the corner shop to buy some fags, Saul looked at the guy behind the counter and thought, 'You don't know what's in my pocket, you don't know what I could do.'

They laughed and chatted but neither of them mentioned the gun.

In the park, they hopped over the fence into the wooded area. Saul shot at and missed a couple of squirrels before they decided to climb a tree for a better vantage point.

' 'Ere, let's see who's the best shot,' said Joss, taking the gun off Saul. 'Look, try 'n' hit that tree.'

'Ner, there's not enough bullets to mess around,' said Saul.

'Come on, it's a laugh. There's fuck all else to hit.' Joss picked out a tree. 'There, that one.' She aimed and fired and hit the tree. 'Ha!' She grinned. 'I did it. You have a go. Bet you can't hit it.'

'Tt, course I can.' Saul took the gun, fired at the tree and missed.

'Ha, ha,' laughed Joss. 'You're crap. That was way off.'

Saul suddenly heard something in the bushes. He pointed the gun and fired it. There was a squeal.

'You hit something. You fuckin' hit something,' said Joss, jumping down from the tree.

'What the fuck was it?' Saul jumped down after her.

They looked around in the bushes until they found it. It was a poodle. It lay in the undergrowth, its legs splayed. It was barely breathing. It quivered slightly as Joss and Saul approached and then looked up at them slowly with deep dark eyes. It was shaved to the skin except for pompom balls of white fur around each of its paws, so it was easy to see where the bullet had penetrated.

The skin looked as thin and delicate as tissue paper. The poodle's haircut looked ridiculous as it lay there dying.

Joss nearly laughed but then she did not. Saul began to walk away.

'Let's go,' he said.

They walked home in silence. Saul did not strut or put his hand in his pocket to feel the gun. He did not look anyone in the eye. He thought, 'That's the second thing you've killed.'

He was walking fast and by the time he reached the flat, Joss was some way behind. He went in on his own, leaving the door open for her. He walked straight to the bathroom for a slash. When he was finished, he turned around and saw his face in the mirror above the basin. He looked himself in the eye.

'You prat,' he said out loud. 'You stupid prat. You can't get anything right. You fuck it all up, don't you?' He looked away in disgust. Christ. Sometimes he hated being himself. He hated having to wake up and look at that stupid face, that face that everyone else seemed to think was so perfect. He hated it. Why couldn't he take a break? Get away from everything, including himself.

He ran the cold tap and lay his hands in the basin. The water poured cool over his hands and wrists. He let it settle in his hand and then flicked it up into his face and over his head to rinse his thoughts clear.

'You are you. There's nothing you can do except be you.'

But he shut his eyes for a second and they filled with the image of the boy lying dead in the undergrowth. The boy was there and then the dog. Both had skin the colour of death – cold, pale blue.

Saul opened his eyes quickly and went into the sitting room.

Joss was back. Saul didn't look at her. She saw his face, pale and distant.

'You alright?' she asked.

'No, I'm not alright,' snapped Saul. 'I just shot that dog. Remember?'

'Alright, Saul, I was only asking.'

'If you hadn't told me to take that gun,' Saul was shouting. 'You and your fucking "can't have a gun and not shoot it".'

'I knew you'd blame me,' Joss shouted back. 'It isn't my fault, y'know. You have got a mind of yer own.'

Saul had known he was going to blame Joss, as well. He had known and he had tried to stop himself. But he had not been able to. The words had tumbled out in her face. It was so much easier to blame her and shout at her, than to be silent on his own and see those faces in his head and hear his own voice cussing him and cussing him, until it became unbearable.

So he blamed her again. 'I wouldn't have been there if you hadn't gone on and on.'

'I didn't go on and on,' said Joss.

' "Can't have a gun and not shoot it." ' Saul imitated her voice. ' "Like a car you never drive." '

'You shot the fuckin' thing. You're only shouting at me cos you feel like shit.'

Saul opened his mouth to shout back. But then didn't. They both knew she was right. They were silent. Joss wondered whether Saul was going to carry on shouting. Saul was trying to work out what he wanted to say.

'I just . . . I dunno.' He wanted to tell her what was going on inside his head. How he was beginning to despise himself. How the face of that boy would not go away. He'd think he was alright. He'd think he was holding it down, staying in control of the voices and the fear he was feeling. Then suddenly it would all come flooding back again. He wanted to tell Joss but he did not know how to untangle his feelings enough to put them into words. 'It was such a stupid thing to do,' was all he could say.

'It was just a dog, Saul.'

Saul thought, 'No, it wasn't. It was him, as well.' But he said, 'I killed it. I shouldn't've killed it.'

'You didn't mean to. It was an accident,' Joss said. Why was Saul taking it so seriously? 'It's not like you saw it and shot it.'

'But what the fuck was I doing? I always fuck up. I always fuck everything up.'

'Don't be stupid.' Joss paused and let out a heavy breath. 'Look, maybe it was kinda my fault. I shouldn't've said to take the gun out.' She laughed half a laugh.

'But I pulled the trigger, didn't I? I pulled the trigger.' Saul looked up and looked Joss in the eye.

'Saul, get it together,' she said firmly. He was freaking her out the way he was talking. 'It's done. You didn't mean to do it. There's nothing you can do about it now. So don't wallow in it. I mean, Christ, it's only a poodle.' She laughed again. 'Think yerself lucky, mate. Could've been some kid. Then we'd really be up shit creek.'

Saul thought, 'But he was a kid.' Jamie lay in the undergrowth and opened his eyes and looked at Saul.

'Donatella,' shouted Tash. 'Donatella.'

Shit, where was that dog? Shouldn't have let her off the lead. Lady Parknell had said don't let her off the lead. But Donatella'd been pulling against it. Full of energy. Tash had found her hard to control. It'd irritated her that Donatella wouldn't listen. And Tash had felt sorry for her which had surprised her. She hated that dog. Always had done. So fucking precious. Not allowed off the lead in case she hurt herself. And fed strictly on sirloin steak. All so she could be strutted around and shown off at namby-pamby dog shows.

Tash had thought, 'Fuck it, why can't she run free for once in her life? Live like a normal dog. Do what she wants to do.' So Tash had let her off the lead.

Now Tash was beginning to regret it. As soon she'd unleashed Donatella, the dog had streaked across the lawn. She'd run so fast, it'd seemed she might never stop. Tash had quickly lost sight of her. She glimpsed her again in the wooded part of the park, sniffing amongst the undergrowth. Tash had called her. Donatella had heard, looked up and then ignored her. Freedom was too good to give up so easily. She was having fun. She'd never known there were so many smells to be sniffed here. She wasn't going to hurry back to the lead.

'Donatella,' shouted Tash again. Shit. What if she never came back? Or if she did come back and there was the slightest blemish on her? Tash would be in deep shit. Whoops. Hadn't wanted to take the dog for a walk in the first place. But Lady Parknell's arthritis was playing up again and she couldn't take Donatella out. Tash's mum had said, 'Tash won't mind, will you, Tash?' She'd said it in front of Lady Parknell, knowing Tash couldn't refuse. God, she could be a bitch sometimes. She knew how Tash hated that dog. Why couldn't she walk it herself, if she was so keen to help out Lady Parknell? She didn't have anything better to do. She was bored stiff at home all day. Polishing and cleaning. Hoovering and dusting. After the Filipina had done it all once already. And then repolishing and redusting. Tash thought perhaps her mum had known something would happen to Donatella. Perhaps she was willing something to go wrong. Because then she'd have an excuse to have a go at Tash.

'Donatella, Donatella,' shouted Tash.

A man came up to her and said, 'Lost your dog, dear?'

Tash looked at the man and wondered why people found it necessary to ask such stupid questions. She felt like saying, 'No, I've lost my false teeth. They're called Donatella. Have you seen them?'

But instead, she said, 'That's right. She's a poodle.'

'Oh, haven't seen her, I'm sorry to say,' the man replied. 'Lovely dogs poodles.'

'If you say so,' thought Tash.

Tash decided that if Donatella wasn't going to come to Tash, Tash would have to go and find her. She hopped over the fence and into the wooded area. She looked about and called a couple more times. It was strange how quickly she found Donatella. It was almost as if she knew where the dog would be. The dog was almost dead. Tash could see that straight away. Donatella was scarcely breathing. Her eyes were nearly shut. She opened them a little more when Tash approached. Tash knelt down beside her. Donatella seemed to be trying to lift her head. She moved almost imperceptibly and then sank back as if resigned to die.

Tash looked at Donatella's body. There was a hole in her chest. 'Shit, she's been shot.' Tash sighed. 'Why did this have to happen to me? How many dogs are shot in Holland Park? And it has to be the one I'm looking after.' Tash thought about giving Donatella mouth to mouth. Not for long. But the thought did cross her mind. What the hell were you supposed to do?

Donatella breathed her final breath and slipped to death.

Tash laughed, a false, forced laugh, and then cried in disbelief. This couldn't be happening. No, this really couldn't be happening. All she'd had to do was take the dog for a walk and look, look what had happened.

'Shit, the stupid bitch,' she said. She wasn't sure who to. Perhaps to Donatella for dying on her. Or to Lady Parknell for having a dog who could do that. Or to her mum for volunteering her to take Donatella out.

Tash closed her eyes for a moment, hoping that when she opened them again, the dog would be gone or would be bounding back through the bushes, alive. Tash opened her eyes. The dog was definitely dead.

'Shit, shit, shit.' Tash stood up and paced up and down, puffing her cheeks up and breathing out slowly. No, this wasn't happening. Really, it couldn't be happening.

But every time she looked down, there was the dog. Living proof. Or rather, dead proof, that it was happening.

'Shit.' Tash was going to have to do something.

★

'Mum, hi, it's Tash. Errr . . .' Tash said when her mum answered the phone. Tash suddenly didn't know what to say. She'd been practising over and over in her head what she would say. Things like, 'I'm sorry but she's dead.' Like they say in films when the hero finally dies after a brave struggle. Or, 'She's been shot. Yes. Shot dead.' But suddenly, when the words were meant to come, nothing came. 'Um . . . er . . . um.'

'Yes.' Tash's mother sounded impatient, as always.

'Er, I don't know how to put this. Er . . . er.' Tash really didn't know what to say and then suddenly the words fell out. 'Donatella's dead. She's been shot dead in the park.' There, it was said.

She had to say it a few more times before her mother would believe her. Finally she did. She found out exactly where Tash was, told her to wait and put the phone down.

It was perhaps fifteen minutes, perhaps half an hour, before the ambulance arrived. Tash was surprised to see it. But not half as surprised as the ambulance men were when they discovered their patient was a dog.

'You shot a poodle in the park?' said Chelsea incredulously.

'Well, yeah, Saul did,' said Joss, wondering whether it really was true or not.

'A poodle in the park.' Chelsea thought maybe it would sound more believable second time round. It did not. 'Why? Got something against poodles, have you?'

'Loopy Liz gave Saul this gun cos she owed him some money.'

'Loopy Liz. What was she doing with a gun?'

'Fuck knows,' continued Joss. 'But anyway she gave it to Saul. So I said, you know, let's go down the park and shoot it. I mean you can't have a gun and not shoot it.'

'No,' agreed Chelsea. 'It's like having a cock that's never sucked.'

'Exactly. That's what I said to Saul.' Joss was glad Chelsea

79

understood. 'So we ended up in the park. It was quite fun really. Like all those 'Nam movies.'

'What, shooting squirrels in the park?' Chelsea was trying to imagine Sylvester Stallone hunting down squirrels in Holland Park.

'Y'know what I mean.'

'Ever thought about joining the TA?' suggested Chelsea.

'No,' replied Joss.

She stopped telling her story until Chelsea said, 'Well, go on then. How did the poodle come into it?'

'I dunno, we were jus' messing around and then Saul fired and hit something.'

'And it was a poodle.' Chelsea was laughing.

'Chelsea, don't laugh,' said Joss but it was a relief to not be too serious about it. 'It was sad. The way that dog looked at me with its big brown eyes. I won't ever forget that.'

'Pity you didn't have a camera with you.' Chelsea held her laughter for a moment. 'You could have sold the picture to Athena for one of those "Why?" posters.' She burst into hysterics again. She laughed so infectiously that Joss had to join in. They laughed until their guts ached. Joss was glad to have the chance to laugh. Saul was so serious at the moment.

Neighbours had just finished. Chelsea flipped through the channels with the remote control and stopped on *London Tonight* when she heard the words, 'Prizewinning poodle was shot dead in Holland Park today.'

'Joss,' Chelsea shrieked. 'Joss, they've got it on the news.'

'Fuckin' hell,' exclaimed Joss.

'No. No way. Imagine getting nicked for shooting a dog.'

'Don't say that, Chelsea. Shut up, I wanna listen.'

The telly showed a man in a suit standing in the wooded area of the park. He was saying, 'Yes, we are here at the, er, scene of the, er, shooting, which took place only this afternoon. The, er, the dog's owner, Lady Parknell, wife of the eminent judge, is too upset to, er, to comment . . .'

'Well, no wonder they've got it on the news.' Chelsea tossed her head. 'The dog only belonged to a fucking judge.'

'Sshhh,' said Joss. 'I can't hear.'

The reporter continued, '. . . head of the Royal Parks Constabulary.'

There was now a policeman standing next to him. 'Well, yes, we are of course, um, doing . . .' He shifted from one foot to the other. He was slightly nervous, seeing as it was his first time on television. '. . . doing all we can to, er, to apprehend the miscreants who perpetrated this, er, felonious crime of proportions, er, disproportionate to that which we, here at the Royal Parks Constabulary, are accustomed . . .' He drew in a deep breath and continued. 'Particularly working and living hereabouts in such beautiful, er, beautiful surroundings – and at this point I would like to say a hearty thanks to all the gardeners here who have, er, been working and are, er, working and will indeed continue to work throughout the summer to make the park what it is – a beautiful, er, oasis in the midst of the metropolitan capital of England . . .' He paused, trying to remember the point he was making. 'And of course not, we hope, er, a place in which people will needlessly gun down innocent animals as sadly happened here today.'

The interviewer looked a little unnerved.

'Er, yes, er, thank you,' he said, regaining his composure. 'That was the head of the Royal Parks Constabulary. And this is Tim Wallaby reporting from Holland Park. Thank you.'

'Oh, my God,' said Chelsea. 'Saul's got all the parks police after him.'

'Well, if that one's anything to go by, he hasn't got much to worry about,' retorted Joss.

'He'd better get rid of that gun.'

'Oh, fucking hell, what a twat!' Joss shook her head. 'How can he've done that? Shoot a fuckin' judge's dog.'

'He'll be alright,' insisted Chelsea. 'They're not seriously going to come looking for him over a dog, are they?'

'Ner, s'pose not,' said Joss. But she still felt uneasy. 'He's gonna lose it if he sees this. He was gutted this afternoon when it happened.' Joss thought of Saul. She was worried about him at the moment. He didn't seem himself, not since finding that kid at Doppingdean. 'Oh, God, I don't wanna go back. I don't wanna see him. He'll only flip out.'

It was dark down by the canal. Dark, except for the headlights driving over the bridge. The light splashed on the water and shattered.

Saul stood under the bridge where the night was darkest. He looked around and, seeing no one, pulled out the gun. He had gone there to get rid of it but now it sat heavy in his hand. He did not throw it.

Saul looked into the water and saw Jamie's face. The ripples twisted the image. Saul's jaw felt tight. His body seemed dead. The gun was still in his hand. Jamie's face rippled. Saul saw the dog, dead in the dirt. He saw its skin torn open.

'You did that,' he said to himself. 'You did both those things.' His teeth pushed hard against each other. His eyes were full. 'It was your fault. You're worth nothing.' He didn't see the light falling on the water as a car drove past. 'Nothing. Nothing at all.' His whole being was tense with anger and frustration. 'Even Joss is beginning to hate you. Even she can't bear being with you.' He held up the gun against his head, pushing it hard into his temple, so hard he thought the skin would split. His head shook in spasms. His mouth opened. 'Can't even do that.' He hurled the gun into the dark and heard the canal swallow and spit. 'Can't even do that, you're so weak.'

Chapter Eight

There was a knock on the door. Saul went to answer it. It was Chelsea.

'Saul, I've been meaning to tell you this for a while.' She looked him in the eye. Her eyes were cold and dark. Almost violet. Saul had never noticed before. 'The thing is, Saul,' Chelsea drew a sharp breath, 'I don't like you. Never have done. Probably never will.'

Saul felt weak. Helpless. Chelsea and him were quite good mates, he thought.

She followed him into the living room, saying, 'Don't know why I didn't tell you sooner. Don't like you at all. Hate you in fact.'

The living room was full of Saul's mates. When he came in, they started nudging each other, winking and giggling. He span around, looking from face to face. They were whispering about him. But loud enough so he could hear.

'Arrogant,' they were saying. 'Selfish . . .' 'Tosser . . .' 'Dickhead . . .' 'Never liked him.' Their voices became louder and louder, till they were shouting. 'Wanker . . . Prat . . . The things he says . . . Thinks he's so cool . . . What a prat.'

Saul screamed. 'But why didn't you tell me?'

'Didn't want to hurt you,' said Chelsea.

'Don't give a shit now,' someone else said. And they all began to laugh.

But Saul knew it was not a joke.

★

When Saul woke up, he looked about in the dark, half expecting them all to be still there. But there was no one except Joss, lying next to him asleep. He touched her softly and whispered, 'You still love me, don't you?'

But he didn't feel sure of anything.

Saul stood at the window and looked down at the street outside. A dog was settling himself to shit on the doorstep. At the same time a couple were letting themselves into the house. They must live in the flat downstairs. The couple clocked the dog and the man kicked out at it. The dog yelped and skulked off down the street.

Saul watched as the couple disappeared into the house. They looked strangely familiar – the woman, scrawny and blonde, the man, small and his head shaven. Had he met them before somewhere? Probably just coming and going on the street. Funny how easy it was to get a false sense of familiarity.

And then Saul noticed it.

The car across the street. It'd been there yesterday too. Saul might be uncertain about the couple but he was sure about this.

There was a man sitting in it now. What was he doing? He didn't seem to be doing much, drumming his fingers on the steering wheel. He took out a notebook and started writing. What *was* he doing? What was he writing? He couldn't be, could he? Not watching Saul.

'No,' Saul said to himself. 'Don't think that. That's stupid. Don't even think it.'

But then what else was he doing? Why had that car been there two days in a row? Saul hadn't seen it round here before. The bloke definitely looked like a copper. The short hair, that 'tache. And the motor was new as well.

The bloke glanced up at Saul and caught his eye. Saul froze.

He *was* watching him. It wasn't such a dumb idea. Pigs did watch people. How else did they know when to bust people? Or whether they should?

Saul moved quickly away from the window. He nearly drew the curtains but then he thought, 'Ner, too obvious.'

He didn't know what to do. He wiped his mouth with his sleeve and went to the stereo to put on a tune.

'Have a spliff. Chill out.' He sat down and rolled a spliff, making sure he was out of view of the window. When it was lit, he went to make himself a cup of tea. But the spliff and the tea did not calm him down. His mind began to race. Thoughts spun chaotically in his head.

'Might not be about dealing. Could be about that dog. Thank God I dashed the gun. But still someone might've seen. They must've done. Maybe I didn't see them, but they saw me.'

Saul wasn't sure what to do. When was he going to get busted? Should he chuck away his drugs? Or keep them? What should he do?

The doorbell rang. It was Ellis.

'Alright,' said Ellis, walking behind Saul into the living room.

Saul suddenly remembered his dream and wondered whether he could trust Ellis. Was Ellis really his mate?

'Don't think about that,' Saul said to himself. 'Don't think about it. It was just a dream. The man outside. The man watching you. Think about him. That's what's important.'

Ellis didn't know what was wrong with Saul. He was in a right state. Kept going on about some bloke outside. Thought he was watching him.

'He's watching me,' Saul was saying. 'He's watching me, I know he is. *You* have a look.'

Ellis took a look out the window. The bloke did look kinda like a pig. That short hair. And he glanced up at the window as Ellis watched. But all the same, Saul was being a bit para. People waited in cars all the time. Didn't mean they were watching you. And a bloke could have short hair without being a pig.

Saul was really in a state, pacing up and down, cussing, pulling at his hair. Ellis had never seen him like this. Saul had always been cool and in control.

Ellis felt himself beginning to be sucked into Saul's paranoia. Saul could be right. He did shift a lot of drugs and he'd been living in the same place for a while. The pigs might know the flat. Quite a few people had bin nicked recently. It could happen to Saul. You never knew.

'Well, how long's he bin there?' asked Ellis.

'Don't know, could've bin there a couple of days,' said Saul. 'I don't know.'

Ellis paused. 'Well, how long've you seen him there?'

'Today, just now,' Saul replied. 'But the car was there yesterday too. What d'you reckon I should do? Do you think I should get rid of my drugs or what?'

'You've only seen it today?' Ellis relaxed. Saul was overreacting. The bloke was probably only waiting for someone. 'I wouldn't worry about it. He'll probably be gone in a while.'

'But this bloke wants some pills,' Saul said, looking wildly at Ellis. 'I can't get 'em with that bloke sitting outside. It's not safe. He might follow me.'

Ellis didn't understand the problem. 'Either get the pills or don't,' he thought.

'Say you can't get them,' he suggested.

'I've gotta get them. He's already given me the money,' said Saul urgently. 'But I can't get them, not with that bloke out there.' He looked furtively towards the window. A voice inside his head repeated. 'Gotta get them. But you can't. Gotta get them. But you can't.' Saul felt like a dog chasing its tail.

Ellis still didn't understand the problem. Why didn't Saul give the money back? He seemed intent on winding himself up. Then he had an idea.

'Why don't I get them for you?' Ellis could help Saul out and earn himself a bit of cash at the same time.

A fog seemed to lift in Saul's mind. That was it. That was the answer. Let Ellis take the risk. The bloke in the car wouldn't be watching Ellis.

'Yeah,' he said. 'Yeah. You can get 'em. I'll pay you for it.'

Saul found the money and counted it out to Ellis. There was a grand there. Saul wanted him to get a couple of hundred. They both knew the bloke who did the pills, so he should be alright about Ellis going round there. Saul gave him a ring just to let him know. There was no problem. Ellis was all set to go.

'D'you wanna take this jacket?' Saul said, holding out a black puffa. 'You can stash 'em in the lining. It's thick enough for people not to notice 'em.'

'Cheers,' Ellis said as he took the jacket.

'Now, don't fuck up,' Saul said as Ellis left.

'Who d'you think I am?' replied Ellis.

When Ellis was gone, Saul suddenly wondered whether it had been such a good idea. He remembered his dream. And he thought, 'Can I really trust Ellis?'

Chelsea's husband-to-be was sat on the bar stool waiting for Chelsea's double gin and tonic and his own Coke. He was a short man and as he sat there his legs dangled uncomfortably in mid-air. Chelsea thought he looked like a child perched on its high chair. The nervous way he talked endlessly also made him seem childlike.

'Oh, yes, Chelsea,' he was saying with his heavy Indian accent. 'Chelsea. It is a very lovely name. Yes. But I was finding it very, very difficult to remember.'

'Really?' said Chelsea, coldly, hoping Deepak, as he was called, would get the hint and stop talking.

Deepak misunderstood and felt encouraged to tell Chelsea a story. 'Oh, I mus' tell you dis. It is very funny.' Deepak chuckled to himself. 'I was finding your name very difficult, so my friend, he was saying to me, "It is easy. Think Kensington and Chelsea and den dere will be no problem to remember." He say to me many times, "Kensington and Chelsea." But dat was not helping me. I keep calling Kensington.' Deepak chuckled to himself again, clearly delighted with his story. 'Ha, ha, ha! Not Kensington, Chelsea', he repeated. Chelsea seemed to be a little slow getting the joke. 'Now, I know, you would not be very happy with me if I was always calling you Kensington, all of de time.'

'Shall we go and sit down somewhere?' said Chelsea, impatiently.

'But Chelsea, we are already sitting down here,' Deepak looked confused. He thought perhaps Chelsea was a little simple.

'Oh, my God,' thought Chelsea. 'The man's an idiot.' She got up, taking her drink with her, and went to find a table.

Deepak followed obediently. Once they were both sat down, he started talking again. 'I have been watching dis film, dis *Green Card*. You have seen dis one?'

Chelsea nodded and took another mouthful of gin.

Deepak continued. 'Very good film. Very funny. She look like you, I tink. What is her name?'

'Andie MacDowell,' Chelsea said shortly. What a compliment! She tried to stop herself smiling. It was always best to act as though people said things like that about her all the time. But now he came to mention it, she could see the similarities.

'Oh, yes,' Deepak said dreamily. 'Just like you.' And then he became a little more serious. 'I have been practising, you know. I am remembering soap. Because dis is how dis man in de film, dis man with big nose. He was forgetting his soap and he was sent home. But I am remembering soap. I will be having no problem dere.'

'What the fuck is he going on about?' Chelsea wondered.

'Ah, you are looking surprised, Chelsea. I know it very, very difficult remembering all dese soaps. Dere are many. But I have big brain.' Deepak tapped his head and laughed. 'Do not worry, I am remembering dem all. Dove. Johnson. Pears. Coal tar. Palmolive. Imperial Leather. All dese I am remembering. Whichever one you are using, I will be remembering.'

Chelsea was confused. Why didn't he just remember the one she used rather than every soap that existed? Still, if he wanted to spend his time remembering the names of soaps, that was his problem.

Deepak settled into his seat with a broad grin on his face. He was pleased with himself. It had taken him a long time to remember so many soaps. She must be proud of him too.

Chelsea thought Deepak had finally finished talking but he lurched forward again and said, quietly, as if confiding a secret, 'But we must not be falling in love like in dis film *Green Card*.'

'I don't think there's any danger of that,' said Chelsea with great certainty.

'Me?' said Deepak. 'I am not so sure.' And he sat there looking at Chelsea with doting eyes in a way that made her feel terribly uncomfortable.

So she gulped down the rest of her drink and said, 'Any chance of another gin and tonic?'

Deepak snapped himself out of his reverie and scurried off to the bar.

The marriage was being arranged by an intermediary, a friend of Chelsea's father. He'd suggested that she jot down a few questions to ask Deepak when they met, so she could begin to form a 'dossier' on him. It was essential that they knew each other well for the immigration interview and the sooner they started the better. So Chelsea had bought a little note pad and had thought up a few questions to ask Deepak. When he came back, she launched into the first question, pen at the ready in order to make a note of his answer.

'Now, Deepak,' she said, sternly, so that he would know that she meant business and didn't want him going off on a tangent once again. 'I'm doing a sort of questionnaire on you so that I can begin to get to know all your likes and dislikes. Right, first question is, what is your favourite colour?'

'Oh, dat question is very difficult, very difficult.' He clasped his hands together to think. 'Really, I am not knowing. Sometimes I am liking yellow best, sometimes red. Oh, dearie me. I do not know.'

'Well,' said Chelsea feeling impatient. 'I'll put down both.'

'But green is really a wonderful colour also.'

Chelsea sighed. Deepak was beginning to get on her tits.

Ellis had the pills. They were safely stashed in Saul's jacket which he had on. Everything was under control. And then – Ellis couldn't see what happened exactly, he was sitting too far at the back of the bus – he just felt the bus jam on its brakes and thirty bodies lurched forwards and he heard a woman shout, 'Could've all been killed.'

Then the bus pulled up on the other side of the street. The driver was talking to a woman stood on the pavement. People were straining to see what was going on. Ellis strained with them but he couldn't quite see the woman.

'Course it's retribution, you know.' It was an old woman on the back seat of the bus. 'The Almighty punishes the wicked and rewards the deserving.'

The woman next to her nodded and tried to smile.

People were getting restless. They began to stand up. But the doors at the front of the bus were still shut, and no one got off.

So everyone simply stood and waited rather than sat and waited.

Then a man-with-a-mind-of-his-own pushed his way to the front.

'What the fuck's going on?' he asked the driver. 'Can't you just drive off?'

'She won't move her car till the police get here,' the driver said. 'Thinks it's my fault.'

'Oh,' exclaimed an old woman still sitting near the door. 'Did we crash, dear? How excitin'! Excitin' things never usually happen to me.'

The driver opened the doors and everyone on the bus fell out on to the road. And there was the cause of all the trouble, a scratch, maybe a couple of inches long and the width of a hair, just above the wheel arch on the side of a gleaming silver Saab.

Ellis looked, and looked again. It was Chelsea's car and there was Chelsea mouthing off about police and no-claim bonuses. 'Trust Chelsea,' thought Ellis.

'What you makin' such a fuss about?' shouted the man-with-a-mind-of-his-own. ''S only a tiny scratch.'

Chelsea stood her ground. 'That's five hundred quids' worth of damage,' she insisted.

'Five hundred quid? What garage d'you go to?' exclaimed the man-with-a-mind-of-his-own. 'I'll do it for a couple've hundred.'

Ellis was wondering whether he should slink off – after all, he did have all those pills on him and he didn't want to be around if the police were going to get involved. Or should he try and help Chelsea out? They were mates.

'Ellis!' cried Chelsea as she spotted him.

His decision was made for him, he couldn't ignore her now. He wandered over to her.

Chelsea thought she'd found an ally. 'Ellis, you know about cars, tell them how much a respray costs.'

'Um, those touch-up paints are very good,' he said diplomatically.

Chelsea was not impressed. 'Touch-up paint,' she repeated.

'I'll even do it for you,' Ellis suggested. He just wanted to get out of there as quickly as possible. He tapped Saul's jacket, where the pills were stashed and nodded knowingly. 'Come on, let's get out of here.'

Chelsea looked at him and took the hint. She moved towards her car reluctantly. 'But don't think I'm going to forget this. I've got your number plate,' she called out to the bus driver as she started the engine.

Ellis got in the passenger seat.

Chelsea was fuming. She wouldn't stop moaning. 'Didn't use his mirrors at all. And then he has the audacity to blame me. Can you believe it?' She didn't wait for Ellis's reply. 'Fucking cheek of it. Should've waited for the police. Why were you so desperate to get away? You got some things on you?'

'Yeah,' replied Ellis. 'Some pills I got for Saul.' He felt the jacket where the pills were hidden, just to check they were still there. Yeah, still there.

'Well, if it hadn't been for you I would have waited. I mean, did you see what happened? Did you see?'

'Couldn't really see from where I was.' Ellis was relieved he hadn't seen. Chances were it had been Chelsea's fault and he'd hate to have to be the one to tell her.

'I've had a dreadful day,' continued Chelsea, not really hearing what Ellis had said. 'Met my husband today. He was such a bore. Couldn't believe it. And thick as two short planks.' Chelsea swerved as she pulled out in front of a car. 'Fucking drivers. See what I'm up against?'

Ellis said nothing.

But he didn't need to; Chelsea carried on all the same. 'Yeah, I can't believe I'm actually going to marry the bloke. Can't fucking believe it.' And then she remembered. 'But he did think I looked like Andie MacDowell.' She smiled at the thought. 'I do rather, don't I?' She lifted her head up so she could see her face in the mirror. When she looked back to the road, she was heading for a parked car. She swerved once more and was beeped at by the car behind. 'What, you fucking wanker?' she shouted at the car. She glanced over at Ellis as she said, 'What did I tell you? These fucking drivers.'

Ellis grunted. He thought he'd better reassure her that he was still listening.

Chelsea sighed. 'God, I could do with a drink. Look, there's a pub. Shall we stop?' Chelsea pulled in and parked, not bothering to wait for an answer.

Ellis wasn't going to refuse a free drink or two. But he didn't want to let Saul down either. Ellis knew Saul was relying on him to bring those pills home safely. Ellis was determined he wasn't gonna fuck up. He kept tapping the jacket, just to check they were still there. Yup, still there. Sound. He should stop worrying. Nothing could happen. It was all under control. But still, maybe he should give Saul a quick ring to let him know the score. Saul'd bin pretty paranoid earlier and Ellis didn't want to give him anything else to worry about.

Ellis got up. 'Just gonna use the phone,' he said to Chelsea.

Ellis dialled Saul's number – he knew it by heart – but there was something wrong with the phone. When Saul answered, he couldn't hear Ellis. But the phone still gulped down the money.

'Fucking pay phones,' thought Ellis. When he got back to the table Chelsea had bought him another pint.

'I feel like getting absolutely slaughtered,' she was saying.

Ellis was halfway down his pint. He was beginning to feel very pissed. Strangely pissed for only a pint and a half. Chelsea was giggling to herself.

'What? What?' asked Ellis.

'Feeling pissed?' she asked. 'There's a double whisky in that as well. And in the last one.'

Ellis really didn't want to get too pissed. He had to sort those pills out. Couldn't let Saul down. Mustn't.

'There's a party later,' said Chelsea. 'Wanna go?'

'Yeah, wicked,' replied Ellis.

'Shit, the pills,' he was thinking. 'Gotta sort them out. Mustn't get too pissed.'

But it was too late, he was already rat-arsed. He kept thinking about going round to Saul's but then couldn't be bothered cos he felt too pissed, or Chelsea would distract him by talking about going to the party. And Ellis was like a puppy following its nose – he followed fun wherever it led him. So, when it came to closing time and Chelsea said, 'How about that party then?', Ellis said, 'Yeah, alright.' And the pills were forgotten.

Chapter Nine

The party was in a disused sports centre that'd been squatted. Ellis and Chelsea had a wander round. It was only just gone midnight, so things were still pretty quiet. The main sound was only just being set up in the sports hall. There were lines on the floor marking out courts for various sports – badminton, tennis, football. The squash courts were empty except for a few people having a spliff and a couple of other people having a . . . were they shagging? Yup, they were. Ellis made an embarrassed retreat. Chelsea shouted out, 'Call that a knob? That's a needle, not a knob.'

The needle-knob wilted at the suggestion.

The chill-out sound was already set up in what used to be the swimming pool. The pool was drained. It was now covered with a thin layer of green algae. People were climbing up and down the stepladders that led into the pool. It looked totally surreal.

'Hasn't really got going yet, has it?' said Chelsea, looking for her wrap of coke. When she found it, she squatted down and chopped them out a line each. They snorted them and then Chelsea said, 'How about we do one of those pills each?'

'Oh, ner, I can't, Chelsea,' said Ellis. He hated these tests of his will-power. 'I can't.'

'Oh, alright then.' Chelsea was irritated and then she thought about it and thought about the position Ellis was in. She mustn't bully him. It wasn't fair. He was so weak-willed anyway. 'I'm sorry. I'll go and buy us some. I won't let you take any of Saul's. You can rely on me.'

Chelsea went off to find some pills.

When she was gone, Ellis suddenly felt worried about the pills. What was he doing at a party with two hundred of someone else's pills on him? What a nutter! He was heading for a disaster. He knew it.

Chelsea came back, mission accomplished. They dropped one each.

'I'd better go and phone Saul,' said Ellis. He'd phone him and if he was in, Ellis'd take the pills round there.

Outside, Ellis had a look around for a phone. He didn't know this area. Wasn't even sure where he was exactly. So he wandered off, hoping to come across a phone.

He found one a few streets away. He was just coming up strong on the pill. Rushing heavily. He lifted the receiver, put in some money and dialled.

BT's computer voice answered. 'The number you have dialled has not been recognized. Please check and try again.'

Shit. What was Saul's number? 969 8537. Or was it 960? Ellis tried again. A Spanish-sounding woman answered. Wrong number. Shit. 969 8375. 969 8373. Ellis couldn't think straight at all now. Loads of variations were going round in his head. They all sounded vaguely familiar. But which one was right?

He tried a couple more times. Two more wrong numbers.

'Fuck it,' he thought. 'He can't say I didn't try.'

Saul was sitting at home. The telly was on but he wasn't really watching. How could he? All he could think about was Ellis and those fucking pills. A grand of someone else's money. Shit, where the fuck was he? Saul should've known Ellis would fuck up. Probably at some party caning them all. How could Saul've done that? How could he've asked Ellis of all people to get them for him?

'You stupid fucking twat,' he said to himself. 'You stupid twat.'

Just cos've that bloke in the car outside. He was gone now. He'd gone just after Ellis left. He probably hadn't bin watching Saul.

'You stupid twat. You're so fuckin' para, you can't think straight. Can't get someone else to do things for you. Let alone Ellis.'

Saul flipped the channel over, suddenly bored of what was in front of him. He relit the spliff in the ashtray.

'I'll fuckin' kill him when I see him. I'll wrap a fuckin' baseball bat round his fuckin' head, the piece of shit. And I'll enjoy every minute of it. Crack his skull open. Put him in fuckin' hospital. That'll teach him to mess around with me. That'll fuckin' teach him.'

The party had really got going now. Chelsea had bought them another couple of pills each. She was by the speakers, jacking. She could feel the bass shuddering through her body. Ellis was off on the blag, chatting to people asking them for money or a bit've hash to skin up with.

Joss was sitting back on her heels, leaning against the wall. She could see Ellis, but he hadn't seen her yet. It was funny watching him at work. He was so good at it. He'd smile so sweetly and dance his eyes around. And squirm like a little kid not wanting to cause any trouble. And nearly every time he got what he wanted. You had to admire him – a master blagger.

Joss'd done a couple of pills and drunk a bit. She was fucked but not totally wasted. She never seemed to get completely off her head any more. No matter what she did, she always remained in control, holding something back.

97

'Not like them,' she thought, looking at some of the kids dancing in front of her. They were dancing manically, making boxes with their hands or skipping from one foot to the other like boxers. Joss noticed one girl in particular. She was not dancing in such a crazy way as the others but still she was moving with incredible energy and a huge grin plastered on her face. As she danced, she gazed around the room with a look of childlike wonderment.

Joss remembered a couple of years back, when she herself had looked like that, when everything about this scene had seemed new and exciting. It had seemed like a new beginning, not just for her, but for everyone. She was part of a new generation with new ideas and new aims. The old institutions, hierarchies and beliefs would be swept aside. And about time too. Change was long overdue. The world had lost its way. It had been distracted by false idols, chasing hollow goals of money and self-interest. People had forgotten to look out for each other, caught up in a stampeding rat race that had become all the more frenetic and selfish during Thatcher's eighties. No one had cared when people tripped and fell. They were the losers. People trampled over them in order to win. And when the money ran out, businesses went bankrupt and houses were repossessed, it seemed people had forgotten how to look after each other. The community was dismantled irrevocably. People were poor again but this time they were on their own.

But things were gonna change with this generation. They were young. Things could be different, better. People could get on together, look after each other. Didn't matter what class or colour you were. That was what Ecstasy was about, everyone being together, getting on with each other. Loving, dancing, enjoying themselves. There were never any fights. There was no need, people were too busy having a laugh.

That's what she had thought. Now when she looked around

the room, detached, it seemed more like a vision of hell than of heaven. The words 'drug crazed' sprang to mind. They did look crazy, these kids, their eyes bulging and their unstoppable limbs swingin'. They looked like clockwork toys that had been wound up as far as they could go and then set free to unwind. They didn't look like the saviours of a lost world. Perhaps it was them, not the world that had lost its way. Joss saw what they were – a load of wasted kids dancing at a party.

'This party is amazing,' Tash thought. A disused sports centre. What a venue! She'd had a couple of pills and was dancing her tits off. She loved this feeling. It was like a spring bubbling up inside her, pouring energy and love into every limb of her body. All she wanted to do was dance, dance, dance. Express this feeling. Hug people and dance. They were all feeling like her. No one could stop themselves dancing. It was such a wicked feeling. She didn't want it to end. Ever. She lived for these moments. Why did you need anything else in your life? Wasn't this enough? How could it get any better? It was like being reborn. Everything felt new and exciting. Drinking water was a pure exquisite pleasure. It'd never felt so good. She'd never appreciated it before. She poured water on her face. It trickled over her skin, tingling in each pore. Enlivening. Refreshing. An echo of the feelings inside her body. How could she ever feel bad again, now she knew how to be so happy? Why wasn't all of life like this? But it could be, couldn't it? There was no reason to stop. Just go on and on for ever. Higher and higher. Like floating away in a hot-air balloon. Up into the clouds. Just as long as the balloon didn't burst.

She loved herself like this. She was truly herself. Free from all inhibitions, irritation, worry. She could just be herself and everyone loved her. She'd always been shy but now suddenly she could talk to people. She didn't think twice about what she was saying, the words flowed and everything came out right. And now, even when she wasn't on E, she had a new confidence, and could talk to people.

And dancing; she'd never danced like this before. Her body had always felt awkward and clumsy. But now she loved it. She was able to dance. Feeling the bass bounce in her body. She could express herself. Her body and herself as one.

The guy had just come and sat down next to Joss. She seemed to be attracting freaks tonight. She had already been accosted by a bloke called Dave the Rave. He was wearing a long mac covered with smiley faces. He had rotten teeth and a balding head. He looked like a pervert on pills. He started going on about how MDMA powder was the answer to the world's problems. He said the word powder with a cockney drawl that made it sound like 'pahh-da'.

He said, 'Pahh-da for breakfast. Pahh-da for lunch. Pahh-da for yer tea. It'd stop all the world's problems. Never be a war again.'

This new freak was not much better. He was dressed from head to foot in orange. Even his hair was orange. He sat down next to Joss and said, 'Aliens. You know there's three sorts of aliens. There's the grey ones. They're the evil ones. They're trying ta fuck things up for us. When things go wrong, it's usually cos a grey alien's had something to do with it. There's the green ones. They're not evil but they're not too cool either cos they're sex maniacs, see. 'N' they're always trying to kidnap people and rape 'em. I got kidnapped by one only the other day. Scary shit, man. Huge enormous green alien cock coming towards me – don't think they know the difference between blokes and girls or they're poofters or som'ing.'

Joss looked at the guy, thinking, 'Are you serious?' He looked stern and slightly scared. He was serious alright.

'So what's the other sort?' asked Joss.

A look of relief passed over the bloke. He smiled and said, 'The other sort are the orange ones. Now, they're the ones that are looking out for us. In fact, they're planning a way to save us from our own planet. At the moment they are preparing another planet for us to live on when they come and save us.'

It sounded like a new religion. Now no one believed in God and heaven, people were beginning to believe in aliens and new planets.

A while later Joss looked round and was surprised to see the orange man had been replaced by a kid with dreads. Must've been 'bout eighteen or nineteen. He too was full of ideas about how we might be saved.

'Dreads,' he said. 'I don't think anyone quite realizes how important they are. Some people think they're just pieces of hair, a fashion accessory or a fad. It really winds me up. They're not just that. There's so much more to it than that. Dreads are a symbol of independence and freedom. In the days of slavery, hair was, like, the only way people could express themselves. So they let it grow free, however it wanted to be. It was a symbol of the struggle for freedom. My dreads are so important to me. Almost spiritual.'

Joss had a sudden wish that she had a pair of clippers on her and could shave off the boy's dreads and leave him with a skinhead, spiritually bereft.

The boy went on, oblivious of his audience. 'I mean my whole life has changed since I grew my dreads. It's like a way of life. Y'know, a direction. They're almost like friends. They have kind've a life of their own that sort've like guides me. I mean, I don't know what I'd do without them. I'd be lost.'

'This place is amazing,' Tash was thinking. There was even a sauna and a Jacuzzi, and they both still worked. As soon as she'd seen the Jacuzzi, she'd stripped off and slid in. She could feel the jets of water pummelling against her back. She moved her back up and down so that the jet of water ran up and down around her spine. What a feeling! What an incredible feeling!

Ellis had also spotted the Jacuzzi. As he stripped off, he remembered Saul's pills. 'It'll be okay,' he thought as he put the jacket down. He'd keep his eye on it. But he'd had another couple of pills and now his eyes were falling half shut. He was so off his head, he was mumbling something to himself, as though he was having some imaginary conversation.

There was a pretty boy in the Jacuzzi too. He was eyeing up Ellis.

'Ever thought've tarting?' Prettyboy asked as soon as Ellis opened his eyes.

'No,' said Ellis defensively. His arse was his own and he wanted it to stay that way.

'No need to get touchy. I was only asking.' Prettyboy tossed his head.

'I'm straight anyway,' said Ellis.

'That doesn't make any difference,' smiled Prettyboy. 'Ever such good money. I get thirty quid for a massage and a hand job. Seventy for a massage and a blow job. And . . .'

'I don't wanna know,' said Ellis.

'Are you sure?' Prettyboy stretched his leg out under the water and stroked Ellis.

'Fuck off,' screeched Ellis. He jumped out of the Jacuzzi and hurriedly threw on his clothes. Fucking poofter.

Tash hadn't meant to end up in bed with the guy. It'd just happened. She wasn't even sure whether she fancied him. She was interested in him, sure. Fascinated by him in a way. But attracted to him? Not really, not sexually anyway. But you know what it's like when you're rushing your tits off. Sometimes you get these urges and whoever's there at the time is who you end up in bed with.

Now here she was, back at his place, with him pumping away on top of her to a frantic techno beat. The music was going faster and faster. As it did, Danny's thrusts came quicker and quicker.

Tash lay beneath him, watching his face grimacing. She was getting a bit bored. Not exactly sensuous sex. Should she just hang on in there till it was over – shouldn't be long now – or should she tell him? Maybe if he changed the music to something slower, he'd slow down too.

But then with one final thrust and strange contortion of his face, he was done. Danny rolled off Tash. Tash sat up.

'Do you want a spliff?' she asked.

'Mm,' grunted Danny.

Tash began to skin up.

'Aah,' he sighed. 'That was som'ing I missed.'

'What?' Tash emptied the fag into the Rizla.

'Sex.'

'When, when did you miss it?' Tash began to crumble the hash in amongst the tobacco.

'When I was inside,' said Danny.

'What, you were in prison?' Tash was excited by the thought. 'What for?'

'Did over a bank.'

'What, armed robbery?' asked Tash.

'Ner, I'm cleverer than that.' Danny smiled. 'Computer fraud.'

'Really? How much d'you get?' Tash rolled the Rizla up and licked it down.

'Half a million quid,' Danny said proudly.

'It wasn't Claybars, was it?' Tash smiled. She lit the spliff and pulled her head back so the smoke didn't float into her eyes.

'Yeah.' Danny looked at Tash. 'How d'you guess?'

'My dad works there,' laughed Tash. 'He's one of their senior executives.'

Danny started laughing. 'What'd he think if he knew who you was in bed with?'

'Fuck knows.' Tash puffed on the spliff. What *would* he think? 'But you did him a favour. He got his promotion because of you. The bloke above him got the sack over that fraud.' Tash took another puff. 'So, how long did you do inside?'

'Five years,' Danny said thoughtfully. 'Not bad though. Five years for half a million quid. Hundred grand a year.' There was no other way he would've got that kind've money together.

'Ner, not bad,' said Tash. But she was thinking how her dad earned half a million quid every year.

'Wouldn't've got nicked either if someone hadn't grassed.' There was a bitter edge to his voice. 'We were workin' with him 'n' 'e grassed.'

'What did you do?'

Danny shrugged. 'Had 'im killed. What else could we do?'

Tash wasn't as shocked as she might've been. It seemed almost fair in a brutal kind of way. Life was like lots of different games, each with a different set of rules. The rules of each game were fair, so long as everyone knew them. The bloke who'd grassed had known the game he was playing. He'd known the rules and he'd known the consequences if he broke them. He broke the golden rule – never grass – and he paid the penalty.

Danny suddenly lightened up. 'But at least I got away with the cash. Stashed it in bank accounts the pigs couldn't get at.'

Tash felt a thrill about what she was hearing. She felt herself falling into some seedy underworld that belonged in books or films. But this was real and it excited her. She loved the feeling of falling.

Chapter Ten

When Alec arrived at the Neopole Hotel, there was still half an hour before he was due to open the conference with his presentation on the benefits of effective time management – just enough time for a quick boot. He took the lift up to the top floor, the twenty-third. The lift doors opened on the twentieth. Two women dressed in dark suits and shoes stood waiting.

'Going to the conference?' one of them asked Alec, seeing his own dark suit and shoes.

'I'm going up,' Alec said, thinking how in fact he was about to ease his mood down. The woman looked momentarily confused and then smiled as she disappeared between the lift doors.

It was not hard to find the door to the roof – it was at the end of the corridor up a small flight of stairs. Usually, when Alec took downers, he took them in the basement of wherever it was he was working, whether it was in a hotel, conference centre or block of offices. It seemed to be appropriate to be down beneath street level in the dark, warm, maybe slightly damp depths of a building, in order to inject his blood or fill his lungs or digest pills that would slow his body, numb his brain and soothe his soul. Basements were usually still, there would be no sudden movements to break his trance, and he liked the techno landscape he usually found in basements. His mind would float amidst the dirty overhead piping and the noise of the heating system or the air conditioning whirring up. It all seemed right.

Conversely, when he wanted to take coke or uppers, he would usually go to the roof and stand or sit as close to the edge as he dared, sometimes with his legs dangling over the side of the building. There he would watch the city streaming with feverish activity, and the streets, like wind tunnels channelling tornadoes of traffic, swirling, swarming and subsiding, leaving in their path a chaos of regurgitated crap.

But today, although Alec felt like some gear, he wanted to be up high on top of the building. As he opened the door on to the roof, the sounds of London cascaded upon him as loud as if he had been down on the streets. Buses growled. A man shouted, 'Out my fuckin' way.' A couple of car horns tooted. The city seemed to heave with a moaning sigh as if writhing in pain.

Alec shut the door behind him and sat, leaning against the wall by the side of the stairs. He opened his briefcase in front of him, collected together the papers that lay on top, and placed them inside the pocket on the lid. He lifted a sheet of velour-lined cardboard that matched the inside of his briefcase. Beneath was an array of paraphernalia – a syringe, spare needles, some needle wipes, a spoon, foil, a few bottles of pills and several packets of powder. Alec had had a friend specially cut a layer of foam so that each piece of equipment lay flush within it, each in its own place.

Alec unfolded a piece of foil and took out a tube and a bag of brown. He tapped a little on to the foil and melted it and then let it slide in a chocolate line, as he sucked at the smoke. Inside him the smoke oozed calm into every pore of his body, every cell of his blood. He let his hands sink into his lap and his head lean against the wall. He drifted with the clouds. There was not a care in his world. London fell away beneath him, its nervous energy dulled.

A few minutes later, he had another boot and then let himself drift once more. His mind was completely still, thinking over slowly what he was going to say in his presentation. There was no panic, no racing thoughts, no fear. His mind was calm, like a pool with not a single ripple to disturb it, only the crystal-clear reflection of the sky above.

When Alec checked his watch, he was five minutes late for the conference. He hurriedly packed up his briefcase and went to find the conference room. The room was full of perhaps fifty suits, mostly male, arranged in three semicircles round a whiteboard. As he walked in, he heard a man say loudly, 'Are we ever going to start, do you think?'

Alec strolled up to the front of the room, set his briefcase down on the desk and turned to the whiteboard. In his immaculate handwriting, he began to write 'Punctuality'. He was not put off by the murmurs that ran through the room. 'Uh, he can talk.' 'What does he know about it?' 'Ten minutes late himself.' No, Alec wasn't put off. In fact he rather enjoyed it. He continued writing, 'is essential'. The murmurs continued, along with a few snorts of indignant laughter.

Alec turned to face his audience, unruffled. 'I couldn't help noticing some of you were slightly disgruntled when I walked in late.'

'Slightly,' said a man in the front row.

Alec continued, 'Right, I want to have a brainstorm on those feelings. Perhaps we could start with you, sir.' Alec indicated the man in the front row. 'What were you feeling? Not your thoughts, just your feelings.'

The man in the front row looked slightly taken aback. 'Well,' he said, 'I was very . . . I mean, it's quite preposterous being . . .'

Alec didn't let him finish. 'Angry,' he said writing the word on the whiteboard. 'That's good. Now, who else?' Alec scanned his audience looking for his next victim. Some of them were looking uncomfortable, trying not to be noticed. Others seemed quite relaxed, they had done this sort of thing before. 'You, madam, what were you feeling?' Alec looked at a woman near the back.

'Um, frustrated,' she replied.

Alec wrote the word up on the board. His audience was getting the hang of this now. He gathered a few more feelings from them – anxious, annoyed, bored – and wrote them up on the board. And then he turned to them and said, 'So, you see how your clients might be feeling if you are late for them. Not only have you wasted their time and your own, you have also clogged their minds with all these emotions, so it becomes all the more difficult for them to focus on the business in hand.'

The suits in the audience relaxed and smiled. This man obviously knew what he was talking about.

Alec was drawing his presentation to a close. 'There's still half an hour to go before we break for coffee. I'd like you to start on your feedback sheets.' Alec handed out the sheets.

'Time for another boot,' he thought to himself. He did not want to go all the way back up to the roof – there was not time – and anyway there were too many people around. So instead, Alec went to the ground-floor toilets, near the entrance hall.

Alec sat on the loo and hovered on a smack thermal, his eyes half shut. Alec had always loved drugs. Now he had the money, he loved being able to control his moods with such accuracy. When he wanted energy, there was a drug for that. When, like now, he wanted to be soothed, he turned (amongst other things) to smack. When he wanted something entirely different from normal life, he could hallucinate.

Alec hated the way people attached such a stigma to heroin. In his eyes it was no better or worse than any other drug in its side effects and it was one of the best in its positive effects. Sure, it could be dangerous but it was not bad in itself. It could be used and abused. It could be a wonderful condiment to life, something to help improve life's bitter-sweet taste, or it could take over and become your staple food, essential to your survival. It was like any other drug. In fact, it was like many things in life – money, food, sex, love – things that are enjoyed by many but for a few become a problem because they are that person's driving force. They dominate them, enslave them, gnaw at their soul until there is nothing left but a hollow heart. Yet that does not mean that others, who do not find problems with these things, who are able to stay in control and keep their passions in check, cannot go on enjoying such things.

Smack enslaves some people. People who have nothing else in their lives, nothing worth being aware of, that is. Lives that drone on relentlessly through inner-city squalor, the worry of bills, of food even, of kids crying and their empty future.

But for Alec it was different. He enjoyed the feeling heroin gave him but he had the intelligence, strength and success not to let it enslave him. He was in control.

Alec could hear two men pissing and talking: 'Awfully good conference, don't you think?'

'Terribly interesting.'

'Bit dubious when he was late but all part of the conference. Good idea that.'

Alec smiled to himself, waited for the men to leave and then returned to the conference room.

Ellis was dying for a dump. He'd woken up earlier in the morning, still at the party. His head had been lodged against a bass bin and he woke up with it pounding in his ear. He had a look around for Chelsea, but she'd gone home. He'd have to make his own way back. Now he was wandering the streets looking for a tube station or a bus that was going in the right direction. But he really was dying for a dump. He wasn't going anywhere until he'd had one.

He ducked into a hotel, crossed the entrance hall and found some toilets. When he went into one of the cubicles, he noticed the smell of gear straight away. It was a deep, rich smell that filled him with empathic calm. And then he saw a piece of foil, folded and tucked behind the back of the toilet. He pulled it out and saw behind it another length of foil, clearly a squashed tube. He unfolded the first piece and noticed the gear was not quite finished. He rerolled the tube and settled down on the bog for the most unlikely boot of his life.

The hotel receptionist had seen Ellis come into the hotel – he was hard to miss. She was new to the job and eager to make a good impression, so without hesitation, she alerted security. 'Security' consisted of Ken, a solid, middle-aged man with equally solid morals and a strong, albeit misplaced, loyalty to his firm. Ken took his job seriously, nothing was going to jeopardize it, certainly not some yob off the streets who was probably just wanting to use the hotel as a place in which to satisfy his craving for drugs. From the receptionist's description of him, Ken had no doubt that Ellis was a drug addict – his type always were.

Ellis was just smoking the tube when Ken pushed the cubicle door open. Ellis looked at Ken and cussed himself for not locking the door. Ken was triumphant. He did not know much about the consumption of drugs but he had a feeling this was a little more serious than marijuana. He grabbed Ellis's ear, pinched it hard and twisted it slightly.

'You're coming with me,' he said, feeling like a policeman (a good feeling).

Ellis was too shocked and caned to put up much resistance until they got out into the corridor. Then he thought he could either run or blag his way out of this one. He soon realized he was in no fit state to run. He'd have to start blagging.

The conference was just stopping for a coffee break and people were beginning to trickle into the corridor. Ellis started making as much noise as he could, in order to cause a scene and embarrass this geezer into letting him go.

'Get your hands off me,' he shouted. 'This is assault.' He turned to a passing gentleman. 'Help me,' he said. 'I'm being assaulted.'

Ken let go of Ellis. 'I was doing no such thing,' he said.

'No, well what's that then?' Ellis pushed his ear forward as evidence.

Alec saw what was going on and, as conference organizer, thought it best that he do everything to see the conference ran smoothly.

'What's all this about, then?' Alec asked Ken.

'I apprehended him consuming drugs in the toilets. Reception warned me about him. I knew he was an addict from the moment I clapped eyes on him,' Ken replied, oozing self-importance.

Alec wanted to slap him and tell him he didn't know what the fuck he was talking about, but he knew this would have been difficult without revealing his own little secret. Instead he looked at Ellis and thought, 'Stupid prat, getting caught with my gear.' But he said, 'Anything you want to say?'

Ellis looked clearly at Alec for the first time. He looked at his eyes and clocked the pupils pinned. 'Ner,' he thought. 'Can't be.' But then it must be. He had a way out.

'I picked up some foil in the toilets. It wasn't mine.' Ellis was looking Alec straight in the eye. 'But I think I know whose it was.' He waited for Alec to react.

Alec was completely calm. He thought, 'Perhaps he's not so stupid after all', and said to Ken, 'I think I'd better handle this. Important to have the utmost discretion in such sensitive matters.'

He led Ellis to a small room down the corridor from the toilets.

Ken was disappointed that he was no longer involved. This event was the most exciting thing to have happened to him in years – except the time when someone rolled into the back of his car while they were waiting in a traffic jam. He would have liked to have milked it for all it was worth. Still, it was something to tell the grandkids, when they were old enough.

Alec shut the door and looked at Ellis and said, 'If you tell anyone what you think you know, no one will believe you.' Then he reached inside his jacket and pulled out his wallet. 'I hope this will make up for any inconvenience.' He handed Ellis a crisp fifty-pound note.

'It should do,' smiled Ellis as he put the note in his pocket.

Chapter Eleven

'Here's some letters for you,' said Ellis as he walked into Saul's flat. He handed Saul the letters and then said, 'Look, mate, I'm really sorry I didn't come round sooner. But y'know how it is . . . I, er, y'know, got pissed 'n' forgot 'n' then ended up goin' out 'n' . . . Y'know.'

'Yeah, right.' Saul'd been so angry with Ellis last night that he'd woken up still fucked off this morning. He'd had visions of beating the shit out of Ellis. Pummelling him and enjoying it. But now Ellis was standing in front of him, all the anger drained away. Ellis was his mate, Saul wasn't gonna hurt him. Saul knew what Ellis was like, how unreliable he was. He should never've let him go off with the money in the first place. Idiot. All this paranoia. He was driving himself crazy. Panicking, forcing himself to make stupid decisions. But Ellis was here now with the jacket. Just as long as the pills were safe and sound, Saul wasn't gonna freak. He wanted to keep himself calm. Start thinking straight again.

' 'S alright, mate,' he said to Ellis. 'I'm just glad you turned up. Thought you might a done a runner.'

'Course I wouldn't. 'Ere, look, d'you fancy a beer? Some bloke jus' gave me fifty quid.' Ellis reached into a carrier bag he was holding, pulled out a beer and handed it to Saul.

'What? Gave you fifty quid?' said Saul, cracking open the beer.

'Sort've a bribe. Bit've a long story.'

'Yeah, later, jus' give us those pills, eh?' said Saul. 'You haven't caned them, have you?'

'Ner, course not. I was tempted but I didn't touch 'em.' Ellis took off the jacket and held it slung over one hand while he felt for the pills in the lining. He could not feel them and he couldn't see the rip in the lining either. Ellis frowned. What was going on?

Saul watched Ellis fumbling with the jacket and saw his puzzled look. He became agitated.

'What you doin'?' he scowled. 'Where are the pills?'

'I . . . dunno.' Ellis didn't understand. He hadn't moved the pills and he hadn't left the jacket alone. Had he? Shit. The Jacuzzi. He'd taken it off to go in the Jacuzzi. Shit. Someone must've nicked the pills. But he didn't leave it alone for long. It was right there, near him all the time. But the pills'd gone. They'd definitely gone. Christ. How was he gonna tell Saul?

'Where are they?' Saul snatched the jacket off Ellis and looked at the lining. No pills. He looked again and realized. 'This isn't my jacket. What've you done, Ellis? A grand. A fuckin' grand. What the fuck've you done?' he shouted.

Ellis squirmed and shifted from one foot to the other, not knowing what to say. He looked away. What could he say? He'd fucked up. He looked back at Saul. Saul was pulling at his hair, his face twisted. The jacket was limp in his hand.

'I, er . . .' Ellis tried to explain. 'There was this Jacuzzi and I, er, y'know, took off mi clothes to go in it.'

'You left my jacket with all those pills in it to get in a fucking Jacuzzi?' Saul was seething, his body burning. He couldn't think. He could hardly speak.

'I'm sorry, Saul. I was off my head. Y'know how it is. I . . . I . . .' Ellis couldn't believe he'd done something so stupid. But it'd all seemed alright. The jacket had never been that far away from him. And he'd got it back. How was he to know it was the wrong one? He'd only been try'na help Saul out in the first place.

'You stupid fucking . . .' Saul found his voice momentarily but then lapsed into silence again. There was nothing to say. This couldn't be happening. It wasn't real.

Ellis was quiet as well. Every time he thought of something to say, he realized it was ridiculous. There was nothing for him to say. He'd lost the pills. He'd fucked up. That was all there was to it. All he wanted to do now was get out of the house before Saul lost it.

'Look, I'll go back to the party and see if I can find the jacket,' he said.

Saul was shaking his head. His eyes were shut. 'It won't be there,' he said. 'It won't be there.'

'Might as well try,' replied Ellis.

He let himself out.

Saul remained on the sofa, his eyes still shut. He was rubbing them with one of his hands. He hadn't seen Ellis go, but he'd heard the door slam. Now he was alone, he thought he might burst into tears. But he didn't. He opened his eyes and his lungs and screamed. His stomach became solid. His hands grabbed at the air in front of his face. Even his calf muscles tightened. The jacket slipped to the floor.

He stopped, running out of breath. But then he tipped his head back and screamed again and again.

'Calm,' he snorted to himself when he'd finished screaming. 'Calm.' He snorted a laugh. He was anything but calm. Every muscle in his body was tense. So tense, he was beginning to tremble. His jaw was locked. His eyes were fired wide. He felt sick with emotion – anger, frustration, despair and failure. Failure. It was all going wrong. Everything. He couldn't do anything any more. It was all fucked up.

He got up suddenly and launched himself at the wall, fist first.

His wrist buckled with the impact. As he took his hand away, he saw the knuckles already blushing blue and grey. Blood was seeping into the wells formed where patches of skin had been scraped away.

Saul plunged his fist back into the wall. His hand throbbed with pain. He cradled it in the cup of his other hand. Somehow by making the pain inside him physical, it made it easier to bear. But there was still pain inside him. A raw biting pain that was gnawing away at him, burning him like acid. A pain so fierce that if he left it without releasing it, there would be nothing left of him. He would become hollow and dead. A rotten carcass.

He flung his arm out at a vase of cut flowers. His forearm slammed against it, smashing it on to the floor. He kicked at the sofa and took a couple of stamping strides to the bookshelves. The books ripped and splayed on the floor. Saul paused for a moment and looked at Joss's records. But there was enough sense in him to turn away from them. Instead he tore a picture frame down from the wall. The wall plug hung out of the plaster like a bloody tooth. The glass shattered as it hit the floor. And in one final attempt to express the hatred and hurt he was feeling, he swung his fist through the window. The glass rained on the pavement below. He didn't care any more how much he hurt his body because nothing could hurt him like he hurt inside. If he could only show his pain, maybe someone could help him. He pulled his arm back and looked at his wrist. The two tendons bulged like railway lines. Above, near the base of his palm, a grid of veins wove blue beneath the surface. But the skin was still intact. It was not even scratched. Saul stood looking at his wrist with disbelief and disappointment. He laughed falsely and then began to cry, sobbing like the mourning mothers of the Middle East. He was shaking, moaning and wailing. His tears came in cycles. Full force, abating and then coming again with renewed vigour and great heavy shudders of his shoulders.

That was how he was when Joss found him. She looked around the room, the flowers on the floor, the wet patch of carpet, the splinters of glass, the window, the books and Saul shuddering as he sat on the arm of the sofa.

'What's going on, Saul?' she asked. 'What's happened?'

Saul couldn't speak through his tears. He didn't try. How could he begin to explain the pain inside him? She could see it in the debris about them. He couldn't put it into words. Words were too small to express the pain and confusion knotted inside him. There was no way forward. That was the problem. There was nothing but dead ends and disappointment.

Joss thought something terrible had happened. A few images flickered through her mind. Someone dead. Saul's sister raped. His father in a coma.

'What's wrong?' she said. 'What's wrong, Saul? Tell me what's wrong.'

Saul forced a few broken words through his tears. 'I . . . I . . . dunno . . . I . . . just . . . dunno.' Saul didn't think to mention Ellis because that wasn't it. Losing the pills had simply been one last twist on the vice that was crushing Saul's spirit.

'Christ,' thought Joss. 'Now what am I supposed to say?' Joss felt her stomach sink. She almost wished someone had died. At least then there would be an actual problem. It would be easier to find something to say. But if Saul couldn't even explain what was wrong, how could she possibly help him?

She tried to hug him. But he was cold and detached, as if he didn't notice her presence. She held him for a moment but then let go. It was hard to hold someone when they didn't react.

What was she supposed to do? Slap him and tell him to pull himself together? Or say, 'Don't worry, it'll be alright'? She wasn't very good at this kind of thing. It made her feel uncomfortable, seeing him upset. She'd had to deal with it a lot over the last few weeks. He was becoming more and more paranoid, more volatile, harder to talk to. Joss didn't want to let herself think it but she couldn't help the words popping up into her mind. Was he losing it? Was Saul going crazy? What the fuck was going on in his mind?

Joss didn't know what to say to Saul or what to do, so she left him alone. She began to pick up the books and put them back on the shelves.

Saul was still sat on the arm of the chair. He had stopped crying now. He was staring into space, silent. How could Ellis have done this to him? How could this've happened?

Joss had the dustpan and brush now and was sweeping up the broken glass. She felt like crying but she kept herself busy so she couldn't cry. Saul was watching her.

'Leave it,' he said. 'I'll do it later.'

But Joss ignored him and carried on. Saul picked up the letters Ellis had brought in and went into the bedroom. He didn't want to talk about it. He wouldn't know what to say. And he thought if he tried to talk, he'd start crying again. He didn't want that.

He lay on the bed wondering why the fuck everything had suddenly become so complicated. A few weeks ago, everything had been sorted. Everything had been simple. It had only been a few weeks ago, hadn't it? Saul wasn't sure. It seemed to him as though all this had been going on for ever. He almost couldn't remember what it felt like to feel good and happy and free. To know what you were about and where you were going.

How could this've happened? How could he've been so dumb to give Ellis the money? He wanted to kick himself. He kicked the bed instead. He'd already done all that violence thing. He sighed. He wasn't gonna start that again. That was all finished.

Shit. The stupid fucking dickhead. Ellis. How could you, Ellis? How could you? He couldn't be that stupid. He couldn't. No, and he probably wasn't. He'd probably nicked the pills. He must've done. Where did he get the money for those beers?

Someone gave him fifty quid. Oh, yeah? Things like that didn't happen.

Saul sifted through the letters, absent-mindedly. And then he noticed his giro wasn't there. It should've come yesterday and it still wasn't there today. And someone else was meant to be sending him some money in the post. That wasn't there either. Ellis must've nicked the giro and that money too. As well as the pills. He must've done. Why the fuck had Saul ever trusted him? He was stealing blatantly right from under his nose. Saul was letting him into his flat and Ellis was stealing from him. The pills, the giro, the money. All gone. All while Ellis was around. Saul knew Ellis was dabbling in gear at the moment. Maybe getting himself a habit. He knew you couldn't trust a junkie. Course you couldn't. And Saul like a fool had trusted Ellis. He'd thought he was a mate. Thought you could trust a mate. Well, you couldn't. You couldn't trust anyone.

But then something didn't make sense. The jacket. The jacket wasn't Saul's. Had Ellis got it muddled with someone else's? Or had that just been a blag? Had he bought another jacket yesterday? He'd had the time to do it. And then pretend that the jackets had been swapped. Make up some story. Had he done that? Was Ellis that clever, that calculating?

Saul didn't know. He didn't know anything any more.

Was life always going to be like this? Was it always going to be so confusing, so full of despair and disappointment? Fuck knows.

Chapter Twelve

'Tash, Tash, are you awake, dear?'

It was her mum, Jane Caroman. Tash had been nearly asleep. She snapped back to consciousness.

'Yeah, yeah, I'm awake,' she said opening her eyes and looking over at her mum.

Her mum was pissed. She'd been out at some dinner party. They were always at some dinner party or other. Almost every night. Business masquerading as pleasure. Her mascara was smudged. Her eyes puffy. A couple of tears lingered in the corners.

'God, those goddamn parties. Those goddamn people. They're all so bloody boring. So false.'

'It's taken you this long to realize,' thought Tash.

She had seen her mum like this before. She often got like this when she was pissed. Emotional and overwrought. Everything would seem disastrous. Intolerable. How could she ever go on? But by morning, she'd've forgotten about it. Nothing would change. Tash could never work out whether alcohol made her mother have a true insight into her life and see things as they really were or whether it distorted things beyond recognition. Perhaps both. A distortion of the truth. Whereas in sobriety things were clear but utterly false.

'So bloody false,' Jane repeated. 'On and on. Same old stuff. Don't think they believe a word of what they're saying. Just regurgitating what they've been told. What they've been told to like. What they've been told is fashionable. God, can't they have any opinions of their own? And you know the only reason they're talking to you is because you're the wife of Mr Caroman of Claybars. And the only reason I'm talking to them is for Thomas's sake because they are some banker or businessman and it helps Thomas and the bank for me to be seen as his good little wife. But no one cares what anyone else is saying. No one's the least bit interested because they're all saying the same things. On and on.'

'They always have done,' said Tash. She never needed to say much when her mother was in these moods. Her mother offloaded without much encouragement. In fact, once she'd started, she was hard to stop.

'And those women,' her mother continued, oblivious to what Tash had said. 'What have they ever done with their lives? Nothing. Been Mrs So-and-so. That's all. Been their husbands' wives.'

Tash felt like saying, 'What have you done with your life?' But she stopped herself.

Her mother went on. 'I know you could say, 'What have I done with my life?' But I have done some things. I'm sure,' she said uncertainly. 'I have, Tash. I'm not like them. I'm not like them, am I?'

'Er, no,' said Tash, trying to sound reassuring but she knew she wasn't convincing.

'Oh, God,' said her mother, with renewed vigour. 'I've done nothing. Except bring you and your brother up. What have I done? What have I done?' She paused and Tash wondered whether she was expected to answer the question. She didn't know what to say, so she stayed quiet and, to her relief, her mother didn't press her for an answer but carried on talking.

'I've been a wife and a mother, that's all. It might seem like

I've got everything. Oh, yes, I've got the nice house. Houses,'
she corrected. 'And nice cars. Still married. Husband's got a good
job. One of the top jobs. But you know what, Tash? You know
what? I'm bored. I'm so bloody bored of it all. I mean what have
I achieved? What have I ever done?'

Tash stopped listening. She'd heard it all before. Why didn't
her mother do something about it, rather than getting pissed and
moaning? Tash wasn't going to let herself end up like that. No
way. She wasn't going to do what was expected of her. She was
going to do what she wanted to do. She wasn't exactly sure what
it was she wanted to do. But she was going to find out. Try
everything until she found what it was that meant something.
That stopped that deadening feeling of boredom. Something
real. Something that would make her feel alive.

Jane was still talking. 'It's all so easy when you're young. So
easy. Everything seems possible. Nothing will stop you. You
have your dreams. So much energy and enthusiasm. Think that's
all you need. So confident. Sure your dreams will come true.'

Jane paused for a moment, remembering herself as a young
woman before she'd met Thomas. She saw herself, beautiful, determined, vital. The clearest image she had of herself was of her dancing. Her body stretched and vaulted, floating on air. Each muscle
tuned with hard-worked suppleness, so that every part of her body
was ready to work for her, with her, in an effortless expression of
music and her own inner self. Streaming to the rhythm of the music
that flowed around her and within her.

It had been easy then. Everything had been easy then. To
express yourself. To move. To feel alive. To have music beating
within you. To be yourself and be proud. To be free.

Jane had been good at dancing. She had known she was good.
Everyone had known she was good. And she had had some luck,
a few breaks. Right time, right place. She'd met the right people.
It was the beginning of something special. She was going to be

the best. She was going to go all the way. She had been so certain, so sure of herself. She had been young then.

Dancing was everything. It was her life, her soul, her breath.

But then she had met Thomas. He was intelligent and handsome with a cheeky grin that made her glow inside. When they had first met, they had talked. Talked and talked. About everything. About nothing. They had laughed and shouted together. They had fallen in love.

Jane had felt more alive than ever; even dancing had never made her feel like this before. When she saw him she wanted to shout out to the world how she felt. Sometimes she did. She didn't care when people turned to stare. Didn't they know what this felt like? This feeling welling up inside her, erupting, overflowing. She had felt as though she was running downhill, her legs tumbling on ahead of her, and she had hoped she would not fall down.

Thomas had been her life. He was all that mattered. Dancing did not seem so important any more. All that mattered was him and their love for each other. She had poured herself into him. Lost herself. They were young and in love. They would conquer the world.

And when she got pregnant, it had seemed almost magical. An independent, living, kicking confirmation of their love. It had been beautiful. She had cried when she had found out, not tears of fear or despair but joy, because now their love was complete.

They got married. Thomas had found a job at Claybars, not much in itself, but a job that might lead somewhere. Her parents, shocked at first, had grown accustomed to the idea of a grandchild. They had never liked the idea of Jane dancing, it had not been right. This was far more acceptable – a child and a husband with good prospects.

Jane had given up the dancing and become a mother, wife

and housewife. And it had remained beautiful – for a time. Until she realized she had lost herself. She had become a shadow of Thomas, of the children, of the house even. All her dreams and hopes were gone. Her achievements were that of her family. Thomas's promotion. Natasha's first words. William's first tooth. And Jane was an echo, hollowing with time.

'Should never have happened,' Jane said to Tash, brushing away a tear. 'Never have happened. None of it. None of it.'

Tash wasn't sure what her mum was going on about. When her mum got in these moods, her thoughts became disjointed. Tash had trouble following them. Sometimes her mum seemed almost crazy, pulling together snatches of bitterness that'd been needling her. Pulling them together in no real order, simply as they occurred to her.

Jane suddenly said, 'It's all fucked up.' She spat each word out.

She didn't often swear and the words sounded strange coming from her. They hung in the air awkwardly as if not knowing where to go.

'It's not that bad,' said Tash. 'Is it?'

'You'll see. Life's not as easy as you think it's going to be when you're your age. You think you'll be different, don't you? You think your dreams'll come true, don't you?'

Tash was silent.

'Don't you?' There was venom in Jane's voice. She stared pointedly at Tash, forcing her to speak.

'Dunno. S'pose,' Tash said reluctantly.

'You think you can make something of yourself. But let me tell you, you can't. You might as well stop dreaming, now. Stop hoping. Because those dreams will die and you'll die with them.'

Tash had had enough. 'Well, then, what's the point, Mum? What's the point, if it all comes to nothing?'

'There's no point, Tash. There's no point at all.'

★

'Come on, Tash, get out of bed, it's nine o'clock.' Jane was feeling panicky. It was her week to host the bridge day. She had the vol-au-vents to prepare and the cheese soufflé, which she was rather worried about but none the less determined to make a success of. Not to mention tidying and dusting the sitting room – the Filipina still didn't seem to know how to dust. No matter how many times Jane tried to show her, she never seemed to cotton on. Jane didn't understand the difficulty; dusting should be easy enough. Didn't they have dust in the Philippines? 'Come on, Tash, get up.'

'Nine o'clock,' Tash thought. 'Nine o'clock.' She'd had fuck all sleep in the last few days. She could do with a lie-in. She opened her eyes briefly and then drifted back to sleep.

Jane came in again five minutes later. 'For God's sake, Tash, get up.' The puff pastry wasn't coming together at all. 'You're so lazy. Why can't you do something with your life? You do nothing with yourself all day. Why can't you be more like William?' Tash's younger brother, William, had a job in the City. He was at work by seven-thirty each morning and was already earning a 'decent' salary. 'He's heading for a good career. What are you heading for? Nothing. You're a disaster. You haven't done anything with your life. Doesn't seem like you ever will. Doesn't even seem like you want to. You're wasting away, Natasha. Your life will have slipped away and you won't have done anything with it.'

'Like you, you mean,' said Tash. Tash didn't have to listen to this kind of shit first thing in the morning. Her mother loved blaming Tash for all her problems. Her mum's life was her problem. Tash's life was her own. No one else's. And, if she could help it, it wasn't going to be anything like her mum's.

'*Get out!*' shouted Jane. How dare Tash be so rude?

'Don't worry, I'm not planning on sticking around to play bridge all day.'

Jane left. She had so much to do.

Tash crawled out of bed. Her mum was such a bitter bitch. No, Tash promised herself, she wasn't going to be anything like her.

Tash tidied up her room a bit while she decided what to wear. She put away her black puffa jacket. She didn't want to wear it for a while. She'd noticed a bloke wearing one just like it the other night at that party. The bloke in the Jacuzzi. She hated seeing people in the same clothes as her. And it was starting to look a bit tatty. She'd never noticed before. Must've got battered at the party.

That party had been a laugh. And she liked that bloke she'd met, Danny. The sex had been a bit mental but she enjoyed his company. He was full of energy. He was funny and his directness was so refreshing. Most of her friends were public-school kids who were arrogant and full of themselves. They never said what they felt. They just said what was expected of them, whatever would cause the least conflict. They said what was expected and did what was expected. They all had neat cosy jobs in banking or advertising or law. Usually arranged through Daddy's connections. Or if they weren't already locked into a career, they were at university. After which they would end up in a cosy job in banking or advertising or law. Everything was laid out for them from the moment they were born. Prep school, public school, career. Each step led without question to the next. There was no risk, no excitement. There was nothing but what their parents had laid out for them to do.

Danny was different. He did what he felt like doing and he did it when he wanted. He had money but he'd made it his way – he hadn't had it handed to him on a plate. And he took risks. He took risks all the time. Sometimes they paid off. Sometimes they didn't. That didn't matter to him. As long as things were changing, never stagnant, he was happy. Whatever happened, life with Danny was never boring.

Tash went out without saying anything to her mum. What was the point?

She bought a paper and read it over a cup of coffee in a French patisserie she knew. Afterwards she phoned up Danny. Why not? She wanted to see him again. He might not want to know but she could give it a go. What did she have to lose?

She felt nervous as the phone rang.

Danny answered. 'Hello.' Danny sounded pissed off and Tash suddenly wished she wasn't doing this.

'Hi,' she said. 'It's Tash here. We met at the party the other night.'

Danny's voice suddenly lightened. 'Tash, alright, luv. How's it going? D'you think I'd forgotten ya?'

'Well, I don't know.' Tash relaxed.

'So, how are you? What you up to?'

'Nothing much. Arguing with my mum.' Tash was surprised she'd mentioned it. But she felt easy talking to Danny.

'Don't worry, mate, happens to the best of us.'

'What you up to today?'

'This 'n' that. Got a few bits 'n' pieces to sort owt,' said Danny elusively.

'Got time for lunch?'

'Got all the time in the world for you, luv.'

'Enough of the sweet-talking,' said Tash. 'There isn't a bucket for me to chuck up in. What do you want to eat? Malaysian sound good to you?'

'Yeah, sounds great,' said Danny although he was a bit unsure. Malaysian? What the fuck was their food like?

'I know a nice place we could go to. Shall I pick you up? That's probably easiest, isn't it? About one?'

'Yeah, sounds good,' Danny replied. He liked the way Tash was taking control. He'd never been taken out for a meal by a woman before.

★

And the meal *was* good. They had a laugh. They both felt strangely comfortable with each other although they were from such different backgrounds. And because they were so different, they each gave the other a glimpse of a totally new world.

Tash stayed that night at Danny's. The sex was better.

'Where are we going?' Tash asked, pulling her shades down from the top of her face and on to her nose so she could see the signs better. It was the next morning and they were driving down the motorway out of London. 'Where are we going?' she repeated when Danny didn't answer.

'You'll see,' he said.

They were just outside London when they turned off the motorway. They were on a road to some place called Laddington when Danny pulled in down a track, turned the car around and stopped. He turned off the engine.

'What are you doing, Danny?' Tash asked. What the fuck was going on? Why'd he parked here? She suddenly felt a little uneasy. She'd only known Danny a few days and what she knew of him wasn't all that innocent. And now here she was parked up with him down some track in the middle of nowhere. And she was on her own.

Then suddenly a bloke came running down the track. As soon as Danny saw him, he turned on the engine and drove slowly forwards to meet him. The bloke jumped in the back of the car.

Danny started laughing. 'You made it, mate. Freedom. What does it taste like?'

'Fucking wicked, mate, I tell ya,' replied the bloke.

'Happy birthday.' Danny was driving off back towards the motorway. 'There's some champagne in the boot. Crack it open.'

The bloke reached in the boot. He pulled out a bottle of champagne, wound down the window and popped the cork out on to the road. He took a swig on it and then handed it to Danny.

'Who's she?' the bloke said to Danny.

'I'm Tash,' said Tash.

'You're a bit posh, aren't you?' said the bloke.

Tash didn't say anything. Who was this knob?

'Oi,' said Danny to the bloke. 'Show some respect. She's my woman.'

'I'm not your woman,' snapped Tash, although she was chuffed Danny thought of them as together. 'I'm my own woman.'

'Y'know what I mean,' said Danny. 'Anyway, Tash, this is Jim.'

'Hi,' said Tash.

Jim ignored Tash.

Danny said, 'So you didn't have no problems, then?'

'None,' said Jim, proudly. 'Piece a piss.'

'Jim's broken out for his birthday,' Danny explained.

'What, out of prison?' asked Tash.

'No, out the zoo,' replied Jim, sarcastically. He didn't like this girl. Posh little bitch. Didn't know shit. Why'd Danny have to bring her along?

'You hungry?' Danny asked Jim. 'You fancy an Indian?'

'Yeah, mate, it's my birthday, ain't it?'

An hour later they were sat round a table in the Balti Basement. They ordered and then Danny went off to the loo.

Jim turned to Tash. 'What d'you do if you see a Paki drowning?' he said loudly.

Tash cringed and turned away.

Jim roared, 'Throw 'im 'is wife 'n' kids.' He laughed falsely.

Tash was quiet.

Jim said, 'What's up with you, got no sense of humour? Too fuckin' posh to laugh, are ya?'

Tash looked at him and stared but still didn't say anything.

What was there to say? The guy was a tosser. He wasn't worth wasting her breath on.

Jim continued, 'So, you're Danny's new woman. He's always got some little tart hanging round him.'

Danny came back and slapped Jim on the back. 'Take it easy, mate,' he said. 'She's alright.' And then he said to Tash, 'Take no notice of him, he's jus' jealous. Aren't you, Jim? You never got in my knickers, did ya?'

Jim grunted.

By the time they'd finished the meal Tash was pissed and the blokes were practically legless. They went to find the car but it was gone.

'What the fuck?' said Danny.

'What? Where izzit?' slurred Jim.

'Fuckin' bin towed away, ain't it?' said Danny, kicking at a lamppost and missing.

'Are you sure you parked it here?' asked Tash.

'For fuck's sake, Tash,' Danny said. 'Course I'm sure.'

'How'm I fuckin' gonna get back now? Gotta fuckin' get back soon,' shouted Jim.

Then he was standing next to another car. Next to the driver's door. He was fiddling in the lock with a piece of metal. Within a couple of minutes the lock slid up. Jim pulled his sleeves down over his hands and got in the car. He ripped out the wires from under the ignition and touched them together. The engine started.

'Come on, let's go,' he said.

Danny and Tash piled in. Danny kept his sleeves over his hands as well, so as not to put his prints anywhere. Jim drove off like a lunatic, accelerating hard and spinning round corners.

'Fuckin' wankers,' he was saying. 'What'd they have to take your fuckin' car for?'

'Fuckin' tossers,' agreed Danny. 'Their job's to fuck up other people's lives, ain't it?'

And then there in front of them was a towaway truck hitching up some other person's car.

'Look, the fuckin' wankers,' Jim said, accelerating and smashing into the back of the truck.

The towaway people looked terrified as Jim reversed and went for it again. One of the towaway lads ran off to call the police. Jim reversed and smashed. Danny was cheering. Tash was getting thrown about in the back. Reversed and smashed until the car was a crushed heap of scrap. Then there was a siren. They tried to get out the car but the doors were slightly crumpled and hard to open. The coppers were out their car and walking over towards them. Finally the door opened and they all jumped out. Jim nutted one of the pigs and he fell away clutching his face where his nose was split. Danny kneed the other in the balls and then caught him on the side of the head with a right hook that sent him spinning to the floor. Tash was just standing watching. Danny shouted at her to run. The pig with the split nose was back in his car calling for assistance. The other was still on the floor when Tash turned to see Jim stamping on his face. She felt sick. She ran on. Jim carried on kicking the geezer till Danny pulled him away.

'Come on, mate, we gotta get out of here.'

They caught up with Tash and flagged down a cab.

'Can you take us outa London?' asked Danny. 'Laddington. I'll give you the cash up front if you're worried.'

'Yeah, alright,' said the cabbie.

They sat silent in the back seats.

'Had a bit've trouble?' the cabbie asked, noticing the knuckles on Danny's hand were slightly grazed.

'Little bit,' said Danny. 'Some geezers starting on us. My mate here's got a bit've a big mouth. Gets 'imself into trouble. Nofin' serious. No one got hurt or nofin'.'

They dropped Jim off near where they'd picked him up. The

cabbie thought it was all a bit strange but what'd he care, so long as he got his money? He didn't often get rides like this.

On the way back, they were still silent. Danny moved up close to Tash and put his arm round her.

'You alright, luv?' he asked and kissed her cheek.

'Mm,' she said. But she felt like shit. She kept seeing Jim's foot coming down, heavy, on that bloke's face.

They got out round the corner from Danny's. He didn't want the cabbie knowing where he lived, just in case. There was still time to go to the off-licence. They went and bought a few beers each. Tash didn't know what she was doing. Did she want to go to Danny's? She wasn't sure she wanted to go back to his. But she certainly didn't want to go back home. There was nowhere else she could go. She wanted to talk to someone but she didn't know who would understand.

She followed Danny back to his flat. When they were inside the door, she cracked open a beer and said, 'You didn't have to do that.'

'How else were we meant to get away?' Danny said gently. 'Jim's menna be inside, for fuck's sake.'

'But he stamped on his face.' Just saying the words made Tash feel ill. 'He was on the ground and he stamped on his face.'

'Look, Jim's not a bad bloke but he's a nutter. Especially where pigs are concerned. But he's got his reasons. You think what he did was bad? When he was fifteen he was put in hospital with three broken ribs. Four pigs, four've 'em beatin' the shit out've him with truncheons. He can't help himself. Every time he sees a copper, he jus' goes crazy.'

'But . . .' Tash didn't know what to say. It was all a bit much. Was it exciting or was it just sick? She suddenly felt she couldn't tell what was right and wrong any more. It should be easy. It should be clear. But it was suddenly complicated and confusing.

'I don't like shit like that,' continued Danny. 'I don't like it.

But that's life. Sometimes you gotta do shit like that jus' to keep your head above water.' He paused. 'You never seen anyone get beaten up before?'

Tash shook her head.

'Well, welcome to the real world. It's not all silver spoons and games of bridge.'

Chapter Thirteen

'How long've I bin workin' 'ere?' repeated the old boy. 'Let me see. I was sixteen when I started 'ere and I'm twenty-one now.' He chuckled and winked at Ellis, who was sitting in the passenger seat of the removals truck. 'You work it aht.'

Since he was sixteen? Ellis couldn't believe it. The bloke was at least sixty. So what was that, forty years or more? Christ almighty. How did he do it? Ellis had been working at Wallace and Simpson Removals for just over two hours. In that time he hadn't done much, except eat a big fry-up in the canteen with the boys and drive halfway round London, but all the same he was beginning to feel the strain of getting up at quarter to seven that morning. Quarter to seven! Ellis was usually going to bed at that time, not getting up. The thought of doing that every day for forty years was outrageous.

'It's not bin bad,' continued the old boy, who was called George. 'It's bin hard work, but then a day's hard graft never did anyone any harm. Some days work all evening 'n' all night till three or four in the morning and gotta be up for work by seven that morning.'

'How much d'you get paid for that, then?' asked Ellis.

'What is it?' said George, suckin' on his lip. 'Time 'n' a half after seven during the week 'n' double at weekends.'

'Fuckin' hell!' thought Ellis. Their normal hourly wage was three quid, so that went up to only four pound fifty an hour if they worked all night. 'That isn't work, that's slave labour,' Ellis thought, but he held his tongue. The boys had already taken a dislike to him because of him and his big mouth. He'd started telling them how he was homeless and that he used to live in a bender on top of an empty block of offices, until he got evicted, and he told them about Doppingdean. These things were normal for Ellis. All his mates went to Doppingdean and most of them squatted but these boys had never heard anything like it. They couldn't work out whether Ellis was making these stories up. It all sounded so weird to them. If he wasn't making it up, then he must be telling them to take the piss out of them, stuck in their council flats with the wife and kids, paying rent, never seeing anything except work, pub, wife, work, pub, wife. Who did this bloke think he was?

'When do we finish tonight?' asked Ellis.

'Dunno, mate. Whenever the work's done,' replied George.

Ellis groaned silently, thinking he wouldn't be able to stand working through the night. Why the fuck did these people do it? Ellis was doing it cos he had to. After he'd fucked up with those pills, he knew he had to sort himself out and start earning. He owed it to Saul. Saul was alright about it in the end. At first he thought Ellis might've nicked the pills. But now he knew Ellis had just fucked up. They'd reached an understanding. Saul'd paid back his geezer and left Ellis to pay him back in his own time. But the sooner the better. Perhaps usually a grand wouldn't have made so much difference to Saul. But now he was trying to stop dealing, Saul was pretty skint. Ellis didn't want to make things any harder for him, so he'd got the first job he could find. He knew it'd be hard work and long hours for shit pay but he'd been desperate. He wasn't gonna stick it out for long, just enough time to get on top of Saul's debt. But these people he was working with were making a career out've it. Why? There had to be better jobs.

'Forty years,' George was saying. 'But it's paid the rent and fed the wife 'n' kids.'

An hour or so later, Ellis was groaning quite openly and very loudly, when the real work had begun. He found himself wedged between a banister and a sofa whose entire weight he was supporting. At least it felt like he was taking the whole weight. The lad at the top of the stairs who was holding the other end of the sofa didn't seem to be doing much except shouting at Ellis.

'Left . . . Right . . . No, no, no, I said left . . . Up . . . Down . . . No, not that way, the other way.'

It seemed Ellis couldn't do anything right. He'd never realized removals was such a complicated business.

By the time they had the sofa safely loaded into the truck, Ellis was sweating like a pig and was ready for a tea break. But there were three more sofas to load up before anyone was talking of having a break. The people they were doing the job for were super rich. Not only did they have four sofas, all antique and covered in pristine cream linen, they also owned an oak table that would comfortably seat ten, not to mention a considerable collection of art. Ellis was no art historian but he knew a Matisse when he saw one and there was a crude but strangely beautiful sculpture out in the garden. It looked suspiciously like one of Henry Moore's.

Ellis was back up in the flat before the other lads. He took the opportunity to take a rest and sat down on one of the sofas. There was a strange object on the table next to him. It was black with a couple of buttons on it and a black string looped around one end as though you were meant to wear it around your neck. Ellis picked it up, wondering what it was. He pressed a couple of the buttons but nothing happened, so he set it back down on the table, none the wiser.

He could hear the boys coming back up the stairs again, laughing and joking amongst themselves. He stood up so he'd look like he was ready for work, and they wouldn't have any reason to have a go at him. But as he stood up, he turned and saw a small black patch on the sofa. He looked at his trousers and saw a matching small black patch on the back pocket. There was a Biro in his pocket. The ink had leaked through his trousers and on to the sofa.

'Shit,' thought Ellis. He had just enough time to flip over the cushion before the boys came back into the room. With luck they wouldn't notice.

'Right, get those cushions off the sofa,' one of the boys barked at Ellis.

Ellis froze and stared at the bloke. Was the bloke taking the piss? Had he seen what Ellis had done?

But then Ellis remembered, they had to take the cushions off before they carried the sofa downstairs. The bloke didn't know what Ellis had done, at least not yet.

Ellis hadn't moved. He tried to speak but no words came out, just a strange noise.

'What?' shouted the bloke. 'Just get on with it. We ain't got all day.'

Ellis felt his body heavy with apprehension. There was nothing else for it, he'd have to get on with it and uncover what he'd done. It was like a visible confession. Slowly he began to take the cushions off. When he came to the one he'd stained, he felt the weight of the boys' gaze pressing down on him, making his movements slower and more deliberate. He pulled it up and . . .

'Fuckin' hell,' said one of the boys. 'Look at that stain.'

'Bet she killed the person that did that,' chipped in another.

'Shouldn't've 'ad a white sofa in the first place. Stupid idea,' laughed another.

The boys crowded round to get a closer look, laughin' 'n' bitchin' about how fuckin' stupid the woman was to have a white sofa. Ellis sighed with relief until the cry erupted, ''Ang on a minute. This ink's still wet.' One of the boys was dabbing at the black blob and looking at the residue of ink on his fingertips. The boys turned to Ellis, sending his stomach sinking once more.

Ellis kept his cool. 'Still wet, is it?' he said, shrugging slightly.

Ellis remained so cool that the boys, to their great disappointment, couldn't believe it was him. They looked back at each other, disgruntled, and one said, 'She must've only jus' dun it.' But he was barely finished speaking when, out the corner of his eye, he saw a black splodge on the back pocket of Ellis's trousers. Triumphantly, he strode over to Ellis and thrust his stubby finger at Ellis's buttock.

'What's that, then?' he exclaimed.

Ellis knew now the game was up. There was no denying it, he had been caught black-bottomed.

'I didn't realize my pen was leaking,' said Ellis. 'Didn't even know I had a pen in my pocket.'

'You stupid wanker. We'll all get our pay docked now.' The bloke prodded Ellis's bum again.

'No, you won't,' said Ellis. 'Put it back how it was 'n' no one'll notice.'

'Course they will,' said the bloke.

'She'll notice sooner or later,' another said, stepping in to support his mate.

'When she does, if she does, I'll say it was me,' said Ellis.

'You're damn right you will, you piece of shit.'

'Yeah, we're not taking any blame for you.'

'Why should we?'

'I'm not askin' you to,' said Ellis. What did they want him to do, commit hara-kiri? Okay, it was a dumb thing to do but he hadn't meant to do it and it was done now, they had to deal with it, which is what finally they did. They loaded the sofa in the truck and replaced the cushions, so the stain was covered.

But the boys weren't going to forget it. They were glad to

have a legitimate reason to hate Ellis. When they stopped for tea break, they sat apart from him but he could hear them bitching about it. He didn't need to sit and listen to that shit. He wandered off back inside the flat. It was incredible to see art in such an informal setting. The stale atmosphere of galleries somehow dulled art, made it seem less impressive, but here it was fresh and real. He could reach out and touch it.

In the corner of the room was an alcove with a small mahogany table. There was only one thing on the table, an egg. The egg was in two halves opening out to reveal a basket of white china flowers. The two halves of the egg were dark red and overlaid with a fine gold pattern. The edges were studded with diamonds. So was the basket. At the centre of each flower was an emerald. The egg was mounted on a small marble stand.

Ellis reckoned the egg must be by that bloke, what was he called? Fabergé. That was it. Fabergé. Something like that must be worth a few quid. A few thousand. Ellis wasn't sure exactly how much but enough to pay back Saul, though. And there it was sitting in front of him in a neat little egg that he could so easily pick up and slip in his pocket. Thousands of quid in his pocket in a couple of seconds. A year's wages at this job, probably, maybe more. And these people had spent that money on an egg, not to eat or drive or live in but to sit on a table in their living room and look good. Or for them to mention it at dinner parties – 'Yes, John bought a superb Fabergé the other day.' It wasn't right. It simply wasn't right. But here was the perfect opportunity to even up the odds a little. Robin Hood stylee. Just pick it up and put it in your pocket. Done. Wouldn't have to worry any more . . . Ellis picked it up and held it in his hand.

'Beautiful, isn't it?' It was the woman who owned the flat.

'Yes, yes,' said Ellis, looking round at her. 'I was just, er . . .' Thinking of stealing it. Did she know what he'd been thinking?

'Yes, it is beautiful. You like art then, do you?'

'Yeah,' said Ellis. She didn't seem to suspect anything. He put back the egg carefully.

'Do you want to see my Constable?' the woman smiled and winked at Ellis.

That was a wink, wasn't it? Ellis looked at the woman again, trying to work out whether he'd seen right but the woman was already turning and walking towards the bedroom. Ellis followed her. Above the mantelpiece there was the Constable – a small chequered landscape with a sky of blended pinks and mauves. They stood in front of it together, the woman slightly behind Ellis, silent and still until – Ellis suddenly felt something touch his crotch. Billy the Willy woke up. He'd thought he'd be having the day off today, seeing as Ellis was at work. Ellis jumped and turned to see the woman's mouth coming towards his own and her hand fumbling its way inside his trousers. This wasn't what he'd been expecting but the woman wasn't bad looking, so he wasn't going to complain. He'd rather spend the afternoon humping her than humping furniture around. She had his trousers undone now and they were beginning to slip down around his ankles when there was a knock at the door and a man's voice called urgently, 'Mrs Pollard, Mrs Pollard, are you alright in there, Mrs Pollard?'

Mrs Pollard pulled her mouth away from Ellis's and looked at him, panic-stricken. Ellis grabbed his trousers and began to pull them up. Mrs Pollard finally snapped herself out of her daze and went to see who was at the door.

It was the police. One rather overweight policeman, to be precise. His bulging cheeks were glowing red and glistening with sweat and he was dabbing his forehead with a handkerchief. In fact his whole body was bulging from the uniform, which seemed a little too small.

'Had a call from the station,' he said, panting, so that the words came out in fits and starts and some were lost completely as he gulped for air. 'Panic . . . Panic button . . . Came as soon as we could . . . Everything alright?'

'Panic button?' thought Ellis and then remembered that funny black thing that he'd been fiddling with earlier. Was that what it was, a panic button? Mad, to have so much money that you're always scared of being robbed. Scared even in your own home. Dangerous business being so rich.

'Yes, yes,' said Mrs Pollard, feeling more relaxed now. 'Everything's quite alright.' She turned and winked at Ellis who was trying to disguise the fact that his trousers were undone and his pants were bigger than they should be.

The policeman looked over at Ellis and looked him up and down. He wasn't sure he trusted him.

'You are sure,' he said to Mrs Pollard, able to breathe slightly easier now, 'there's definitely nothing wrong.' He had a fantasy that Ellis was holding Mrs Pollard captive but that she was too scared to say anything. There was definitely something awkward about the way Ellis was standing and what was that lump down his trousers? Was he trying to conceal a weapon?

'Yes, yes, I'm fine,' said Mrs Pollard, impatiently. 'Must've been some kind of mistake.'

The policeman still felt uneasy. How could he ever forgive himself if he were to leave and she was harmed?

'Everything's fine,' Mrs Pollard repeated when the policeman still made no attempt to leave. 'I'm quite alright.'

He put his feelings of unease to one side. Mrs Pollard *did* seem alright, in fact she was beginning to sound a little annoyed at his presence, as though she had more important things on her mind. He asked her one last time, just to be sure, and then left.

'Better get back to work,' said Ellis, sure Mrs Pollard wouldn't want to continue after the interruption. She was probably a little embarrassed by the way she'd jumped him. But not a bit of it.

She stormed back over to him and said, 'I don't think you are going anywhere,' before launching herself back at him with renewed vigour.

Billy, who had begun to recede, picked himself up again, ready for round two. Before Ellis knew it, they were on the bed and their clothes were on the floor. They were tossing and turning, prodding and poking, moaning and groaning and then, with a few shrill yelps and one final poke, it was all over.

Mrs Pollard pulled herself off Billy. Ellis looked up at the ceiling, thinking, 'My first honest day's work.'

Mrs Pollard was saying, 'Thank you, thank you. That was my first orgasm in five years.'

The boys were beginning to wonder where Ellis was.

'Couldn't take the pace, could he?'

'Lazy bastard, slopin' off.'

'Couldn't do a hard day's work.'

Ellis lay back in the bath. It was full and deep and the bubbles bounced up against his cheeks. The bathroom was the size of a small flat and done out completely in white marble. There were two basins – his and hers. The bath was also white and huge. The taps on both the basins and the bath were gold – real gold.

Ellis was playing with one of them now, running his big toe along its curve and easing it up inside the tap.

'Aahhh, this is the life.'

Ellis tugged at his toe. Like so many things in life, it seemed the tap was easier to get into than get out of. He tugged again. He could feel his toe swelling inside the tap, as he yanked at it. He tried again, more gently, with a little twist and wiggle of his foot. Uh, er. No go. But his toe wasn't stuck. It was just being awkward. It definitely wasn't stuck. It couldn't be. Ellis wouldn't even let himself think it. A bit of soap. That's what he needed.

He managed to pull himself up to the taps. It was quite awkward to do with one foot suspended in mid-air. He felt like a meditating yogi. He lathered his toe with soap and pulled at it again, gently at first and then more fiercely when it still didn't move. He twisted it and yanked it and added a bit more soap, although there was plenty there already. But the toe wouldn't budge.

Fuck. Ellis felt his stomach sinking. For a moment he thought he might vomit. 'Bastard,' he said to his toe. 'What did I ever do to you?'

It was then that Mrs Pollard came in with the news that Ellis had better hurry up and get out of the bath as her husband would be back soon. Off to Hong Kong, you see. Early evening flight.

Ellis looked at his toe and looked at Mrs Pollard and confessed with a whimper that made him sound like a guilty dog. 'I, er . . . It's stuck. My toe.'

'Don't be so ridiculous,' said Mrs Pollard. 'Have you tried some soap?'

'Yeah.'

'Let me try.' Mrs Pollard strode over to the bath, lathered the soap vigorously and plastered Ellis's toe with suds. She grabbed his foot with two hands and pulled as though she were pulling on a bell rope.

Ellis slipped and disappeared into the bathwater. When his head popped back up, he saw his toe, red and throbbing and still stuck in the tap.

'Yer see,' he said. 'It's stuck.'

'What were you doing putting it in the tap in the first place?' screeched Mrs Pollard.

'I dunno.'

'How ridiculous. You stupid idiot.'

'This isn't my fault,' replied Ellis, defensively. 'You started this. I didn't ask you to jump me.'

'My husband! My husband!' Mrs Pollard screamed. 'What will I say?'

The boys were about to take the grandfather clock downstairs.

'You hear that?'

'I'd be deaf not to.'

'Sounds like a lovers' tiff.' A laugh.

'Having an affair right under our noses.' Another laugh.

But they didn't twig who lover boy was.

When the fireman saw Ellis, he nudged his mate and nodded and they both started laughing.

It had been Mrs Pollard's idea to call out the fire brigade. Ellis hadn't wanted to. Hadn't wanted to make a fuss and the boys to work out what was going on. But Mrs Pollard had insisted. They had to do something. It was getting late and her husband would be back soon.

By the time the firemen arrived, Ellis had managed to swivel his toe around inside the tap so that he could sit up on the side of the bath and Mrs Pollard had given him a towel to wrap round his waist. So things weren't as embarrassing as they could've been but they were bad enough.

It took the firemen a few minutes to recover their composure.

'Right,' said one when finally he could speak. 'Angle grinder.'

Ellis looked up at him. 'Angle grinder,' he repeated.

'Don't worry. It'll all be over soon enough.'

That wasn't the point. Ellis wanted to know whether, when it was all over, he'd still be left with his toe.

When the fireman returned with the angle grinder, he gave Ellis a pair of goggles to wear and told Mrs Pollard to stand back.

'Leave enough space for my toe,' shouted Ellis as the angle grinder came closer. 'Don't touch my toe. You don't know how long . . .' His voice was lost as the angle grinder cut into the metal. 'Be careful,' he was still crying out as half the tap and all his toe clunked to the bottom of the bath. It took him a moment to realize he was alright and no longer attached to the bath.

'Thank you so much,' Mrs Pollard was saying to the firemen. Her problem was solved, but Ellis – Ellis still had the end of a tap stuck on his toe. He had nothing against toe rings but this was a little OTT.

'Now what?' he said.

'Soap,' said the fireman.

'Soap?' said Ellis. 'But I've tried that already.'

'Not from this end,' said the fireman.

'Come on,' said Mrs Pollard, still agitated. 'My husband will be back soon. Get out of my house.'

'That's all the thanks I get for your first orgasm in five years,' retorted Ellis.

The firemen looked at each other and smirked. Mrs Pollard blushed and remained quiet after that.

Ellis tried the soap trick again and the firemen were right. The soap could get right underneath the tap and it slid easily off. He kept hold of it and when he was dressed, he popped it in his pocket. Had to be worth a few quid and he wasn't gonna get paid for his first (and last) day at Wallace and Simpson Removals.

Chapter Fourteen

Chelsea had been looking forward to her wedding day. She had been getting quite excited and a little nervous. But when she woke up on the day, the only feeling she had was one of being kicked in the head. She had been dreaming some bloke was launching a steel-toecapped boot into her head time after time. When she woke up, she realized her assailant was just a dream but the vicious throbbing in her head was real – a real hangover.

Chelsea had planned to get a good night's sleep. No such luck. Joss and a few other mates had been round giving it, 'It's your hen night, Chelsea. Gotta party.' They'd bought some beers and a couple of bottles of tequila. Chelsea had ended up chopping out lines liberally. No one had got to bed till six in the morning.

Chelsea slammed her fist down on the alarm clock. She had an hour and a half to calm down, get ready and get to the registry office on time.

'Bollox,' she said as she looked around the kitchen. No aspirin and no milk. Chelsea snarled and kicked one of the bodies that was strewn on the floor as she went out to the shops.

Two cups of tea and four aspirins later, she was feeling a little more relaxed. She went to run a bath and sat on the loo watching the water run. She had just finished a fat crap when she looked around and saw – no bog roll.

'Bastards,' she screamed, as she wiped her arse with a layer of cardboard she had peeled from the inner tube of the loo roll. She slid into the bath, saying to herself, 'Calm down. Take it easy.'

But Chelsea was far from calm as she tottered into the registry office ten minutes late. She didn't wear a watch and was clutching her alarm clock instead.

'Out of my way. Can't you see I'm late.' Chelsea pushed past a couple who were holding hands and smiling inanely at each other. She held out her clock as proof and repeated, 'I'm late. I'm late . . .' but faltered as she looked up at the big circular clock, stuck up on the registry office's wall. It said ten past eleven. Her own clock read ten past twelve. 'Your clock's slow,' she barked at the receptionist. 'Stupid. How can people be on time when the clock's wrong?'

The receptionist shrank into her seat and checked her own watch, almost guiltily. It said ten past eleven.

'Erm,' she said. 'I think it's ten past eleven. My watch says it is.' She smiled feebly. Perhaps if she was nice to this woman, the woman would be nice to her.

'Well, then they're both wrong,' snapped Chelsea.

The woman was thinking something. She wasn't sure she dare say it but she took a breath, hoping to inhale a little courage and, without looking at Chelsea, mumbled, 'Perhaps it's your clock that's wrong.'

Chelsea looked through the receptionist as though this was the most preposterous idea she had ever heard.

'Well, we'll see, shall we?' Chelsea yanked at the sleeve of a groom who was passing. 'Excuse me, do you have the time?'

'Certainly,' the groom smiled and looked at his watch. 'Ten past eleven.'

'Ten past eleven,' Chelsea repeated incredulously. 'But, but . . .'

'That's right, ten past eleven,' said the man. 'Haven't missed

147

a wedding, have you?' He grinned as he saw Chelsea's mouth hang open.

'No, I haven't. I'm an hour early,' replied Chelsea, coldly.

Chelsea sat in the waiting room in a worse mood than ever. All that rush. All that panic this morning. For nothing. Because of that stupid alarm clock. How could it be an hour fast? And why hadn't she seen the clock in the car? Stupid little thing. It was too small to see.

In the waiting room with Chelsea was a young bride dolled up in a white dress, veil and loads of make-up. She was sitting on her own.

How old was she? wondered Chelsea. She looked about fifteen.

'You don't look old enough to get married,' exclaimed Chelsea. 'What are you doing throwing your life away?'

'But . . . but I'm in love,' smiled the girl.

'Love!' exclaimed Chelsea. 'What's love got to do with it? You think you love him now but you wait and see. He'll be bored of you soon. Chasing off after other women.'

'But . . . but . . .'

'I mean, I'm not trying to put you off or anything. Just don't want you to make a mistake, that's all.'

The girl got up suddenly and ran out with a sniff and a squeak as though the floodgates were about to open. Chelsea felt a little pang of guilt. Had she been a bit harsh on the girl? Had she been taking out her mood on her? No, she was simply saying what she thought. You had to, didn't you? Couldn't keep your thoughts boxed inside your head. Anyway, she was right. Little girl like that shouldn't be throwing away her freedom.

Chelsea sighed and looked up at the clock. She still had three-quarters of an hour to go before the wedding. Enough time for a couple of gin and tonics. That'd sort out her hangover. Hair of the dog and all that. Hair of the dog? Chelsea had never understood. What good is a dog's hair if you've been bitten?

When Chelsea came back from the pub, she was in a much better mood. The gin and tonics – she'd had three doubles – had calmed her down and dulled her hangover. Ellis was there in the waiting room and Joss and Saul and a couple of other mates. Deepak was surrounded by a whole posse of Indians. Chelsea scampered up to Joss.

'Joss, didn't think you'd make it,' she said, glad to see her.

'Course, mate, it's your wedding day, ain't it?' replied Joss. 'I wasn't gonna miss this for the world.'

Ellis was glugging on a bottle of whisky. Even Saul was looking relaxed. He took a swig on Ellis's bottle and smiled at Chelsea.

'Looking good,' he said.

'Do you think so?' said Chelsea, looking down at her dress. It was the sky-blue dress she'd nicked from Fitzroy's. 'I was a bit worried it didn't suit me.'

Deepak was standing biting his nails.

'Oh, Kensington,' he said when he saw Chelsea. 'You are looking very lovely.'

'It's Chelsea, not Kensington,' said Chelsea.

'Oh, yes, yes,' said Deepak, looking even more worried. 'Yes, Chelsea, not Kensington.'

'Don't forget,' said Chelsea.

The strap of her dress was slipping from her shoulder. Chelsea went to pull it up and felt Deepak's hand on her shoulder, also trying to pull up the strap.

'Don't touch me,' she snarled at him and then smiled sweetly as she saw the registrar coming towards them. Had she heard? Just in case, she said to Deepak, 'At least not till after the wedding.'

Deepak looked confused.

The registrar also looked a little confused. 'Hello,' she said to

Chelsea. 'I'm the registrar who'll be marrying you. Just a little query that needs clearing up. Your initials, F.C. What do they stand for exactly?'

A blush shot through Chelsea's face. 'Nothing. It's just F.C. That's it,' she said.

'I'm terribly sorry. I'm not trying to be awkward.' The registrar had noticed Chelsea blush. Some people could be so touchy about their middle names. 'Only, I have to have your full name.'

'I don't see why.' Chelsea sounded irritated. 'I mean this is my special day. I should be able to do what I want.'

'I'm sorry but those are the rules,' smiled the registrar.

'Alright, if you must know,' said Chelsea, sighing. 'It stands for Football Club.'

'Football Club?' repeated the registrar. This woman wasn't seriously called Football Club, was she?

'Yes, my dad was a fan.' Chelsea felt hot and pissed off. Why did her dad have to have given her such a stupid name? It was so embarrassing.

Deepak was roaring with laughter and seemed to have forgotten Chelsea was meant to be the love of his life and he was meant to know all about her already.

'Chelsea Football Club,' he laughed, glad to have some way of releasing his tension. 'Oh, dearie me, I am marrying Chelsea Football Club.'

Chelsea had had enough. He was really getting on her tits and her hangover was back in the vicinity. She turned to him and slapped him across the face. He stopped laughing and stood clutching his cheek. The registrar looked aghast.

'Are you sure you want to go through with this?' the registrar asked, tentatively.

Deepak looked as though he was about to burst into tears. Chelsea still wore a stony stare.

Joss, who'd seen what'd happened and knew how much

Chelsea hated her middle names, stepped up and said, 'It's alright.' She smiled at the registrar, reassuringly. 'She's just a little nervous, that's all. Aren't you?' She put her arm around Chelsea's shoulder.

Chelsea pulled herself together and remembered the blag she was trying to pull off. They had to look more convincing.

'Course I am.' Chelsea smiled at the registrar. Then she smiled at Deepak. 'Darling, I'm so sorry. I'm just a little nervous. Still hung-over from the hen night. You know what I'm like.' She took Deepak's hand and kissed him on the lips. 'I love you.'

Deepak still looked shell-shocked and all he could say was, 'Yes, Ken . . . Chelsea.'

The registrar seemed satisfied. The ceremony was about to begin. They all filed into the registry office. Ellis sat at the back of the room, still glugging surreptitiously on his whisky.

'We are gathered here today to join in matrimony Deepak and Chelsea,' said the registrar once everyone was settled. 'Deepak, will you repeat these words after me?' The registrar looked at Deepak. Deepak looked as though he was about to be sent to the front line. 'I do solemnly declare.'

Deepak repeated, 'I do solemnly declare.'

'That I know not of any lawful impediment,' the registrar continued.

'That I know not of any lawful impediment.' Deepak's voice was shaking. He kept looking at the registrar, checking he was saying the right thing, rather than looking lovingly at Chelsea.

'Why I, Deepak Mahajan.'

'Why I, Deepak Mahajan.' Deepak looked relieved. That part was easy. At least he knew his own name.

'May not be joined in matrimony.'

'May not be joined in matrimony.' Deepak was staring at the registrar.

'To Chelsea Football Club Minnoela.' The registrar bit her lip as she spoke. She mustn't laugh. She really mustn't laugh.

This was the part Deepak was dreading. 'To Chelsea Foot, Foot.' Deepak knew if he continued, he'd burst out laughing. He paused, trying to control himself.

The registrar thought perhaps Deepak, amid his nerves, had forgotten the name of his bride. 'Football Club,' she prompted.

Deepak tried again. 'Foot.' He got no further before his mouth crumpled into first a smirk, then a chuckle and then outright laughter.

Chelsea glowered at him. 'It's not that funny, Deepak,' she snarled. 'Just get on with it.'

Deepak pulled himself together, remembering the slap Chelsea had given him earlier.

The registrar looked at the couple. She'd seen some strange weddings in her time, like the one when the couple had dressed up as Charles and Diana, but at least that couple had seemed in love. These two didn't seem ready for such a commitment.

Deepak finally managed to say the words, 'Chelsea Football Club Minnoela.'

Deepak had further problems when he was trying to put the ring on Chelsea's finger. He would've put it on the wrong finger, had Chelsea not steered him to the right one.

Finally the ceremony was over. Everyone was gathering their things together, ready to leave. Ellis leant forward, belched and vomited on the person in front of him, an old Indian man with white hair and beard. Ellis then slid to the floor, unconscious. The old man was calm and dignified. He went quietly to the loos to clean himself up.

Chelsea exclaimed loudly, 'Ellis, can't take you anywhere.'

Saul went over and kicked Ellis gently. 'Oi, mate, get up.'

The next couple in line waited nervously, each hoping the delay wouldn't give the other the chance they needed to back out. The registrar looked equally nervous. The office had a very tight schedule to keep.

'Come on, Ellis,' said Saul. Ellis didn't respond. There was only one thing for it. Saul lifted Ellis and took him out to Chelsea's car.

The registrar sighed as they left. Thank God not all couples were like that.

Chelsea couldn't wait to get home and have a couple of lines and some gin and tonic. Deepak was really bugging her. A few people came back with her to celebrate. Saul bundled Ellis out of Chelsea's car and left him unconscious in the corner. The others were getting a chillum together.

Saul puff, puff, puffed on the chillum and passed it on. He felt the air, hot, deep inside his lungs. He sat back and felt a shiver of tobacco run right through his body.

A moment later, a fog enveloped him and he wished he hadn't taken a toke. The fog hung heavy about him, dampening each of his senses. The images on the TV and the faces of the people around him felt distant and yet strangely vivid, as colour intensified. His ears seemed plugged, sounds dull. His mind was clumsy. He couldn't speak. With senses like these, he didn't trust himself to say anything intelligible. He sat alone, marooned in a cocoon.

Everyone else was talking. They were talking about him. He could feel it. He could sense it. He couldn't hear exactly what they were saying but he felt sure it was about him. Every now and then, he heard his name being mentioned. And he was sure Joss was joining in too. Dave kept turning and looking at him and grinning. Saul knew he was trying to mock him. Saul tried to smile back but his mouth set solid on his face. How could he smile? It would be as though he was agreeing with what they were saying about him. It would be as though he didn't understand that they were making fun of him, bitchin' about him. And not even doin' it behind his back. Doin' it right there in front of him, as though he were a fool. As though he were weak.

'Saul, Saul,' he tried to snap himself out of it. 'What are you thinking? What the fuck are you saying? Stop it. Stop it. Are you crazy? They're not talking about you. You're just stoned.'

The mirror was coming round with a rack of lines that Chelsea had cut for everyone. He wasn't sure he wanted to take it. He saw himself breathing too heavily and blowing the coke in the air. He didn't feel he could do anything right. Not now. But he couldn't say no. He didn't want anyone asking him why.

'Just do it,' he said to himself. 'What are you worrying about? How many lines of coke have you done before? Just get on with it. Stop thinking so much.'

Saul took the mirror and the note, tooted his line and passed them on. He sat back in his seat and felt the coke slide, viscous, down the back of his throat. He gulped. His body was tight with dead-end energy. He wanted to speak, just to hear his voice, but they were still talking about him.

'. . . Saul . . .'

There it was, he'd heard them say his name. And Dave's sly smile again. Never felt comfortable with them. Always knew they didn't really want me around. It's just like in my dream. Why, why *would* they want me here? No good. No good to anyone. They all know about that kid. Probably still hold it against me. And the giro and the money that's gone. It was someone that's been round the house. Maybe not Ellis. But someone. Someone took those letters. Someone did. Thought I wouldn't notice. Thought I wouldn't care. Rich dealer. Look at Dave smile at you now. Thinks you're a fool. And them all laughing at you. Giggling to themselves. Whispering. Laughing at you.

'What the fuck?' Saul snapped at himself. 'Are you going mad? Stop yourself thinking like that.' He closed his eyes and shook his head. 'Mad. You'll drive yourself crazy.'

Crazy. You know you're already crazy. Talking to yourself

like this. Who else talks to themselves like this? They don't. Only you. Only you. Because you're mad.

'Stop it.' Saul stood up suddenly. He had to get out. He went to the loo although he didn't need to go. He pulled his jeans down around his knees and sat on the loo with his elbows resting on his thighs. He looked at the red walls of the room. The red bellowed at him, hot like hell.

'Why did Chelsea paint it red of all colours?' he thought. He closed his eyes, breathed deeply and did not let himself think. His body was taut. He tried to relax.

'Breathe slow, relax,' was all he would let himself think. He felt his muscles soften slowly.

After a couple of minutes, he stood up, carefully did up his button flies, as though it was important to get it right, and then flushed the chain, for no real reason. He went to the basin and let the cold water run over his wrists. He splashed his face and looked himself in the eye.

'Take it easy. It's okay.'

Saul walked back into the lounge. As he walked in everyone seemed to stop and Si glanced at him over his shoulder and said, louder than he needed to, 'Yeah, a right dickhead', and then he looked back at everyone else. Joss giggled.

Saul felt the energy surge in his body, his chest hot and his heart beating. Before he knew it, he was standing over Dave.

'What the fuck are you saying?' Saul hears himself say. And then he has Dave up against the wall, twisting the top of his shirt tight around his neck. Dave's eyes are flickering with shock and disbelief, dancing from Saul's face to the others and back, trying to work out what is happening. He nearly starts to laugh. Is this for real? But it is. Saul begins to shake him.

'What the fuck?' Saul is saying. 'What the fuck? Talking about me like that. As though I don't know what you're saying.' Saul's voice sounds hoarse and high as though he's forcing the air out from his throat. He's shaking Dave. Dave's head begins to flop against the wall. Before Saul knows it, he's swung his fist round into Dave's face. The cut isn't deep but the blood is bright. Red like the walls of the loo.

Joss came up behind him. She looked at Dave. He was dabbing the cut on his cheek and looking at his fingers as though he had never seen his own blood before. Joss looked at Saul. His eyes were glassy and wild.

'Saul, what you doin'?' she said, touching his shoulder. She looked at him but it was almost as if he wasn't there.

'What the fuck's wrong with you?' shouted Dave. 'Are you mad?'

Saul didn't speak. He shrugged Joss off and walked out the door.

Outside it wasn't any better. His mind was still foggy as fuck. The air was dark. Choking diesel. It wasn't any better. He was still himself. He was still Saul. He was still there inside that same crazy head. It *was* crazy. He knew it was crazy. He knew *he* was crazy. Why else would those questions chase each other round in circles inside his head?

What the fuck are you doing? Who the fuck do you think you are? Think you're cool? Think you're clever? You're not. You're shit. *Shit. Shit.*

The voices were talking at him. *That* was mad. That was what madness was. Talking inside his head. He couldn't handle it. That voice. The one that whispered to him.

You're shit. You're shit. You're worth nothing.

He'd come outside to clear his head. Get away from all of that. Leave what had happened behind him. But how could he? Because what was happening was happening inside his head. He couldn't get away from it. Everywhere he went the voice whispered.

Crap. Shit. Can't do anything.

And he was beginning to believe it. He couldn't be on his own because then he could hear the voices most clearly. But how could he trust himself to be with other people?

Saul saw himself hunched and mumbling as he walked down the street in the dark. Suddenly he remembered the ragga he'd seen a few weeks ago, calling out, 'Charlie, don't jump. Don't jump out the window. Charlie, don't do it.' He'd seen the ragga and known he hadn't been mad. But look at him now. Mumbling down the street. They were the same, crazy as each other.

You're fucked, Saul. You've lost it. Can't ever sort it out.

Saul wanted to hurt something. Break something. Maybe then something would change. At least it wouldn't all be inside his head any more. It'd be out there. Not trapped inside here.

And then there was a black kid standing there. Just hanging out. Not doing anyone any harm. Waiting for someone, perhaps. Waiting for a cab? Whatever, he was there. Wrong place, wrong time. Saul didn't wanna hurt him but the kid was just there. And Saul couldn't help it. He turned and punched him. And punched him and punched him and punched him.

Chapter Fifteen

Danny punched the geezer. And punched him again and then swung round and ducked as someone tried to punch him.

Tash was standing watching, not sure what to do. So was the rest of the pub. Even the barmen and the landlord. No one wanted to get involved. It'd all flared up so quick. One minute they'd been sitting round drinking and then suddenly they were fighting. Something about some sunglasses that'd been nicked out've Danny's mate's flat. But how the fight proper had started, Tash couldn't tell. No one really knew. They were all just fighting now because someone had lamped them or their girlfriend, or someone'd cussed them. Some bloke had tried to break it up but something'd been said that he couldn't ignore and then there he was, lashing out with the rest of them. And it was spreading. More and more people getting involved for no reason except that they were pissed.

Everywhere Tash looked it was kicking off. A kick in the head. A knee in yer balls. A bottle breaking on the skull. And she watched as a hand held a pint glass. Saw it breaking against the bar. Heard it smash and felt it slash against her gut. And she looked the geezer in the face and then saw the glass swinging into her forehead. It happened in slow motion but was all over so quick. She had a second to think, 'It's coming at my face.' She screamed at the thought. And then it was done. There was a gash in her gut and another above an eye and across the bridge of her nose. It didn't really hurt but she called out again in shock, at the thought of it more than anything else.

She felt nauseous in the pit of her stomach. She knew she had to get out. She couldn't really see straight. Blood streaming above and into her eye. She fell past the people, still fighting all around. Out on to the street. Blood-blurred vision. Thought she might vomit. Stumbling. Dabbing at her face with her T-shirt. And then walking out into the road. The car couldn't stop.

And it was all going slow again. The weight of the car driving into her body. Flying through the air. Almost floating. And then crumpled on the road, unable to move. Her leg was pounding.

'Jesus Christ,' shouted the driver and jumped out his car. He looked at Tash's body. The bone in her leg stuck out through her skin. 'What the fuck have I done?' he thought.

'Got some coke. D'you want a line?' asked Danny.

'Yeah,' Tash smiled. 'Cheers.'

It was a few days after the accident. Tash was in St Charles's hospital. She'd been operated on to straighten out the bones in her shin and was now in a room of her own so the doctors could keep an eye on her.

'Gotta look after you, ain't I?' winked Danny. He racked out a couple of lines and sniffed one. Then, feeling restless, he got up and began fiddling with a strap that was hanging loose off Tash's traction.

'Danny,' screamed Tash. 'Leave that alone. This isn't some Carry On film.'

'Fuckin' hell, can't do anything right,' Danny muttered as he sat back down on the bed. He fidgeted with the cuff on his shirt for a moment before grinning up at Tash. 'Sorted it out for you.' Tash looked inquisitive, so Danny continued. 'The bloke that put you in 'ere. Sorted him out.'

'I don't want you sorting him out,' said Tash. 'There's nothing to sort out. I walked into a car. That's how I got in here. It wasn't anyone's fault.'

'Don't talk shit. That bloke that glassed you. If he hadn't done that, then you wouldn't be in here. Can't let 'im get away with it. Glassin' a woman, it ain't on.'

Tash was tired. She didn't want to listen to gangster shit now. And she didn't want Danny doing anything dumb on her account.

'Leave it, Danny,' she said, firmly. 'I don't want you to do anything.'

'You don't understand, do you?' Danny was pissed off. 'They're fuckin' takin' the piss. Stealin' off us. Then fuckin' puttin' my woman in hospital.'

'I told you, I'm not your woman.'

'You're in hospital, though, ain't it?' Danny sniffed. 'Can't have 'em takin' the piss. They'll think our firm's a loada poofs. Can't 'av' it. They gotta know who they're dealin' with.'

'For fuck's sake, I'm the one who's in hospital and I'm telling you, I don't want you doing anything.' The thought of the fight made Tash feel ill. She wished it'd never happened. She didn't want it to keep on going. Some petty feud over a pair of shades that was nicked in the first place.

But Danny went on. 'Gotta be taught a lesson. Can't let things like that go. Takin' the piss.'

'Piss off, Danny,' shouted Tash. 'I don't wanna know.'

Danny was silent. He stared hard at Tash and then walked out. Women just didn't understand.

Thing was, it was already sorted. Danny'd found out who'd glassed Tash. A mate of the geezer that'd nicked the shades. Danny knew who he was, so him and a few mates had sorted him out.

They knew where he lived. Caught him as he was coming out his flat. Coshed him on the head. Bundled him into a car and they were away. They took him to the wasteground. Strung him up from a tree by his ankles. He was whimperin', the fuckin' pussy, and they hadn't even started.

One of the lads picked up a piece of wood and hit him across his back.

'Can't fuckin' mess us around.'

'We ain't gonna take no shit.'

He was swinging like a punch bag. They were punchin' him and kickin' him. Danny thought they'd bin at it for ever. Thought they'd never stop. The grass and dust beneath the geezer was damp with his blood.

Then Danny said, 'He's had enough.'

'You're lucky. This time.' Kicked him one last time.

Someone cut him down. They left him in a pile on the wasteground.

Yeah, they sorted him right out.

Tash's mum had come to visit her.

'Now, really, I think you should've gone private. I mean look at this place.' She ran a finger along the window sill. 'It's covered in dust.' She inspected the tip of her finger disapprovingly, expecting to see a layer of dust. She was a little disappointed to see that her finger remained clean, except for a piece of fluff that had lodged itself under her nail. 'This is the state of the NHS. No wonder the Tories are encouraging people to go private. It's embarrassing, Tash, to have you here. I can't believe it.'

'When it's an emergency, you don't get a choice,' sighed Tash, wondering what was the point of bothering to explain. 'They just take you wherever's got beds.'

'But you should have insisted,' Jane continued. 'What on earth do you think BUPA's all about?'

'Mum, I was unconscious. How could I insist on anything?' Tash was getting annoyed.

'I don't know why BUPA don't give out cards or something, like kidney donors have or those bracelets diabetics wear to let everyone know they need insulin,' Jane continued. 'But don't worry, Tash, I've arranged for you to move first thing tomorrow morning.'

'Mum, I'm alright here.'

'I don't care what you think, Tash, I want you receiving the best care possible.'

First Danny, now her mum. Couldn't they leave Tash alone? She was ill. She felt like shit. She just wanted some peace.

Her mum was babbling on still. How they'd been burgled. All the silver had gone. Even the necklace Tash's dad had given her mum. How could people do such things? How could they?

Tash thought, 'You've got enough money. Too much. You don't need it all.'

And her mum was going on. Terrible, it was, really ghastly. And the police didn't have much hope of recovering any of it . . .

And then Tash wasn't sure where the words came from, but they just popped out.

'Mum, just fuck off, will you?'

Jane was too shocked to be angry. 'I expect you're tired, Tash,' she said and left.

Tash thought, 'Yeah, tired of you.'

'Alright, Tash. Um . . .' Danny stood awkwardly in front of Tash's bed trying to think what to say. He couldn't think of anything, so he swooped down and gave her a kiss.

Tash knew that was Danny's way of saying sorry.

'I'm sorry,' she said.

Danny grinned. ''S alright. Look, 'ere, I got you som'ing. Som'ing special.' Danny reached in his pocket and pulled out a scrumpled bit of tissue paper. He handed it to Tash.

Tash began unwrapping the tissue paper. She felt something

heavy inside. She caught a glimpse of it. It wasn't, was it? It couldn't be. She carried on unwrapping it. When she saw what it was, she burst into hysterics.

'What, what?' asked Danny, feeling a bit paranoid. Was Tash takin' the piss outa his taste? He'd been sure she'd like it. It *was* real silver. 'What, what's so funny?'

Finally Tash managed to speak. Through her last gulps of laughter, she said, 'It's my mum's necklace. You've given me my mum's necklace!'

Chapter Sixteen

'I'm really worried about Saul, Chelsea,' said Joss. She and Chelsea were at Chelsea's flat. 'He beat up some kid last night when he left here. He's really losin' it.'

'He beat some kid up?' repeated Chelsea. That wasn't like Saul at all. Saul was usually pretty mellow. It was usually him who was stopping fights, not starting them. What had happened with Dave was one thing, that was strange enough, but to go out afterwards and beat up someone he didn't even know. What was going on? 'Why? Why did he do it?'

'I don't know. I don't understand,' said Joss. She was so confused about it herself, it was hard to explain it to Chelsea. 'I just don't understand.' She paused and rubbed her hand across her face, hoping she wasn't about to cry. Her body felt heavy. Inside, she was tired, drained of all energy. 'He said he didn't understand.' Joss sighed. 'The kid was just there and he laid into him.'

'What, for no reason?' asked Chelsea. 'The kid hadn't done anything to him or said anything?'

'Ner, he hadn't done anything. He was just standing there, hangin' out,' said Joss. 'Saul didn't understand what he was doin'. He said he felt so angry. He said he was scared of himself. Of what was goin' on inside his head 'n' scared of what he might do.'

'Why?' asked Chelsea, gently. 'What *is* going on?'

'I dunno. I tried to ask him about, y'know, why he felt angry and shit but he didn't wanna know,' replied Joss. 'He clammed up and walked out. Said he didn't wanna talk about it.'

'What are you supposed to do if he won't even talk to you?' said Chelsea.

'I dunno, Chelsea.' Joss looked at Chelsea. She thought she might cry. She could feel her mouth trembling as she tried to hold in the tears. 'He's losin' it. He's losin' it.' And a few tears seeped from her eyes. She looked away and clenched her teeth and surreptitiously wiped the tears away.

'Don't say that,' said Chelsea, vehemently. 'Course he's not.'

'He says he hears voices in his head,' Joss explained. Saul had told her the other night. But she'd known that things hadn't been right with him for a long time. She hadn't bothered talking to anyone about it. She'd hoped it would just go away and Saul would come back, the real Saul. Come back and be himself again. But it wasn't happening. It was just going on and on. She couldn't stand it any longer. 'Voices in his head,' she repeated, barely believing she was saying it.

'What sort of voices?' asked Chelsea.

'Telling him he's shit. Telling him he's worthless. I don't know what to do. I don't know what the fuck to do.' Tears began to trickle from Joss's eyes again. Her face began to crease and her voice to crack. 'He's not himself. He's been so down since that kid died. He just, he doesn't know what he's doing with himself. Or why he's here. But I don't know what to do. I mean, what can I do? He's got to sort it out for himself. But I can't just sit back and watch him. He's getting worse. He's going crazy. Voices in his head. He's losin' it.'

'Stop saying that, Joss,' said Chelsea. 'Don't say it. Don't even think it.'

'But it's true, ain't it?' Joss looked up at Chelsea.

'He's just depressed,' insisted Chelsea. 'He doesn't know what he's up to. He's got no direction. Lost.'

'But voices inside his head?' Joss emphasized the words. 'That's, like, schizophrenic.'

'Everyone has voices inside their head,' Chelsea said reassuringly. 'Don't you ever talk to yourself?'

'Yeah, s'pose.' Joss had to agree.

'So do I,' said Chelsea. 'Everyone does. It's the way we are. There's nothing weird about voices inside your head. What are stories, if they aren't voices inside your head? Or day-dreams? That's people talking inside your head. And when people write music, where does that come from? It's all voices, isn't it?'

'Well, yeah, sort've.' Joss hadn't thought've it like that before. 'But what about when they're tellin' you you're shit the whole time? Sometimes he doesn't want to be on his own because the voices talk too much at him. I mean, what's going on?'

'It's all the same thing, isn't it?' said Chelsea. 'When you're feeling down, those voices are bound to say shit things to you.'

'You reckon?' Joss still didn't feel convinced.

'Imagine sports people. Imagine a tennis player.' Chelsea loved tennis. 'You know at Wimbledon and they play a good shot. You see them, don't you? You see them talking to themselves, psyching themselves up. That's a voice, isn't it? And what's it saying? It's saying good things. It's saying, "That was a great shot, keep it up." But you know what they're like when they do a shit shot. They're not telling themselves how great they are then. They're saying, "That was crap, come on, sort it out." Now, what's the difference between that and what's going on in Saul's head?'

'I s'pose.' Joss could see what Chelsea was getting at. And it did make sense. 'So, you don't think he's losin' it?' she asked, earnestly.

'Losing it? It doesn't mean anything,' said Chelsea. 'We're all losing it. We've all lost it. He's still the same old Saul. He's just going through a rough patch. He'll sort it out.'

'I dunno,' said Joss.

'You just need to get him out of this rut he's stuck in,' said Chelsea. 'Give him a chance to see things a different way. Get those voices inside his head telling him good things about himself.'

'And you know what else, what hasn't bin helpin'?' said Joss. 'I haven't told you, have I?'

'What?'

'Someone's been nickin' off us,' replied Joss.

'What, out of the flat?' Chelsea asked.

'Yeah, well, sort've. Jus' letters. Saul's giro. Some money someone'd sent 'im. Um . . .' There was something else. She tried to remember. 'Oh, yeah, and my credit card, a new one they'd sent me in the post. That's gone too.'

'Well, who'd do that?' asked Chelsea.

'I dunno, but it doesn't help things,' said Joss, coldly. 'Saul's paranoid enough as it is without shit like that. It gives him a reason to be paranoid. It makes him really believe people don't like him or respect him.'

'Well, who would've done it?' Chelsea repeated. 'You must have some idea.'

'I don't want to point a finger.' Joss shook her head.

'But who, who do you reckon?' insisted Chelsea.

'Well . . .' Joss didn't like to say. 'Ellis.'

'Ellis? No way.' Chelsea didn't believe it. 'Why him?'

'It's just he's bin there every time something's gone missing. He's always there,' said Joss. 'And those pills that he was meant to get Saul.'

'Yeah, but you know Ellis.' Chelsea didn't think Ellis would've done it. Ellis wouldn't hurt anyone, not intentionally. 'That was always going to happen if you sent him off with a load of pills. And I was with him that night, he was trying really hard not to take any. Why would he do that if he was about to nick them?'

'I dunno. But he's into his gear at the moment, isn't he?' said Joss. 'And you can't trust anyone that's involved with gear. They'll always put their next bag before their mates.'

'I dunno,' said Chelsea. 'I know what you mean but still I can't see it. He hasn't got a habit or anything. Not really.'

'Well, I dunno either.' Joss sighed. 'I'm jus' sayin' what came into my head. I hate to think he might've done it.'

'Yeah, right. If you can't trust your mates, then who can you trust?' But Chelsea didn't want Joss getting down again. She brushed the subject aside. 'Don't think about that now. You've gotta concentrate on getting Saul's head straight.'

'Yeah.' Joss sounded weary.

'Take him out for a meal or something,' suggested Chelsea.

'We haven't got any money for that.'

'Don't worry about it. I'll give you some money,' said Chelsea.

'No, you don't have to,' replied Joss.

'I want to,' insisted Chelsea. 'It's important. You two need to have a laugh together. Remember how things used to be. You always said about him that you had a laugh together. That he wasn't just your boyfriend, he was your best mate. So, go and have a laugh.'

Joss opened her mouth to speak.

Chelsea wouldn't let her. 'I don't want to hear any excuses. I'm going to give you some money and you're going to go and have a laugh. Okay?'

'Okay,' Joss smiled. 'Cheers.'

''S alright.' Chelsea was just glad to see Joss smiling. 'I know, why don't you go down to the cottage for a few days? Dad wouldn't mind.' Chelsea's dad owned a cottage outside London that he sometimes used at weekends. 'I'll check when he's going to be there. You can go and have a holiday. I'll give him a ring now.'

Chelsea rang him and there was no problem. They could go down any time in the next week. Chelsea had her own key and she handed it over to Joss with a hundred and fifty quid.

'Now, go and enjoy yourselves,' she said to Joss.

'Cheers, Chelsea,' Joss shook her head. Sometimes Chelsea knew just what to do. 'I'll sort you out sometime, I promise.'

'Shut up, Joss,' said Chelsea. 'You don't have to do anything except enjoy yourself. And have a good shag.'

Chapter Seventeen

Ellis sat back in the sofa. The foil drooped in his hand. It was 3 a.m. *Bassline* was on TV with that woman, Arabella Minty, the one who thought she was sexy. Ellis was sure they'd been watching the same shit this time yesterday. Hadn't they? It all seemed pretty familiar. The short skirt, the flick of the hair.

He asked Ish, 'Weren't we watching this yesterday?'

'Mind control,' replied Ish. 'They know you haven't got a job if you're up watching TV at this time. Control you. Keep you down. That's why they show this shit.'

Ish was full of funny ideas. He was a poet. That's why he did gear. For inspiration. Apparently loads've writers used to cane opium. De Quincey. Coleridge. Oscar Wilde. Junkies the lot of them. Coleridge had even written one of his masterpieces in an opium-induced trance. But then the postman'd knocked on the door and interrupted him. Couldn't get his concentration back after that, so he never finished the poem. Ish himself hadn't written much. He had plenty of ideas though, but was always too fucked to write them down. And by the next morning he'd forgotten them. Ellis wondered whether gear was really helping Ish fulfil his literary ambitions.

The woman on the TV carried on flicking her hair and pouting at Ellis. He let his eyes slide shut. Ish's eyes were flickering too but he was still talking, in a low constant drone that Ellis found easy to ignore.

'Religion is like heroin. An answer . . . stops all the confusion . . . Questions running round in your head . . . Why am I? What am I doing? . . . Is this right? Is this wrong? . . . Questions . . . cacophony of questions . . . always why? Why? Why? Religion is an answer . . . set of answers laid down in a book for you to follow . . . No need to think . . . all the answers in a book . . . Catholic's catechism . . . Who made me? God made me. Why did he make me? To know him, love him and serve him . . .'s easy . . . No doubts . . . faith, gotta have faith . . . Life's simple, straightforward . . . Same with gear . . . Life's black and white. Either you got gear or . . . you haven't . . . you have – 's okay . . . No doubts – you're okay . . . soft and sweet like honey slightly warmed – too good to doubt . . . too good to worry about anything . . . and when you don't have it . . . you're clucking . . . still, no doubt what you need . . . Opium of the people – religion . . . Marx said so . . . And drugs religion of the young . . . need something to stop you searching for all those answers . . . searching all your life for the answers . . . spinning round, trying to find the answers . . . because there is nothing . . . Nothing . . . no reason . . . no plan . . . nothing.'

'Thought the answer was 42,' said Ellis, opening his eyes and smiling at Ish.

Emily laughed but she didn't open her eyes, she remained slumped on the floor, leaning against the sofa. Emily was Ish's girlfriend. She was a tall wiry woman with bleached blonde hair.

The three of them were sharing a squat together. It was a flat in a council block. The flats were built around a courtyard. One half of the courtyard was a building site – the flats were being done up. Their side would be refurbished when the other side was finished, so most of the flats were empty or being squatted. A few council tenants remained, waiting to be rehoused. There was another building site round the back of the flats, a road on one side and train tracks on the other. There was noise and dirt and dust all day and night. Builders' whistles and shouts. Trains blasting past, rattling the tracks. Kids hanging out, pissed and stoned, jeering, shouting, fighting. But Ellis didn't care. It was a place to live, wasn't it?

Ellis suddenly felt his stomach lurch. He stood up to go and vomit. But his legs buckled beneath him and he fell to the floor. Ish laughed and Emily opened her eyes to slits.

'Sort it out, Ellis,' said Ish.

Ellis pushed himself up from the floor and tried again. He took a few steps, steadied himself and then plunged to the floor.

'Ellis,' chuckled Ish.

'Y' alright?' asked Emily.

Third time round, Ellis managed to make it to the bog. But he wasn't quite in time. He chundered half on the seat, half on the floor. He turned and, leaning against the basin, rinsed the dregs of vomit from his mouth.

'Fuck it,' he thought, looking at the puke on the floor. He couldn't deal with that now. He just wanted to lie down and gauge out. He found his way back to the sofa, had another boot and sprawled. His eyes were shut. He could hear the woman on the telly talking about clubs and records and some DJ. A bloke Ellis knew. The DJ's words and the woman's words came and went. 'Great new track . . . very pleased . . . out on Super Elephants.' Ish was off again too. 'All to do with art . . . music . . . art . . . another kind of poetry.' And his words mingled with the telly. 'Post-modernist art . . . fantastic bass . . . particularly like the colours . . . not too vocal.' And then Ellis's own thoughts merged slowly with the other words. So that what he was hearing and thinking became muddled and made a new sense of their own, not belonging to anyone. 'Those pills . . . really can move to it . . . away from installation . . . whoever's got them havin' a laugh . . . at some great new clubs . . . full of stuffed dead animals.'

'What d'you reckon?' asked Ish.

'I'm up for it,' said Emily.

Ellis opened his eyes. They were looking at him, waiting for an answer.

'What?' he asked.

'Sha' we go 'n' score, sum more?' asked Emily.

'Yeah, alright,' replied Ellis. 'You driving?'

'Yeah,' said Emily. 'You'd better stay 'ere. 'S not so good if we all pile round there. Johnny won't be up for it.'

'Well, I'm not giving you my money if I can't come, am I?' said Ellis.

'What? Don't you trust us?' Emily was getting hectic.

'It's not that I . . . y'know what it's like.' Of course Ellis didn't trust them. 'I just wanna check what deal we get.'

'How long've I known you, Ellis?' said Emily.

'Let's just go without him,' said Ish. 'If he can't even trust us.'

'Come on,' implored Ellis. 'I don't trust anyone. Not worth it, is it?'

'Tt, alright then,' said Emily.

So they all went in her car. Ellis looked out the window as London swept past. The street lights smudged against the sky. The streets were mainly empty except for a few bums huddling up in doorways for the night, some trendies coming out a club wondering where to go next, lads walking out the kebab shop with brown paper bags full of beer.

Emily pulled up into a side street. The three of them piled out. Ish rang Johnny's doorbell. They'd all known Johnny a few years. Since before he was a junkie. Johnny's gaunt face appeared in the shadows of the window upstairs. He opened the window and chucked the keys out to them. They let themselves in and went upstairs to Johnny's flat.

It was just one room with a separate scabby kitchen and a tiny bathroom. They cotched wherever they could find a space – on the floor, on the edge of the bed and on an old wooden carton.

173

'Alright,' said Johnny, sounding pretty relaxed. 'How's it goin'?'

There was a syringe and a couple of needle wipes lying on the floor next to him.

'This is Gary,' Johnny said waving up at a bloke who was sat on the corner of the bed. 'Gary – Ellis, Emily 'n' Ish.'

'Alright?' said Ellis.

'No, I'm fuckin' not alright,' shouted Gary, holding up a syringe in one hand. 'Can't find a fuckin' vein anywhere.'

Ellis looked away and wished he hadn't bothered asking.

Gary pumped the fingers of his hand and plunged the needle into his forearm, which was covered with lumpy abscesses. 'Fuckin' hell,' he said as he pulled the plunger back and still didn't draw blood. He gritted his teeth. 'Fuck's sake.' He got up off the bed, nearly stepping on Emily, and went out to the bathroom to give it another go.

'Fuckin' junkie,' said Johnny when Gary was gone. 'He's bin lookin' for a vein for twenty minutes. He wants to take it easy. See, me I'm alright.' Johnny pulled up his sleeves and put out his arms for them to see. There were needle marks down each forearm. 'I'm alright. I take it easy.'

'Yeah, yeah, right,' said Emily.

And Ish and Ellis nodded in agreement.

'So, how's it goin', then?' asked Johnny, his eyelids slippin' shut.

'Yeah, 's alright,' said Ellis. 'Yeah, jus' got this new squat up near Kingsmead.'

Johnny didn't respond. His eyes were totally shut now.

Ellis carried on anyway, 'You know where I mean? Up by the meadow?'

Johnny nodded and opened his eyes. 'Uh?'

'Up near the meadow,' Ellis repeated. 'Yeah, 's alright, ain't it?' He looked at Emily and Ish.

'Yeah,' said Ish.

Emily was gettin' impatient. 'Oi, Johnny, that geezer downstairs, what's he saying? Has he got anyfing?'

Geezer called Phil lived downstairs. Johnny didn't sell gear. He just bought it off Phil.

'Yeah,' said Johnny. 'Phil's there. He'll av' som'ing.'

''S alright if I jus' go down there, ain't it?' asked Emily, standing up.

'Yeah, s'pect so, replied Johnny. ' 'E knows who you are, dun 'e?'

'Yeah, course 'e does,' said Emily. She turned to Ish and Ellis. 'So, what shall I get, then?'

'Ellis, what d'you wanna put in?' asked Ish.

'Well, I've only got twenty quid.' Ellis felt in his pocket and pulled out two tenners. He held them out to Emily.

Emily took 'em. 'So what shall I get for us two, Ish?'

'See if he'll do us a gram for sixty.' Ish handed her thirty quid. 'You got some money, ain't it?'

'Yeah.' Emily went downstairs.

There was silence and then a shout of 'For fuck's sake' from the bathroom. Gary was still in there trying to find a vein.

'See,' confided Johnny. 'I wouldn't be doin' all this if it wasn't fer mi gut. But it gives me such grief, what else am I supposed to do?' He wasn't looking at them, but he carried on talking. 'An' the doctors are shit. I mean, the painkillers they give you, they're shit. Don't do a fuckin' thing.'

There was a shriek of delight from the bathroom. Gary came dancing in.

'Found one,' he grinned as he skipped about the room. 'Fuckin' found one in my cock.' He punched the air and then settled himself on the bed to let the gear kick in.

Emily was back upstairs a while later. She handed Ish a wrap. Ish undid it.

'What's this meant ta be?' he said, indignantly.

'A gram,' Emily replied quietly.

'That ain't a fuckin' gram,' Ish retorted. 'What d'you reckon, Ellis?'

'Don't look like a gram to me.' Ellis peered at the powder.

'What about you, what d'you fink?' Ish held the wrap over in Johnny's direction.

'Ner, no way that's a gram,' said Johnny, having a good look. 'You've bin had, mate.'

'You done any of this, Em?' Ish sounded irritated.

'Ner,' said Emily. 'I had one little toot. That's all.'

'You sure?' Ish looked her in the eye, tryin' a work out whether or not she was lying.

'Doesn't look like a gram to me,' repeated Ellis.

'Go 'n' say it won't do,' Ish said to Emily. 'Did you av' a look when he weighed it out?'

'Well, yeah, sort've,' said Emily. 'Couldn't really see.'

'Go 'n' sort it out, said Ellis. 'No way that's a gram.'

'He's not gonna change it now, is he?' said Emily. 'He'll think we've bin at it.'

'Well, go 'n' give it a go,' said Ish.

Emily took the wrap and went back downstairs, like a little girl being told to redo her homework.

When she was gone, Ish said, 'Bet she had a go at it. That's why it's under.'

Ellis laughed, 'Yeah, right. What's she gonna say to Phil?'

But Emily was back up before long with a much healthier-looking wrap. Johnny didn't have digital scales so they had to divvy it up by eye. Ish emptied the wrap on to a book and took a card out his pocket. He divided the powder into thirds.

'You 'av' that one, yeah?' he said to Ellis, indicating one of the piles.

But Ellis wasn't happy. 'That one? No way, that isn't a third.'

Ish redivided the powder but Ellis still didn't think it was fair. 'Here, I'll do it,' he said. He took the book and card from Ish and fiddled about with the powder.

Ish seemed happy but then Emily said, 'You're havin' a laugh, Ellis, that ain't right.'

So Emily took the book and the card and Johnny was elected referee. Emily cut the powder. 'What d'you reckon, Johnny?'

'Dunno, I reckon that one's a bit bigger than the others.' Johnny pointed at one of the piles.

Emily took a little powder off the pile and divided it between the other two. 'What d'you reckon?'

Johnny said, 'Yeah, s'pose that's as good as it's gonna get. But you cut; let Ellis choose.'

Ellis was about to choose the pile he wanted but then Ish suddenly felt uncertain because, after all, Johnny'd known Ellis longer than he'd known him and Emily. He was probably on the blag. So Ish took the book and the card and redivided the powder. Emily suddenly got bored.

'Oh, come on, for fuck's sake,' she snapped. 'I'm really clucking.'

Ish gave one of the piles to Ellis and him and Emily took the other two piles. They went into the bog to jack up.

'What d'you 'av' to go in there for?' asked Johnny. 'Why don't you just do it in 'ere, like everyone else?'

'Cos we wanna do it on our own, alright?' barked Emily. But the truth was she couldn't jack up for herself. Couldn't stand seeing the needle sinking into her arm. The whole thought of jackin' up was kinda sick. So she always got Ish to do it for her. That way she could keep her eyes shut. But she didn't ever want anyone knowing that. She'd feel a right twat if anyone knew. She was menna be tough.

So Emily and Ish retreated to the bathroom. Ellis had a good long run and sat back, rushing.

'Don't know why you don't jack up,' said Johnny.

'Waste a money not to,' agreed Gary.

'Jus' don't wanna,' said Ellis. He knew why he didn't want to but he didn't want to talk about it. When Ellis was a kid he'd walked in on his dad jacking up. Ellis's dad'd looked up but he didn't say anything. The woman he was with giggled. Ellis ran out knowing something wasn't quite right. He'd always promised himself he wouldn't get into gear. He didn't want to end up with nothing, like his dad. And then when Ellis'd tried gear, he'd promised himself he wouldn't jack up. It was all alright, he was still in control, just so long as he didn't jack up.

'Y'know,' said Ellis. 'If you jack up the nicotine in a fag, it'd kill ya.'

'Well, it's lucky we're only jacking up gear and not fags, ain't it?' replied Johnny.

When Ellis woke up, he was back at the squat. It was three in the afternoon. They'd stayed round Johnny's till about five and hadn't got to bed till six or seven.

Ellis stretched his back. It was really stiff and his arms and legs felt tight with cramp. He lay in bed for a while and thought about going back to sleep. But his body ached too badly. He wasn't gonna be able to sleep. He got up to go for a piss. The vomit from last night was still splattered on the loo seat and the floor. He peed over the top of it into the bowl.

He wasn't gonna do any gear today, he promised himself. He'd see the cramps through. They weren't that bad. He really should lay off it, just for today.

He found some newspaper and cleared up the puke and then ran himself a bath. That'd ease his cramps.

In the living room there were a few empty cans and some odd bits've foil. Ellis checked them to see if there was anything left. Yeah, there was a little bit. Jus' a little. That didn't count as doin' any, not really. So he chased the last few bits and then did the tube.

There was a knock at the door. Ellis wandered out. It was old Mrs Johnson from downstairs.

'You running a bath?' she shouted. She was a bit deaf and couldn't hear what she was saying unless she shouted.

'Shit, yeah.' Ellis remembered his bath.

'Turn it off,' replied Mrs Johnson. 'You've flooded my living room. We've only just been moved because we got flooded. Some kids nicked our pipes. Flooded the whole flat.'

'Sorry.' Ellis shut the door and went 'n' turned off the water. He undid the plug and let some water drain out. The bath *did* ease his cramps. A bit. But by the time he was up and dressed again he was feeling just as shit.

'Little bit've gear,' he was thinking. 'Just a little bit wouldn't hurt.' But he didn't have any cash left anyway. He wandered back into the living room. And then there was a tenner on the floor. He hadn't seen it before. Must be Ish or Emily's. But they were asleep. They wouldn't know, would they? They'd bin caned last night, they wouldn't know how much money they'd had. Anyway, might be Ellis's. He might've dropped it out his pocket. Maybe. A tenner. Perfect for a bag. Just to see him through. Wouldn't hurt, would it?

Chapter Eighteen

'Wha' cha doin'?' Saul shouted down the hill to Joss.

They were trying to launch a kite they'd found in the cottage. Saul was at the top of the hill, holding the strings. Joss was down the bottom, holding the kite.

'Come 'ere,' Saul shouted. 'Ner, move that way.' What was Joss trying to do? Hadn't she ever flown a kite before?

'Hang on,' shouted Joss. The string was caught around her finger. 'The string's caught.'

Joss could hear Saul perfectly. It was a pity he couldn't hear her. The wind caught her words and tossed them back in her face.

'I can't hear ya,' he shouted back. He was walking backwards, pulling the strings of the kite taut, not realizing he was also pulling them tighter around her finger. What *was* Joss up to?

'Waaaiiit. The striiiiing's caught.' Joss heaved her lungs. Effortlessly, the wind puffed her words away. Saul continued walking backwards, tugging at the strings of the kite.

'They've gotta be taut,' he called out, helpfully.

The tip of Joss's finger was beginning to look as though it didn't belong with the rest of her hand. She grabbed the string and yanked it out of Saul's hand. Saul stormed down the hill.

'What d'ya do that for?' he snapped at Joss.

'My finger.' Joss sucked on her finger.

'Don't be such a pussy,' replied Saul. 'You take the strings and I'll launch it.'

Joss walked back up to the top of the hill with the strings. Saul took the kite and held it up into the wind. He released it as a gust of wind caught the kite and shot it into the sky. Joss tugged at the strings. The kite was way above her head. She pulled on one string and the kite swooped downwards. She tugged at the other string and the kite swivelled back into the sky once more. The wind was strong and Joss was able to lean back against the pull of the kite, putting all her weight into controlling its movement.

Saul came running back up the hill, grinning up at the kite.

'Wow, it's wicked, ain't it?' he said.

'Totally,' smiled Joss.

They watched as the kite danced in the sky. Behind, the sky was a clear blue, swimming with clouds.

'Here, d'you want a go?' Joss offered Saul the strings.

He took them and leant back as the kite pulled. He let the kite swing one way, as near to the ground as he dared, and then pulled it back and sent it zooming off in the other direction. He felt a strange sense of freedom. It was almost as if he was up there with it. Floating up there in the sky. All the real world was weighted to the ground but Saul was flying with the kite. Nothing to worry about. Nothing to think about, except its broad, sweeping movements. And the sky, open and inviting. It was such a contrast with the way he'd been feeling in London. There he'd felt squashed. Felt the world closing in on him. Here, it was him going out to the world. He felt a great feeling of space. He felt like himself again.

'Give us a go,' said Joss, snapping Saul from the sky.

He handed over the strings and lay down in the grass next to Joss, letting himself slip away once again. He felt tension released from his body. Felt it draining away. London's noisy racket sliding into the peaceful chatter of the birds. The city's dull greys repainted in a palette of lush verdancy. The harsh lines of streets and buildings softened into fertile curves.

'You ever seen that film *London Kills Me*?' asked Saul.

'Yeah, why?' Joss replied, concentrating on flying the kite.

'Well, it does, doesn't it?' said Saul.

'Does what?' Joss was only half listening and didn't really understand what Saul was going on about.

'Does kill you,' replied Saul. 'London kills you.'

Saul had had a sudden insight. It was a feeling he had inside him rather than something he could explain to Joss. Everything in London seemed crazy. None of it seemed to make much sense. All the rush and the noise and clutter. What was it all for? Where was it going? It boxed you in and fenced you off. It didn't free you. And it'd been doing that to him. Slowly choking him. Now here was air. He filled his lungs and breathed deeply.

The kite came crashing down to the ground.

'Shall we give it a rest for a bit?' asked Joss.

'Alright,' said Saul. He took one of the strings off Joss and began winding it in. Joss wound in the other. They met down by the kite. Saul pulled the supporting pole apart and rolled up the kite. He felt good for the first time in a long time. He felt full of life and energy. He ran to Joss and dived at her legs, in a rugby tackle. He lay on top of her, squashing her into the grasses which rose about them in mauve-tinged streaks.

'I love you,' he said.

'Do you?' asked Joss.

'Of course.' Saul kissed her.

'I love you.' She kissed him back.

'I'm surprised,' replied Saul. 'Thanks.'

'What, thanks for loving you?' laughed Joss.

'Just thanks for being there for me.' Saul kissed Joss again. 'I really thought I was going mad for a while. Really losing it. I thought that was it.'

'Yeah, I wasn't sure either,' replied Joss. 'But you're not mad?'

'Ner, I'm not mad,' smiled Saul. And he knew he wasn't. He'd left all that shit behind him in London. He kissed Joss. And they lay there in the grass and made love.

'You're a cunt,' the bloke said to Saul.

It was evening now. Joss and Saul were in the village pub trying to buy a drink. The bloke was a local lad with short blond hair. He'd just come up to Saul and called him a cunt for no reason. Perhaps because he knew he wasn't from the village. Saul didn't reply and for a moment Joss wondered what he was going to do. She thought he might flip out like he'd done the other night. She thought he might lay into the bloke.

'You're a cunt,' repeated the bloke.

Saul didn't seem angry at all. He seemed like his old self, cool and calm. He looked at the bloke and said, 'Why's that, then? Why am I a cunt?'

The bloke looked a little unnerved. This wasn't the response he'd been expecting. 'Well,' he said, looking around. 'You're just a cunt.' He suddenly pounced on a reason. 'Those trousers. Only cunts wear trousers like that.'

Saul looked down at the trousers he was wearing. 'Yeah, you're right. I don't like them much either.' Saul smiled.

The bloke looked suspicious.

'You fancy a drink?' asked Saul.

The bloke couldn't refuse. He seemed to relax suddenly. He began to chat with Saul. Joss wondered how Saul had managed to turn the situation around. Saul, it seemed, was back. He was himself again.

It turned out the bloke had lived all his life in that same small village. Saul couldn't imagine it. Imagine seeing that one way of life. The same few people day after day. The same pubs. The same few jobs. Imagine never seeing anything else. Nothing new. It all spelt stagnation and boredom. Narrow-mindedness.

But then what was the difference between that and Saul in London? Wasn't he just as enclosed in his world as this bloke was in his?

But somehow it was different. The life Saul had been living, had given him an insight into all kinds of lives. Windows on worlds. Much more than if he'd plodded along in yer average job, in yer average town. He'd seen some crazy things. He'd met some crazy people. He'd been given a taste of freedom. A sense that anything was possible. It was only up to you to make it happen or let it happen without being scared.

Although now he was feeling restless within his world, Saul didn't think these past few years had been a waste of time. He knew it was time for him to move on in his life, to find a new focus. It was all about learning. He'd learnt a lot and he'd seen a lot. He had no regrets.

Chapter Nineteen

It was the second time that week that the police had been round. Michelle could see them as she peered through the kitchen window. There were three of them and a manky-looking dog. One of the pigs reminded her of her old headmaster, who'd always thought he knew exactly what the kids were up to but in fact didn't have a clue. One of the younger officers looked nervous. He was chewing his fingers and looking behind him as though he expected something or someone to jump out at him. The other looked like a psychopath.

Michelle let the curtain drop and went back into the living room. She took the bag of rubbish and hurled it over the balcony on to the tip in the yard below. She picked up a couple of pieces of hash and a wrap and tucked them in the turn-up of her jeans. She kicked Jack.

'Get up, the pigs are here.'

O'Connor, the pig that looked like Michelle's headmaster, said, 'Right, they have failed to answer the door. We now proceed to make a forced entry. Make a note of that, lads.'

The psycho jotted something down in his notebook. The nail-biter looked worried. He stopped chewing his fingernails and chewed the end of his pen instead.

'What exactly should we write, Sarge?' the nail-biter asked and shoved his fingers back to his teeth.

'Now come on, Russell,' said O'Connor. 'You must learn to make notes by yourself. Are you a mouse or a man?'

Russell looked uncertain. 'Was that a rhetorical question, sir?'

'I wrote, "The fuckers won't come out. We're going in after them",' said the psycho.

'Er, yes, Colin,' said O'Connor. 'But try not to make it sound like something out of a Vietnam war film. Next step, we force entry.'

'Batter down the door, sir,' Colin the psycho's eyes glinted.

'Who wants to try this?' asked O'Connor, ignoring Colin – he could be a little overenthusiastic at times.

The nail-biter shrank back.

'Russell,' said O'Connor. 'Why don't you give it a go?'

Russell looked behind, hoping perhaps there was someone else called Russell. He looked at the door nervously and then at his feet as if wondering how the two might ever connect. It seemed to him that if they did, his foot would be the first to give.

O'Connor, sensing Russell's hesitancy tried to give him some words of encouragement. 'Remember what you did in training.'

Russell had been trying to forget what had happened in training. He had been the only man in the section who had failed to make any impact whatsoever on his door. The lads had found it a constant source of amusement for the next few weeks, asking him at all possible opportunities to open doors for them – that was, if he could.

Russell breathed deeply and tried to blank those humiliating memories from his mind. He lunged forward and kicked the door. But somehow he bounced off as though he was made of rubber.

'Put your weight behind it,' said O'Connor.

Russell kicked again. His foot sprang back. The door stood solid.

O'Connor sighed. He was about to ask Colin to kick down the door but before he had a chance, Colin had already knocked down the door with a single well-executed kick, which left Russell in no doubt as to the answer to O'Connor's question – Russell was indeed a mouse.

Jack was going to get the door when the door came to get him. Without so much as a word, the door leapt forward and smacked him on the nose. He doubled over, clinging to his nose, as though trying to hold it in place on his face. And then some guy with glassy eyes and a steely body stormed past him, muttering, 'Out of my way, scum.'

O'Connor stood over Jack and continued the lesson. 'Now, having gained access to the property, we continue by . . . Anyone? Who can tell me what comes next?'

The psycho looked confused. He was thinking, 'Beat the shit out of them all.' But he didn't think this was quite the right answer.

'Shou . . .' Russell began to say something but then decided against.

'We look for evidence,' said O'Connor, encouragingly.

'Shouldn't we deal with the injured?' Russell plucked up the courage to ask his question. He was looking down at Jack.

O'Connor smiled. 'When you've been in the game as long as I have, son, you start to learn the tricks people like this can play. You know the difference between real casualties and Hollywood.'

Jack's nose throbbed. He could feel the blood ooze between his fingers. He'd heard what the pig had said and he wanted to say, 'What the fuck d'you think this is, ketchup?' But the room swam, turned white and was gone.

The police meanwhile had moved into the living room, where O'Connor was saying, 'No, what we do is look for evidence. Make a note of that, lads.'

'Oh, my God,' thought Michelle. 'We've been busted by Police Academy.'

O'Connor continued, 'Yes, we look for evidence. This is where the dogs come in.'

'Dog, sir,' corrected Russell. 'Er, there's only one dog.'

'Yes,' smiled O'Connor, glad to see Russell was feeling a little more confident. 'That's right, Russell. But one dog is all we need. These highly trained dogs can sniff out anything from the smallest piece of marijuana to a single grain of cocaine.' O'Connor took out a large slab of hashish from his pocket. 'Give the dog the scent.' O'Connor waved the hash in front of the dog's nose.

The dog licked the hash and then stood there, his tongue hanging out as he panted.

'The dog thinks it's for him,' thought Michelle.

'Now, seek,' said O'Connor. 'That's right, seek.' He flung his arm out and pointed. The dog ran in the direction of O'Connor's outstretched arm as though he thought something had been thrown for him to fetch and then, realizing nothing had been thrown, he stopped and looked at O'Connor and continued panting. 'There seems to be a little, er, technical hitch with the dog.' O'Connor laughed. 'We will have to gather evidence ourselves, lads. Now, does anyone have any ideas where we might begin to look?'

Michelle had about seventy or eighty pills stashed in a sock in the bedroom. But she wasn't worried. There was no way these idiots would find them.

Colin the psycho scratched his head, pondering O'Connor's question. 'How about down the side of the sofa?' he suggested. His own sofa seemed to have an insatiable appetite for small items like lighters, cigarettes or keys. It was always the first place he looked when he lost something.

'Yes,' said O'Connor. 'But try to be a little more imaginative. Russell, do you have any ideas?'

Russell winced. He hated this kind of pressure. 'Erm, erm, how about in clothing? Say in the pockets of things or, er, in socks?'

Michelle groaned silently. Why did he have to say that? She edged her way slowly to the bedroom, found the sock and tossed it out the window. She turned around to see Russell standing watching her.

Ellis was walking down the street. He'd wanted to get out of the squat. Ish and Emily were already on the gear. Ellis didn't have any money and there was nothing worse than watching people get a hit when you couldn't yourself. So he'd gone out. He wasn't sure where he was going. Perhaps he'd check out the market. Maybe he'd bump into some mates.

Ellis could see something falling from the sky. At first he thought it was a bird dive-bombing him. When he realized it wasn't a bird, Ellis reached out and caught it. It was a sock. He could feel something inside it but he knew now was not the time to stop and look inside. He shoved the sock down his boxers and carried on walking, glancing around to check no one had seen.

By the time Russell went down to the street to look for the sock, Ellis was down the end of the road and round the corner.

The trouble with Ellis was he never knew when to stop.

As soon as he'd realized what was in the sock, he'd thought of paying Saul back. He gave him a ring. But Saul was out, down in the country with Joss, Ellis remembered. So Ellis left a message on the answerphone. And then he'd taken a pill, just one, to celebrate and before he knew it, he was propping up some shabby bar listening to an Irish bloke gabbering on about how his brother had been cut in half with a chain-saw – straight down the middle, cut his nose in two and his cock as well. All thought of Saul had slipped to the back of Ellis's mind. It all might've worked out alright, except that one, one was never enough. It was the rush of coming up that Ellis loved; after that died down, he was ready for another and with a pocketful of pills, who could stop themselves gobbling another couple? Somewhere along the line he'd bumped into some mates and, like a modern-day Milky Bar Kid, the pills were on Ellis. He had so many, he didn't care. Let his mates have a good time on him for once; after all, they were always treating him.

A load of pills later (Ellis had lost count of exactly how many it was), Ellis was in a club, crouched on the floor, his head slung back against the wall. He lifted his head and opened his eyes slightly. Jarring images flashed with the strobe. Ellis wondered how long he'd been sitting there. Where was everyone he'd come with? His head slipped back against the wall.

'Hash,' he was thinking. 'Spliff. Get a spliff together. Darren. Darren's got some. Find Darren.'

Darren was one of the people Ellis had come with. Ellis pulled himself up unsteadily and went to try and find him, pushing past people, walking into them, tripping over his feet. And suddenly he was falling against a door. The door opened. Ellis stumbled through. He was out of the club and in a corridor. There was silence and in the silence, Ellis could hear his head buzzing. Ellis looked around him uneasily, as though someone was playing some kind of trick on him. The corridor was clean and white with a lino floor.

What the fuck was going on? Where was he? There were some signs up ahead, too far ahead to read. He walked closer. The signs read, 'X-ray', 'Physiotherapy', 'Chemotherapy', 'Wards 6-18'. He was in a hospital. What the fuck? This wasn't real, was it? Ellis felt like he'd just fallen down Alice's rabbit hole or walked through the wardrobe that led to Narnia. One minute he was in a club, the next he was in hospital. Was someone trying to tell him something? Ellis wasn't sure he liked this. It was kinda freaky.

He was thinking of going back when he saw a door open a little further down the corridor. Inside he could see a glass-fronted medicine cabinet. His sense of adventure and love of chemicals got the better of him. He crept up to the open door and peered inside. Images of Matt Dillon in *Drugstore Cowboy* flashed through his mind. No one was in the room. Ellis could see bottles and packets of pills stacked up in the cupboard, all different colours and sizes. He felt a sudden thrill jerk through his body, like the beginnings of an orgasm. He tried the cupboard door. It was locked. Fuck it. He could smash the glass. What was the point of a lock when the doors were made of glass?

He went back to the corridor and looked both ways. The coast was clear. The glass smashed easily with a quick nudge of his elbow. He crammed as many pills as he could into his pockets and down his socks. He didn't want to stop to find out what they were, he wanted to get on with it and get out.

But then he heard a door swing open and a woman say, 'Oh, you didn't, did you? Oh, no, so what did he say?'

Another woman replied, 'Well, then he said . . .'

Ellis was crouched by the drugs cabinet. Just ahead of him was a table, so the women couldn't see him. He peered round it to have a look at them. They were two nurses. They'd come through another door at the other end of the room. One of the women was yabbering on about some bloke she fancied. The other was nodding and saying 'Yes' or 'Really?' at appropriate intervals. Her gaze was fixed on the door nearest to Ellis.

'Shit,' he said to himself as he wondered what he could do. He couldn't get out the door without the nurse seeing him. His best bet was to sit and wait for the nurses to go. They'd probably be gone soon and with any luck they wouldn't spot him.

Ellis huddled himself up as small as possible and tried to stay as still and quiet as he could. He suddenly became very conscious of the noise of his breathing and his heartbeat. He hoped it wasn't as loud as it seemed to him.

Ellis wasn't sure how long he'd been crouched there. It seemed a very long time. It reminded him of a game mums make kids play at birthday parties – sleeping lions. The one where you have to lie as still as you can. When you move, you've lost the game. Ellis had never been very good at that game.

The drone of the nurses' gossip went on.

'Course I always *did* fancy him.'

'Did you? You never told me.'

And then the drone was suddenly interrupted by a shrill squeal. 'Oh, my God, there's been a break-in.'

Ellis knew it wouldn't be long before they spotted him. He was gonna have to run for it. He didn't wait to hear any more. He dashed out through the door and down the corridor. But Ellis knew the nurses would have seen him and would come to look for him, so he slipped into another room a little further down the corridor to find somewhere to hide.

Tash was trying to get some sleep when in stumbled some geezer. He didn't see her at first. He kept looking at the door, kind of paranoid, as though he expected someone to be following him. He looked off his head and vaguely familiar. Tash was sure she'd seen him somewhere before. Probably at some party or other.

Ellis had the door ajar and was looking down the corridor to see if the nurses were following him or not. There was no sign of them for a while but then one of them appeared and came strutting down the corridor. Ellis turned to find somewhere to hide. He was surprised to see a girl in bed, her leg in traction – he hadn't noticed her when he first came in.

'Sorry, I just, er . . .' Ellis was going to explain. But then he couldn't think how he could begin. Instead he dived under the bed – and it was just as well because a second later, the nurse rapped on the door and came in.

'Is everything alright?' she asked Tash. 'Only there's been a break-in.'

'A break-in,' repeated Tash. 'Really? I haven't seen anything.'

'Well, press your buzzer if you see anything,' said the nurse. 'Sorry to disturb you.'

'Course,' said Tash.

Ellis heard the door shut and scrambled out from under the bed.

'Cheers,' he said to Tash and then went up to the door to check the nurse had gone. He saw her little white uniform disappear round the corner at the end of the corridor. He wanted to get out and work out a way to get back to the club. But before he did, he reached into his pocket and put something in Tash's hand. The door banged shut and Tash blinked at Ellis's bizarre whirlwind visit. She opened her hand and looked down at an E.

'Alright, Ellis,' Ish said as he came into the squat.

Ellis was curled up on the sofa. The TV was on. He opened his bleary eyes and said, 'Alright.'

Ish assumed Ellis had been doing a bit of gear but he looked down on the floor and saw a pile of pharmaceuticals.

'Christ, Ellis, what've you been doing?'

'Hospital.' Ellis squeezed the word out. 'Hospital.'

'What? You need to go to hospital?' asked Ish, urgently. Ellis wasn't looking good. 'Are you alright?'

'Hospital,' repeated Ellis, unable to string a sentence together.

'Shit. What? Shall I call an ambulance or something?' Ish was beginning to panic.

Ellis heaved himself up, grinned at Ish and said, 'Drugs. Got drugs . . . hospital.' He flung a finger down at the floor to indicate the drugs he'd nicked.

'What, you nicked 'em in hospital?' Ish laughed.

Ellis nodded slowly, his eyes falling shut with the movement. He slumped back into the sofa and his own hazy world.

When Ellis woke up, he still felt serene, as if he'd woken from one of the best nights' sleep he'd had in a long time. He was serene until he was conscious enough to feel the squelching of shit between his butt cheeks.

'Erh,' he groaned and got up, walking with his legs splayed, in an attempt not to spread the shit even further.

It didn't really work. By the time he got to the bog, the shit was squashed against the tops of his legs and the seat of his trousers. It was his only pair. He'd have to try and blag a pair off Ish.

He cleaned himself up, scraping the shit off his arse with newspaper and washing the rest off. When he was done, he chucked the newspaper and the trousers in the bath. He'd seen a bottle of white spirit next door in the living room, sitting on the mantelpiece. Didn't know whose it was or how it'd got there but he remembered it was there. He emptied it into the bath, watching it soak into the trousers and then lit another piece of newspaper, stood back and chucked it on. The bath burst into flames. Ellis stood and watched.

'What you doing?' It was Ish, coming in for his morning pee.

'Burning mi trousers,' explained Ellis. 'You got a pair I can borrow?'

'What happened to those ones?' asked Ish. He stood and pissed, watching the fire burn. 'You shit in them?'

'How d'you know?'

'You only took a load've laxatives last night,' Ish smirked, as he shook his cock.

'What, how d'you know that?'

'I looked it up in *Medicines*.' *Medicines* was a book that listed pharmaceutical drugs, their applications and effects. Essential reading for junkies.

'Oh,' said Ellis, wishing he'd thought've that last night. But he'd been too fucked to think that straight. And too excited. He had pills galore, he didn't care what they were, he just wanted to take as many as he could and see what happened. Looking back, he thought he was lucky to be alive. Perhaps he should try and be a little less enthusiastic next time.

'So what happened, then?' asked Ish. 'You nicked them all from hospital?'

'Yeah, and I found a load've pills in a sock,' said Ellis. Yeah, last night had been pretty good. And now he'd got all those pills, he'd be able to pay Saul back. That debt had been on his mind for a while now. But the pills, where were they? He felt himself lurch as he thought for a second, perhaps they'd been in the pockets of the trousers. That would be something, wouldn't it – find a load've pills and then watch them burn. No, not even Ellis could do something like that. But where the fuck were they?

Ellis wandered back into the living room. Ish went back to bed, still half asleep.

Ellis sat himself down on the sofa and tried to tug a few memories of last night back from the Lethean depths of drug abuse. It was hard. He knew he'd taken a lot of pills last night. And he knew he'd given away a fair few. And no doubt he'd lost a load too. But where were the rest? There had to be some more, didn't there? There had to be. He couldn't've caned all of them, could he? Not in one night.

So where were they? He'd put the hospital drugs in his pockets and he was sure the pills had been down his socks. But he didn't know for sure. How could he know anything for sure?

He scrabbled around on the floor amid the pharmaceuticals but there were no pills. He looked in his socks – it took a long time to find them – but when he did, there were no pills. No pills down the side of the sofa. No pills in his shoes. No fucking pills anywhere.

And then it dawned on him. Slowly and dimly at first and then more and more clearly as flashes of last night's debauchery came to him and he knew it had to be true – he'd caned them all last night. That whole sockful of pills had been gobbled between him and his mates and probably numerous passing beneficiaries of Ellis's generosity. There were no more pills. They were all gone.

Chapter Twenty

Monday, Tuesday, Thursday. No, Monday, Wednesday, Thursday, Friday. Monday, Tuesday, Thursday, Friday. Friday, she's coming. And it's Monday, today, Monday. Monday, Tuesday, Friday.

The old woman counted on her fingers, yellowed with nicotine.

Monday, Tuesday, Friday.

She knew it was not quite right. Something. Not quite right. But she didn't know what it was and so she couldn't put it right. Things were often like that now – inexplicably wrong. No hope of putting them right. Right was lost a long time ago. Her brain didn't function as it should. But, almost to spite her, it worked well enough for her to understand that she was making mistakes, yet never well enough to put those mistakes straight. Like some cruel joke.

Tuesday, Friday. Said she would come. Friday? Friday? Eleven o'clock. Friday.

A sudden panic. How could she know what day it was now? Think hard. She squinted at the clock. Got up with a seized body. Slow grinding steps. Close to the clock. Tired, glazing eyes, peering close. The green numbers, square. Blur in front of her. Nine o'clock. Could be. Focus. Concentrate. Eight? And the image is lost. Slow stiff steps across the dirty lino and half fall into the chair. Wooden.

Just got up, didn't I? Did I? What for? Sam should be here

soon. Been gone a long time. Very long time. Be here Friday. Wednesday now. Tomorrow. Tomorrow. Sam's coming.

Lost in time, no point of reference. Like a diver in the middle of the sea. All around is sea. Dull, thick sea. Above, below, all around, water closing in. And for her, all there was was time. Meaningless time behind her, before her and no way of ever knowing where she was. Which way to go. Except down, down to death.

She was not even sure when Sam had gone. She pretended to herself that she knew. She needed at least some sense that she was not totally useless. Some point of reference. An anchor. But she didn't really know. She didn't know how long she had been sitting here, sucking nicotine. There were three butts in the ashtray. Did that mean something? Perhaps.

She could not tell whether Sam had been there today or yesterday or days ago. Each day dragged on the same. Cigarettes, tea and time, time, time.

The curtains were shut. Always. She was ugly now. Her hair thinning and white. Her skin sagged loose. Her teeth were stained and crumbling. She was ugly. Ugly Mary. No one must see her. She never went out. Never, not for a long time now. Inside, she kept the curtains shut, so no one would see her. Day fell into night and night walked into day but she never knew. Day night day night. It was all the same. A dark confusion of cigarettes, tea and time. So slow and painful. All she looked forward to was death.

'Right, Mum?' It was Sam. She was back. Must be Friday.

'Sam, Sam.' Mary turned her head slowly to look at her daughter. 'Is it Friday? Friday.'

'Friday? It's Tuesday, Mum. Get it together.'

'Bin long time,' said Mary quietly.

'You what?' said Sam. What was her mum going on about?

'You. You. Bin long time. Monday, Tuesday, Friday. Mus' be Friday now. Long time waiting.'

'For God's sake, I've only bin half an hour. Is that what you mean, I've been a long time?' Sam shouted with irritation.

Sam looked at her mother, her face tight with disgust. It made her feel quite ill to watch her mother so pathetic and useless. She didn't even know what day it was. And people argued against euthanasia! They should take one look at her mum. What was the point? Sitting inside all day long. Curtains shut. That was no life. She was already dead.

Sam went into the living room and took out a wrap of brown. She'd forgotten the foil and so went back to the kitchen. Her mother was trying to light a fag. She lit the lighter. The flame swayed a couple of inches from the end of the fag. She seemed unable to connect the two. The flame went out. She tried to relight it. Again and again. But her thumb didn't roll hard enough on the wheel to make a spark. Or it slipped from the button that released the gas.

'I hope I die young,' thought Sam. 'All she does is smoke fags all day and she can't hardly light them. But then, at least it gives her something to do.'

Sam had found the foil and went to leave but then glanced at her mother. She had put the cigarette down now and was concentrating hard on making the lighter work. Still she could not do it. Sam felt a strange pang of pity. She went to her mother and took the lighter and lit the cigarette and handed it back to her. Mary looked up slowly and nearly smiled.

In the living room, Sam sank back into a cloud of smack. Nothing mattered except that feeling of warmth. It was like a breath of life, soothing, calming her body and mind. Womblike – warm, content and complete. Nothing was needed except this feeling. This was the essence of life.

Mary concentrated and finally made her limbs move. She snailed across the floor and down the corridor. It all took so long. Everything. And time went so very, very slowly. She hated her body. When she reached the doorway of the living room, she saw Sam slumped, her head bent back against the sofa. In her lap was the foil, lighter and tube.

'Heroin,' muttered Mary. 'Heroin.'

Sam opened her eyes and looked at her mother. Her lids flickered. The image of her mother wavered and blurred and then came into focus.

'Piss off,' Sam mumbled.

The doorbell rang. Sam got up unsteadily and pushed past her mother, still standing in the doorway. Mary swayed and then turned to walk back to her fags in the kitchen. She coughed and phlegm gurgled up into her mouth and then slid down her throat as she swallowed.

Sam moved slowly. The bell rang again.

'Alright, alright,' she shouted, opening the door to the flat and walking through to the hall. She could see a man, distorted, through the crinkled glass of the door that led out on to the street. 'Trev, is that you?'

She opened the door. A man stood in front of her, hollow eyes and a coarse face.

'Trev.'

'Alright, Sam,' said Trev, stepping inside. 'D'you get any gear?' he asked as Sam shut the door.

'Yeah, course.'

Trev, seeing he was standing on some letters, stooped and picked them up. He opened them.

'Nuvva cheque,' he said and handed the letters to Sam.

The first time they had stolen one of the cheques, Trev had felt uneasy. Mary was an old woman and she was Sam's mother. Sam was an only child. Mary had no one else to take care of her. It didn't seem right to steal from her, especially as this was the money for her rent.

Trev had mentioned how he felt to Sam. But Sam, strong-minded as ever, had screamed back at him, calling him a wimp and a poof.

'You don't understand,' she'd said. 'You just don't understand. Who are you to stand there and judge how I should treat my mother? You don't know. You don't know how she treated me. Left me when I was ten years old. Never phoned. Never wrote, nothing. Told me it was my fault and then left me. Her sister had to look after me and she never wanted me neither. Blamed it all on me. But it wasn't anyfing to do wiv me that she left. It was cos've that man. Just cos of that man and that stupid selfish bitch following him. Going wiv him before she thought to stop and look after me. So don't fucking stand there and tell me that I can't get something back now. I'm here, aren't I? Don't fuckin' try 'n' make me feel bad.'

Trev had backed off. He began to look at Mary in a new light. Maybe she was just getting what she deserved. The next time they stole the cheque, it wasn't so hard.

And there was the gear. It was about then that it began to tighten its grip on them both. He was not sure when it'd happened exactly but he suddenly realized that he no longer did it in order to feel good, he did it so he wouldn't feel bad. When those cramps gripped his muscles nothing else mattered except getting that gear. Everything seemed to stop. His mind was fixed on one thing only, oblivious to everything else, only gear, gear, gear.

'Where's the gear, then, Sam?'

Chapter Twenty-one

Saul and Joss were back in their flat. Saul felt good, refreshed and ready to get on with life. He wasn't gonna let things get him down like that again. He was gonna be strong, stay in control. He could do it. He could get his shit together. He knew he could.

The answerphone was winking at him. He pressed play. There were a couple of messages from some mates and then there was the message Ellis'd left the other night. His voice was loud and he was talking fast.

'Saul, you don't have to worry. It's all sorted. Don't worry about a thing. You wouldn't believe what's happened. You wouldn't believe it. It's . . . it's fuckin' . . . it's a miracle. That's what it is. It's a miracle.' There was a pause. 'It's Ellis by the way. Or did I already say that? Anyway hope the countryside was good. Come and see me when you get back and I'll tell you about this miracle. Take it easy.'

Yeah, Saul knew it was all gonna work out alright.

'What the fuck was all that about?' said Joss. 'He sounded completely off his head.'

'I'm gonna go 'n' find out,' replied Saul.

'You only just got back.'

'Fuck it. I wanna find out what he's going on about.' Saul felt so full of energy, he didn't want to sit around. He just wanted to get on with it.

*

Joss thought she'd heard a noise, a quiet knock on the door. But the music was up loud so she couldn't be too sure. She turned it down and waited and listened. There was nothing. But then just as she was about to turn the sound up again, she heard the knock again. It was quiet and slow but there was definitely someone at the door.

When Joss opened the door, there was an old woman standing before her, looking down at the floor. Her skin was thin, like scar tissue, almost translucent and tinged with blue. She was wearing a nightgown and polyester dressing-gown which was quilted and decorated with sprigs of tree and various birds. On her feet was a pair of faded purple slippers.

Joss felt herself soften at the woman's vulnerability. The old woman was fragile. Fragile like a china doll, thought Joss. No, not like a china doll. A china doll is precious, valuable, something that commands respect and so, although fragile, it won't get broken easily. But this woman was certain to break, if she wasn't already broken. More like a cheap toy, played with, abused and tossed aside once the kid is bored.

The old woman was looking at her feet and mumbling. Joss could only hear a few of the words she spoke.

'Downstairs . . . fag . . . left me . . . left me . . . fag . . . no money . . . no food . . .'

Joss couldn't make any sense of it. But the one word that came out clearly again and again was fag, so Joss said, 'Do you want a fag. Is that what you want? A fag?'

Still the old woman did not look up but she stopped talking and nodded slowly. Joss went inside to find a fag. She lit it and gave it to the old woman. Mary inhaled deeply and looked up at Joss.

'Cheers,' she croaked.

Joss saw her eyes clearly for the first time. They were hollow and dull. Something about them made Joss lurch inside with a feeling of horror. What was it about them that seemed so terrible? What was it? And then she saw, there was no light in them. They were flat, empty of all spirit. They seemed like unconvincing false eyes. But they weren't false. They were real.

Mary stood and smoked. It was like watching someone who has walked thirsty through the desert for days, drink their first gulp of water. She pulled her dressing-gown up around her shoulders as she felt it slip a little but all the time she carried on sucking on the cigarette.

Joss was not sure what to do. She couldn't shut the door on the old woman. Not now. But the woman was silent and Joss didn't know what to say, so she stood there for an awkward moment before saying, 'Fancy a cup've tea?'

Mary looked at Joss. Her lips quivered as though she was trying to smile. Her head darted a quick nod.

'Come on, then,' said Joss and turned to walk into the flat, looking behind her as she went to see how the old woman was getting along.

Mary walked slowly with deep wheezing breaths, already tired from walking up the stairs to Joss's flat.

'Stroke, you see,' she said. 'Had a stroke.'

Joss nodded. 'Doesn't matter. There's no rush.'

When finally the old woman was sat down with a cup of tea and her fourth fag, she began to talk more freely.

'Live downstairs,' she said. 'Fifty years. Downstairs. Fifty years. I've lived there. No fags, no food and I'm hungry. She takes my money, my money. She does.' Mary suddenly sounded frantic, as though Joss was accusing her of lying. 'She steals my money.'

''S alright,' said Joss. 'I believe you. But who, who steals your money?'

'Her,' replied Mary. 'My daughter. And Trev. Trev as well. Thinks I don't know. I know. Now they've gone. No food, no

204

fags. They've been gone days. Weeks.' Mary wasn't exactly sure how long it was but she knew she was hungry. She knew she hadn't eaten today. And she knew she hadn't eaten yesterday. In fact she couldn't remember when she'd eaten last. 'What day is it now? What day is it?'

'Saturday,' replied Joss.

'Saturday, Friday, Monday. They've been gone a long time. Monday, today you said? Monday?'

'No, Saturday,' said Joss. 'It's Saturday today.'

The old woman looked at her as though she couldn't understand what Joss was saying. Hadn't the girl said it was Monday only a second ago? No, it was probably her brain letting her down. What had she been saying again? What was it?

Joss reminded her. 'So, she left you with no money? Your daughter.'

The woman paused, waiting for the words to filter through into her brain.

'Heroin,' she rasped finally.

'Heroin?' repeated Joss.

'Heroin.' Mary waited for a moment. She had been going to say something and then it had gone. 'Words,' she said instead. 'I know. I know. They're inside here.' She touched her head. 'Such a long time for them to get out.' She sighed, as though giving up.

'There's no rush,' said Joss. 'There's no rush.' She waited for the woman to speak again but she didn't, so Joss asked, 'Fancy some food? Beans and mash, sound alright?'

The old woman was still quiet. Perhaps still searching for the words that were clogged inside her mind.

Joss repeated, 'Want some food?'

'Yes, dear, food,' Mary said without looking at Joss.

Joss wondered whether Mary had understood. Or was she simply repeating what Joss had said? But Joss went into the kitchen anyway and began to make some food for both of them.

Mary was left alone with her thoughts. This wasn't Sam's fault. It was her fault. Mary knew it was. It was all her fault. She deserved all this. She'd abandoned her child. And now her child was abandoning her. Stealing from her, leaving her to starve half to death. All the pain, all the hunger, what else was Mary to expect? She'd done wrong and now she was paying. You never got away with anything in this life. You paid for it all.

When Joss came back in with two steaming plates of beans and mash, Mary was talking quietly to herself.

' 'S all my fault,' she was saying. 'All my fault.'

'What's all your fault?' asked Joss.

'Leaving me like this. My daughter. All my fault. I left her. I loved him. He loved me. He did. And I left her to be with him.'

Joss wasn't sure she understood what the woman was talking about. She seemed to speak randomly. Could Joss believe anything she said?

But when Joss walked back downstairs with the woman, she took her some food and some fags all the same. She put the food away in the cupboards and in the fridge. Both were bare, except in the bottom of the fridge there were a few bits of mouldy veg. And suddenly Joss realized what the old woman had been saying must be true. Joss felt heavy and slightly sick as she shut the door on the old woman. What was happening if a woman left her own mother to starve? What the fuck was going on? Life was hard enough, the least you could expect was to die in peace.

Joss knew the daughter and her boyfriend, at least she'd said hello to them a couple of times when they were leaving or coming in. How could you do that to your own mother? Heroin. The old woman had mentioned it. Joss hadn't ever noticed them pinned. But then she'd only seen them a couple of times before. It must've been them that'd nicked the money out've Saul's letters and Joss's credit card. It made sense. They shared the same hallway. All the letters came in together. Why hadn't Saul and her thought of that before? They'd been too preoccupied blaming Ellis. Well, at least that let him off the hook. Joss had hated the idea of Ellis stealing off them like that.

Things were beginning to come into focus for Joss and Saul now. Ellis was about to sort Saul out with his 'miracle' and he wasn't a thief. Saul was happier, back to his old self. Yeah, things were coming together. Everything was gonna work out.

Chapter Twenty-two

'You what?' exclaimed Saul. 'You're taking the piss, aren't you?'

'No,' said Ellis. 'I swear I had them. I had them and I was gonna give them back to you. Ask anyone. Well, you got the message, didn't you? On your answerphone. Oh, mate, I had it in my mind all night to save them and give them back to you. But it was only when I woke up I realized I must've caned them all. I'm really sorry. It's a bit've a wind-up for you, ain't it? But I'll sort you out. I swear I'll sort you out.'

A bit've a wind-up? Saul couldn't believe it. Ellis was enough to drive anyone crazy. But Saul wasn't gonna let it affect him. No, he wasn't. Those few days in the country had got his head straight and he wasn't gonna get back on a downer again. No way. Fuck it. Don't think about it. He hadn't expected to see the money again for a while yet at least.

Joss had been out at the shops. When she got back, she could see Mary's door ajar. She called out.

'Hello, hello.' But there was no reply.

What was her door doing open? It didn't make sense.

Joss called out a couple more times and when there was no answer, pushed at the door. But it wouldn't open. There was something jammed against it. She pushed at it, leaning her shoulder into it, and putting her foot right up against it, to lend extra force.

She couldn't see Mary's body lying on the other side of the door. Curled up, dead, blocking the door. Every time Joss pushed the door, Mary's body rocked and slid back, rocked and slid back.

The door wouldn't give. Joss was only able to push it a few inches further open, enough to peer round the door into the hallway. Now she could see what was blocking the door: Mary's body, a crumpled wreck on the floor.

When Saul came home, Joss was in tears. The ambulance had been round to collect Mary's body. Joss felt strangely affected by her death. She'd only met the old woman that day, so it was not as though she could miss her. But still she was gutted. It was perhaps more the way the old woman had died, than just the fact that she was dead. Half starved to death, neglected by your daughter. It made Joss feel sick. What was it all about? What was going on?

Saul hugged Joss. 'What's wrong, baby? What's wrong?'

But it took Joss some time to explain it all to him. It came in fits and starts, not in one continuous story. She kept thinking about her pushing against the door and Mary's body on the other side of it.

Saul felt heavy once again. What was it about London? Every time you thought things were sorted, it turned around and kicked you in the teeth. Was that London? Or was that just life?

Saul was in the street. He was just walking, didn't really know where he was going or what he was up to. He was just walking. Joss had gone to see Chelsea. She seemed to feel a little better now. It was shock mainly. Seeing someone dead, right there in front of you.

Saul knew him when he saw him. It was Trev. And Sam was there with him too. They were hanging out outside the chippie near the square. Saul knew it was them, though he didn't know their names.

Saul couldn't help himself. He felt a sudden rush of anger welling up inside him. It was something he couldn't control. He hurled himself at Trev, like he'd done with Dave.

'You piece of shit,' he said, gripping Trev by the collar and twisting it. Pushing him up against the wall. Sam just stood there. Thought she was tough. But she just stood there. 'You fuckin' piece of shit. Stealin' off me. What the fuck do you think you're doin'? Fuckin' junkie.'

It took Trev a moment to clock who Saul was. But then he remembered. He was the bloke that lived upstairs from Sam's mum. What did he want? Oh, yeah, they'd nicked that money off him, hadn't they? Shit. How come he was havin' a go at them now?

'What, what you talkin' about?' Trev tried to sound innocent. He wasn't convincing.

'You know what I'm fuckin' talking about,' shouted Saul. He was holding himself back. He didn't want to punch Trev. He didn't want to. 'And you,' he said to Sam, still holding on to Trev. 'Your mother's dead. You half starved her to death, you bitch.'

'Piss off,' said Sam. What was this bloke talking about? Her mum wasn't dead. What a load've shit. She wasn't dead.

'She's fuckin' dead, alright?' Saul shook Trev and then released his hold on him. 'Don't come near my flat again.'

Saul walked away. Trev and Sam did nothing. They stood there, outside the chippie. Trev pulled his jacket down where Saul had messed it up.

And then Sam shouted after Saul, 'Tosser.'

Saul kept walking. Was this going to go on for ever? All this shit. Piling up around Saul. He'd felt alright in the country. He'd felt himself again. He and Joss had got on with each other. It'd been a laugh. But now, as soon as they were back in London, this had to happen. He could feel his mind crumble. He could feel the walls that had been blocking him in, build up again. Closing in on him, ready to crush him like some scene in *Raiders of the Lost Ark*. Would it, would it go on for ever? The walls closing in. Would he ever escape? Would he find a way out or would the walls crush him?

'Excuse me, hello,' a voice said to him.

Saul turned around to see an old Indian man, tall and majestic. He had white hair and a white beard. Saul recognized him from Chelsea's wedding. He was the bloke Ellis'd puked on.

'Bloody Paki,' thought Saul.

'Indian, sir, not Pakistani,' said Ashok.

Saul looked at the bloke. Saul hadn't said anything, had he? How had this old man known what he was thinking?

'It is not so difficult,' said Ashok. 'Once everyone was able to do this. Now many people have forgotten. Especially in dis country, your people have forgotten many things.'

Saul looked at the old man. Around his eyes and mouth, the skin was puckered, almost like a map of his life, marking the rivers of laughter and mountains of sadness. His face wasn't bitter, like so many old faces scarred with disappointment. It was a face that had seen and now finally grown to understand. In its presence, Saul felt his own anger melt and seep from his body. This old man seemed to know something, something Saul needed to learn.

'D'you fancy a drink?' asked Saul. 'A chat?'

'I don't drink alcohol,' replied Ashok, smiling. 'You want a coffee?'

'Yeah, okay.'

Over coffee Saul began to talk. He talked about everything that had happened over the last few months. How he had felt lost and full of self-hate, as though he was going crazy.

He was not really sure why he was talking to the old man like this, except that it felt the right thing to do. It wasn't awkward or embarrassing. Inside, Saul felt himself lighten.

While he talked, the old man said very little. He simply nodded and smiled and occasionally spoke the odd word of encouragement – just enough to keep Saul talking.

'I don't know,' said Saul, suddenly coming to the end of what he was saying. 'I don't know. I just . . . I don't know what I'm doing, where I'm going.'

'Many people do not know,' said Ashok. 'Only some people are better at hiding their ignorance.'

'But some people do know, though, don't they?' said Saul. 'Some people are born with a burning passion to write or draw or sing. And they don't feel good unless they do those things. They know where they're going. D'you know what I mean? They know where they're *trying* to go, at least. Even if they don't get there, like, reach the top of whatever it is they're tryin' to do, it doesn't matter, because they just enjoy doin' it for itself. Like, my girlfriend sings. Now, even if she doesn't ever release a record, at least there's something there for her that makes her feel alive. It gives her a meaning, doesn't it? A reason to get up in the morning. But me? I don't have anything like that. I don't know. I don't know why I'm here.'

'Sometimes, in order to understand something, it is necessary to go away from it, to look at it from another direction. Then perhaps you see answers and problems you could not see from where you were standing all this time. If I had a problem when I was a child, my grandfather used to tell me to stand on my head.'

'Did that help, then, did it?' Saul smiled.

'Sometimes, yes. I saw something different and I understood,' Ashok said and then laughed. 'Sometimes I only got a headache.'

'Well, d'you reckon it'd help me, then, if I stood on my head?' asked Saul.

'At home our holy men stand on their heads in other ways. They give up everything they have in order to travel and be close to God.'

'I don't believe in God,' replied Saul.

'Everyone believes in God. But some people do not understand the word 'god'. They know God but they do not realize it.'

'Like what? When've I ever seen God?' Saul asked, hoping this bloke wasn't going to turn into a Bible-basher and start trying to ram religion down his throat.

'This is the problem,' said Ashok, shrugging slightly. 'Putting big God into little words. What do you call him? Luck? Fate? Creation? Love? Destiny? Justice? Who knows? You know God. That is all. You know him.'

Saul wasn't sure.

Ashok continued. 'The holy men in India, they travel to find their answer. They see new things. Meet new people. New answers to old problems.'

'You reckon I should travel?'

'It is your life. Your problem. You must find your own answer. Not my answer. But stand on your head. Any way you can. If things are not working now, change some things, see if things get better. If it's better, then good. But if not, change some more things. Stand on your head.'

'Next week?' exclaimed Joss. 'You've bought a ticket to India for next week?'

'Yeah, I bought two; one's for you,' replied Saul.

'What, you mean go to Goa for a couple've weeks?' said Joss. She didn't mind the idea of a holiday.

'Ner, they're one-way tickets. I wanna go for a long time.'

'What's all this about?' Joss wasn't sure she was up for this.

213

'You know I haven't felt happy about things, about myself for a long time. I need to snap out of it and get on with my life.'

'You think going to India's the answer?' asked Joss, unconvinced. 'Isn't that just putting it off longer?'

'Maybe,' replied Saul. 'But the thing is I can't get on with my life if I don't know what it is I want to be doing. And I'm not doing myself any favours sitting on my arse here, that's for sure.'

'But why's it gonna be any different out there? Half West London's out there caning it. Why's it gonna be any different? It's the same old scene, different climate. Why're you gonna feel any different out there?'

'It's a big country, I don't have to travel the tourist route,' said Saul. 'I know what you're saying but, shit, I don't have to go to Goa. I can't lose if I go away. I can always come back and, whatever happens, I'll've learnt something,' Saul insisted. 'So are you gonna come with me?'

'I don't know.'

'I'll pay for you to go,' said Saul. 'I should get a few grand for the car. And we've got that housing benefit cheque. We can just pocket that and go.'

'I don't know,' Joss said, her head racing with possibilities. 'I'll have to think about it.'

Saul wanted Joss to go with him, of course he did. But his mind was set, whether or not she decided to go with him. He was going.

'Yeah, alright,' said Joss. It hadn't taken her long to make up her mind. 'Fuck it, I'll come.'

Chapter Twenty-three

The wind blew. A can rattled down the street sending scared pigeons flapping into the sky. A strange series of cause and effect.

Ellis was watching.

So was a boy. The boy looked at Ellis, 'You see that?'

'Yeah,' replied Ellis.

'Funny, ain't it, how one thing leads to another?'

'What d'you mean?' asked Ellis.

'Dunno,' said the boy casually. 'It's just funny, ain't it?'

'What, you mean the slippery slope?' Ellis laughed. Ellis had just been thinking about it. He'd been thinking about jacking up. He'd never thought he'd do it. But now it kind've made sense, didn't it? I mean, he wasn't rich and you had to get the best hit you could for your money. You didn't want to watch it go up in smoke, did you? But there it was, that slippery slope. One thing leading smoothly to the next. And before you know it, there's a needle in your arm. Because it makes sense. Well, it does, doesn't it?

'Listen,' said the boy. 'I don't reckon you should go home today.'

'You what?' said Ellis. Ellis had just met this kid and now he was telling him what to do.

'Don't go home today,' insisted the boy. 'I can't explain it. But jus' don't go home, alright?'

'What the fuck are you going on about?' exclaimed Ellis.

'Here, look, take this and go and get pissed.' The boy handed Ellis a tenner. 'I'll catch ya later, I can't hang around. Don't go home, okay.'

'What the fuck was all that about?' wondered Ellis. Was it some kind've scam? Was the kid gonna go back and burgle the squat? Wouldn't do him much good, Ellis didn't have anything to steal anyway. Was the kid gonna come back with his mates and say Ellis had nicked that tenner off him, so they could beat him up? Fuck knows. Didn't seem that likely. If the kid had wanted trouble, why hadn't he just started on Ellis there and then? Ellis didn't get it. But he was a tenner better off, so what did he care?

He held the note up to the light. Yeah, it seemed real, alright. Well, the kid was right, what better way to spend the day than getting pissed on someone else's money? Ellis headed for the Diver's Tavern.

It was when Ellis was buying his pint that he remembered who the boy was. It was Jamie, that kid who'd died at Doppingdean.

Ellis thought, 'Shit, I've just seen a ghost.' He should've felt shocked but he didn't really. He reckoned Jamie was pretty cool, as ghosts go – not that he'd met many other ghosts. But Jamie'd sorted Ellis out with a tenner, so fair play. Ellis wasn't complaining.

There was no one in the pub that Ellis knew, except that girl, the one sat over there in the corner. She looked pretty familiar. Now where was it that Ellis had seen her? Shit, yeah, she was that girl in hospital. The one whose room he'd hidden in. Ellis wandered over to her.

'Alright, how's yer leg?' asked Ellis.

Tash looked up from her paper. 'Yeah, 's alright,' she said, trying to place the bloke. 'Still pretty painful. I'm only just out of hospital.' Tash still couldn't work out who this guy was.

'D'you remember me?' Ellis saw Tash's confusion.

And then Tash clicked. 'Yeah, I remember you. You gave me that pill when I was in hospital.'

'That's right. I started that night with about eighty pills and I ate half've them and gave the rest away.' Ellis rolled his eyes at the ceiling.

'Didn't you break into the hospital?'

'Yeah, you heard?' Ellis felt a little glow of pride. 'Yeah, got shit loads've drugs.'

'I bet,' said Tash. 'What did you do?'

'Well, actually,' said Ellis. 'I took a load've laxatives by mistake. Woke up and I'd shat my pants.'

'Ner.' Tash laughed.

'Yeah, it wasn't funny.' But Ellis was laughing too. And then Ellis spotted Tash's jacket – a black puffa jacket slung over the back of her chair. Ellis thought about Saul's jacket and the fuck-up with the pills. He looked at Tash again and suddenly clicked where else he'd seen her. 'That party. Did you go to the one in the sports centre?'

'Yeah,' said Tash, wondering why Ellis sounded so excited.

'Did you have a Jacuzzi?'

'Yeah,' said Tash. 'Why?'

'I don't think that's your jacket. I think it's my mate's,' explained Ellis. 'Only I was wearing it that night and I lost it by the Jacuzzi. I put on another puffa when I got out.'

'What, so you reckon this is yours?' asked Tash. Was this bloke having a laugh? 'How do you know it's yours?'

'There's something in the lining, unless you've taken it out,' said Ellis.

'I haven't taken anything out,' said Tash.

'Have a look and see if there's something there,' said Ellis.

Tash took the jacket off the back of the chair and felt around in the lining.

Ellis was thinking, 'Please, please, please can she be telling the

217

truth. Please can the pills still be there. Please. If they are, I swear I won't fuck up this time.' It occurred to him that if the pills were there, Tash might refuse to give him the jacket back. But he didn't give a shit. He'd just punch her, grab the jacket and make a run for it. She was only little, what could she do?

Tash felt around and finally felt the pills.

'I think it *is* your jacket,' she said. She handed the jacket over to Ellis.

Ellis took it and checked for himself that the pills were there.

'Yes,' he said, clutching the jacket. 'Cheers, you don't know what this means to me.'

Ellis put the jacket on. He wasn't going to take it off until he was with Saul. He practically ran over to the phone and called Saul. Just in case something went wrong, Ellis didn't tell Saul he had the jacket. He only said he was on his way over and Saul should make sure he was in.

'I've gotta go,' said Ellis, although his pint was only half drunk. 'Here, have this.' He reached in his pocket and handed Tash a fiver.

But Tash wouldn't take it. 'Don't be stupid, I was only giving you back what was yours.'

Ellis left the pub with the jacket. Perhaps this was what Jamie had been going on about, when he'd told Ellis not to go home. Had Jamie known Tash and the jacket would be there? Perhaps.

Back at the squat, Johnny had just popped round.

'I was in the area,' he said. 'Got this great new gear. It's shit-hot. Thought you'd want some.'

Emily and Ish were both up for it. Of course. Now the three of them were there. Ish shovelling a little gear on a spoon. Johnny ripping up a piece of cloth so they each had a tourniquet. Emily took one've the strips and wrapped it round her arm. Pumping her hand. Watching the veins rise to the surface. Ish was filling two syringes, one for Emily, one for him. So he could get his hit straight after he gave her hers. The gear and the citric were on the spoons and a little water. Johnny and Ish were heating it slowly. Watching it melt together. Emily's hand still pumping, nervously. Anticipating. The syringes sucking up the fluid. One, two, three of them. Tapping the bubbles to the top. And then the needle diving into Emily's arm. Pulling out, drawing blood and plunging back in again. The tourniquet tight around Johnny's arm. A dig. Blood. Plunger down. And a second later, Ish finding his vein. He pushed the plunger down.

So Saul was going away on a one-way ticket. Ellis had just been round there. Given him back his pills. A good going-away present. And finally Saul had no reason to hate or distrust Ellis. He realized it had all been a mistake, a stupid mistake. They were mates again.

Saul was going away. All of life was a journey, he'd been saying, and now it was time for him to change direction.

Well, if life was a journey, Ellis had been travelling in the wrong direction the last few weeks. Stepping down a track beaten by his dad. The road to junksville. One look at his dad and he knew he didn't want that. And you could choose. It didn't just happen to you – not unless you were young or blind. You went in with your eyes open, knowing the dangers. They were all around you. Your mates hollowed and thin. Needles lying around their flats. You knew what being a junkie was all about and you could choose that, if that was what you wanted.

It wasn't what Ellis wanted, he knew that now. But at the same time he knew he couldn't ever quite leave that world. It was his world. It was him. He was at home among that dirty, seedy life. Something in him craved debauchery and was never satisfied until he was wallowing amid it. He'd tried jobs. He didn't mind a bit've work. But he wasn't ever gonna get a steady job. It just wasn't him. He was kidding himself, if he thought he'd ever stick that out. It wasn't gonna happen. No way. Because a part of him (if not all of him) would be craving something crazy and uncertain. That was what kept him alive.

So Saul was set, rolling in a new direction. And Ellis, what would he do? He'd carry on being Ellis with his one set of clothes and fuck-all money. He'd wander on through life taking his chances and always doing what he felt to do. Because that was him. That was what he enjoyed. That was who he was.

Ellis opened the door to the squat. Humming to himself. Walking down the corridor. The sound of the TV. A tap still running. And in the sitting room. A spilt can of Brew. A half-eaten bag of chips. The ketchup congealed. The *Sun* flapping in the wind. The news . . . the news on TV.

And they were dead. One, two, three. Dead. Johnny slumped in a chair. A little dribble sliding from his mouth. Emily curled on the floor. Like a baby. Ish next to her. Leaning against the sofa. The needle still drooping from his arm.

The second hand on the clock was ticking and slipping. Ticking and slipping. Time stood still.

Ellis walked out the flat. Walked, walked away.